thePleasureTube

"Riding thePleasureTube without a trip to the sun is like...jumping from a cliff and never reaching the sea,"- the woman says.

"We're talking about direct electrical stimulation of the orgasmic center of the brain," Collette says. She smiles.
"But that could...kill you."
"Some people never come back. Perhaps they never want to."

"Come with me to the sun," the woman says. She shows her teeth, and touches them with her tongue.

The Pleasure Tube

Robert onopa

A BERKLEY BOOK
published by
BERKLEY PUBLISHING CORPORATION

Berkley Publishing Corporation
200 Madison Avenue
New York, New York 10016

SBN 425-03941-2

*BERKLEY BOOKS are published by
Berkley Publishing Corporation*

BERKLEY BOOK ® TM 757,375

Printed in the United States of America

Berkley Edition, MARCH, 1979

Pleasure is itself unlimited and belongs to that class of things which does not, and never will, contain within itself, or have derived from itself, either a beginning, a middle, or an end.

Plato, *Philebus*

Still image: a woman frozen in space, fixed in inky blackness, the funnel of infinity pierced by diamond points of light, stars in the celestial sea. She floats as a swimmer, her palms flat and forward. Her hair streams behind—yet no breeze. Her expression intense and incomprehensible, lips slightly parted to show the glistening edges of teeth—a kiss or a cry—silent in the void.

The Pleasure Tube

PART I:

EVENT HORIZON [=df the practical limits of a black hole, the sphere within which its gravity does not permit the escape of light; a point of no return.]

CHAPTER 1
Recovery

DAEDALUS SEQUENCE 33.2871//
SPLASHDOWN//
12 August 06:42:19//

We hit the water and penetrate for what seems a minute and surge back up, as if pushed by an immense hand.

My stomach cringes and folds, snaps into a knot. I black out for the blink of an eye.

I think: four years ago.

Salt-rich air spills in as the hatch is blown. How I know we are upside down, not the entering divers: my spittle ascends; hints of my digestion swirl on the roof of my mouth.

The motion of the sea is weather of a heavy medium. In the reentry capsule's aquarium light, I am lowered like a child from the liftoff rig by four hands, guided through the hatch to a rubber boat.

Huge sea, small voices, wind in the face, the light enormous.

Helped into the launch. There is a large, sleek carrier on station kilometers off.

I try my voice: "Everyone all right?"

"Pretty much, sir, welcome back. We do have one anomaly in the first rig we are listing as a psychotic episode. One man is in very bad shape."

"Who? Is he hurt physically?"

"Negative, they're only listing psychotic episode; his name is Cooper. Which one are you?"

An image of Cooper runs through my mind, his large frame hunched in dim light. "My name is Voorst," I tell the J.G. "Rawley Voorst."

"You're the other one they want to talk to, sir. They're waiting for you on deck. Prepare to winch up."

We were almost four years out on the Daedalus; now four years have passed since then. Yet those days stay with me: a looping program whose features I also recall in daydreams, nightmares, sudden visions which paralyze me with their simultaneous confusion and clarity. During those days time itself seemed to coincide with computer-maddening formulas for conic distortions, whirlpools, spirals of decreasing radius and increasing range—a terrifyingly simple future compounded now by its existence in the past. SciCom's report identified in our point of entry an incipient parabola of return. That seems only information produced by the channel to contain it, the wormhole's shape the girth of the worm. There must be more to it: consider the formula for a single wormhole which leads simultaneously to the worm's both ends. Spooked then, spooked now.

/////thePleasureTube///thePleasureTube///thePleasureTube/////

light sensuous sauna   fantasy co-op
lubricious service personnel   foods of the world
aquaplease paradise garden   tactile videon

/////thePleasureTube///thePleasureTube///thePleasureTube/////

"Let's put it this way," Taylor says loudly into the wind, pointing with the stem of his pipe at a hull section being towed in between hovering tugs. "Who punched the code for impact event after the blow? Just who made the decision?"

The carrier deck is landlike, a metal field on the sea

with only the slightest roll. I am still wet from the transfer, my feet sog in my boots, my flight suit clings to my thighs. "Look," I say, "you'll have to ask Werhner, he does those things. I was busy with the ship. Or ask Cooper."

"Yes, but..."

"The investigation was finished on range close to four years ago. You have those tapes." I squint into the sunlight in the direction of the hull section and the tugs, watch an intense gold-silver reflection that rolls to show a wide swath of charred metal along the hull section's side.

"We'll debrief on Guam at SciCom—Agana Base," Taylor says. "What you're going to need is patience, this is a slow process. Maybe think about the event, just what you were doing at the event, we'll start from there."

"That's all in the log," I tell him. "I put everything I know into the log. What I *need* is a vacation. I've got it coming."

"Your hand is bleeding."

"What?"

"You must have cut your hand," Taylor says, pointing his pipestem to my side. "How did that happen?"

I look down and see a trickle of blood spreading onto my palm, the heel of my hand is nicked open, I lick it with my tongue. "Must have jammed it on a vane key when we splashed down," I tell him, tasting the salt of my blood, the salt of the sea. "That's happened before."

He is still looking at me. I notice the bushiness of his eyebrows, the thickness of his lips. "How do you feel about being back?" he asks flatly. "All that relative earth time, eight years your own—how do you feel?"

"Fine," I say. "Just fine." I am still thinking: *four years ago.*

RETRIEVE//
R/V Daedalus//
Flt Vane Eng Class 2//
Station/Rawley Voorst//
Log Entry 1441-44//
Flt yr 3/Day 349+//
Codex 292-1441-1444+//
RETRIEVE IN FULL BEGIN BEGIN BEGIN BEGIN BEGIN BEGIN BEGIN

Proper Time: 16:23:08// Awoke to another day of severe turbulence, the dome instruments in the console room reading macroweather storms in all spectra. The ship continues to pitch and yaw. Almost everyone is under with motion sickness, this is day eight of instability. Thrusters, vanes, microweather ports—all our control systems are again slow to respond to Maxine's programs, Cooper in and out of the dome. We have been compensating with manual systems for vane/lift/drop, using microweather entirely for propulsion, the work almost all mine to do, though Werhner is lending a hand when he's able. At the moment we curl in a far, snaky arm of the Crab nebula, along a front we have been chased by since the Pleiades. There are endless debates in SciCom, endlessly repetitious; the grav field of the huge ghostly star we first saw six months ago is only days—my own guess is perhaps thirty hours—ahead. Its diminishing light makes it the almost certain field of a black hole; still no conclusive approach from SciCom, nothing yet on tangent angle. I continue to work its macroweather front with retrievable microweather on the face of the larger system. If that front signals the well-formed cyclonic depression it appears to, today, I repeat, today, we should reach a lull. Theoretically, SciCom reports, well off any grav field or event horizon, well off our point of no return. In the last hour the Committee Pilot abdicated again at a painful briefing—sick men—in SciCom the endless debate goes on. I am the only one holding my rations—is it the work I do? Stiff watch ahead; at least manually the ship is responding well.

I fly by default another day. I wonder who really knows.

Shift one/neg grav intrudes//
CONT. 1442 CONT CONT CONT CONT CONT CONT CONT CONT

Proper Time: 20:17:53// We have crossed into the lull. Becoming apparent why Maxine's programs are working slow—Werhner detecting time slip between field of

information and control—reading into proper time—
how can that be? SciCom meeting again with Committee
Pilot. I can't go.

Shift one/time distor//
CONT. 1443 CONT CONT CONT CONT CONT CONT CONT CONT

Proper Time: SEE CODEX// Dome more brilliant than
I have ever seen before along starboard, spectrum yellow-
white—yet that acts like the lull—port inky, muddy
violet, but that is where the other front is, approaching by
grav and mag sensors, otherwise blind. Werhner behaving
as if he hadn't been dead sick for the past week, eating at
the console. We have decided that he goes back to
SciCom for choice range and decision. As if there were
any other choices, I see only two. First: to tangent this
front and use it to propel us back and free. Second: to lay
on the thrusters and go through. SciCom circuits
overloaded, Committee Pilot patching out for more
room. I have never seen such a lull. At least our console
terminal . . .

END R$_1$//CODEX??//SEE CODEX SEE CODEX SEE CODEX SEE CODEX

ALARM ALARM ALARM ALARM ALARM ALARM ALARM ALARM

EVENT INTRUSION EVENT INTRUSION EVENT INTRUSION EVENT
ALL AUXILIARY SYSTEMS A & B SEQ ALL AUXILIARY SYSTEMS
DAMAGE CONTROL DAMAGE CONTROL DAMAGE CONTROL

ALARM ALARM ALARM ALARM ALARM ALARM ALARM ALARM
EVENT INTRUSION EVENT INTRUSION EVENT INTRUSION EVENT

The Guam sun floods through the dusty window.
"Why can't I see Cooper?"
"Partly it's quarantine, standard procedure. Partly it's
because *today* he's in Houston. He's been transferred to
Houston."
Smug bastard; I have been asking to see Cooper for a
week. He wrote the report; I cannot imagine what

SciCom is after that's not in the report. Cooper and I avoided one another on the way back—there was the affair with Maxine, and he always seemed to me odd, reclusive, a huge, bearded man who never said what was on his mind—but I never saw him break. Where was he in the ship then? Does it matter?

It has taken me a day to see this information officer. Guam is a morass of requisition systems, authority flows, activity program officers; bad enough before, incredible now. The island landscape—lazy, flapping palms, eroded red hills patched with dusty green scrub, an absolute sun—only fertilizes my growing boredom. Houston. Werhner will sigh and shrug.

/////thePleasureTube///thePleasureTube///thePleasureTube/////

reserve now   fourteen days and nights
a world of your own   twenty-eight to two-eighty credits
orgo-toto   three separate program classes

CONTINUOUS MOVEMENT

LasVenus   suborbital/deep space
LA SoCal   olde earthe/moonloop

TRIP TO THE SUN

risk venture vector   symphonic synesthetic harmonics
the EnergyWest grand prix   megastars in sidereal concert
NoAm biosphere reserve   SoPac tropical reserve

THE PLEASURE TUBE

dial from any codex terminal//106pleasuretube//dial from any codex terminal tubes daily//1.a. trans-port//tubes daily//1.a trans-port//tubes daily////thePleasureTube//thePleasureTube//thePleasureTube//thePleasureTube////

It is Taylor I see one day; his dark, bushy eyebrows never move. He alternates with Knuth, an intense little man who acts as if he were a foot taller—I wonder if his neck hurts sometimes. Today Knuth.

"The exact sequence," he begins, tapping his pencil. Several times before he has asked the same question, in precisely the same way, with the identical emphasis on *exact*.

I tell him what he can read in the log, what he has read in the log, everything is there. I remember hearing Werhner saying, seeing the silver-blue ball of earth, how lucky we were to have come back. Lucky?

RETRIEVE//
R/V Daedalus//
Station/Rawley Voorst//
Log Entry 1446//
Flt yr 3/Day 350+//
Codex 292-1446+//
RETRIEVE IN FULL BEGIN BEGIN BEGIN BEGIN BEGIN BEGIN BEGIN

Proper Time: See Codex//Postevent record. Something terrible has happened, we have blown part of the ship. Three dead, we have lost port pontoon and program, hatch seared at the console room, Damage Control has secured the ship, we are on auxiliary. I don't think they had a chance. There just wasn't any warning. SciCom reading data, Committee Pilot reading data, I am holding at powerdown but we are screaming—we are still being propelled by the shock—I am going to use that to ride through this sector and use the vanes for what's ahead. What instruments we have now read impact event, unanalyzed interstellar material, data on what we hit must have gone in the blow. My recollections: I was holding vane angle in the lull, taping the log and watching Werhner eat. I felt myself become violently ill, I first thought it was from watching him, then focusing on the panel I saw lull figures then everything going red—instantly, don't know if it was a trick of vision, but the red seemed to sweep the panels right to left along with the first strong jolt I felt even in my bones. I don't remember anything else. I blacked out quickly, Werhner says that happened to him, too. It happened so incredibly fast, falling, my perceptions seemed to become detached, then a chill, as if I were diving into darkness. When I came to, I had a gash on the heel of my hand—and this is the strangest thing—it had coagulated. I mean almost healed. It must have been a vane trigger key I fell against, or a whole row. I immediately began resetting instruments, we were just getting auxiliary, when I noticed Werhner lying in a pool of vomit, coming around. Then the rescue attempt. There were only small fragments. Trace. The bodies, the debris, must have just been blown away, vaporized. The ship is responding well, under full control, but we still have no program and damn near lost. Repeat, I am going to retain propulsion from the shock to ride through the weather ahead, we are just getting navigation. When we blew there was nothing showing, absolutely nothing, other than that lull, that zero condition. Nothing.

Werhner is lying on his back, staring at the ceiling in the cottage we have been assigned on Guam. The air is heavy, the light trade winds ripe. He is still wearing his bathing suit. Sweat beads on his chest, runs as he raises himself on his elbow.

"Somebody went through my things," he says. "Somebody went through your things. Nothing missing, but somebody was in here."

I have just returned from another series of encephalograms, kinesthograms, redundant examinations. My torpor dissipates. I fold through my clothes, my books, my papers. . . . "What the hell?" The cover of Dean's *Deep Space Transpositions* is creased; my clothes are in disarray.

Werhner is sitting on the edge of the cot now, popping a pinkish pill into his mouth, swallowing it without water.

"I'm going to get out of here," I tell him. "This is too much. We've been here three weeks."

"Cooper's the only one who's left the base," Werhner says flatly. "I don't know what the hell is going on—these goons spend half their time questioning each other about procedure, the whole dome crew is still here on Guam—Tamashiro, Levsky, Dawes. I think . . . Look, Rawley, I

CHAPTER ONE: RECOVERY / 11

think they're trying to set us up, to stick the blow on *us*. What did your tests show?"

"Nothing abnormal. The same readings as last week. And the week before. And the day after we landed."

"Still having those nightmares?"

"Werhner," I say, "they go away. *This* is a nightmare, this place. Who can live this way? The same questions, steamed food, and look at that cot, that cot's killing my back. I'm going to get out of here."

"Me, too," Werhner says—he is picking up his diving mask and snorkel and fins. "To the reef? Utama Bay?"

"Not now. I've got something to do."

"No swim? Gonna watch the vidi?"

"I wish I were flying," I tell him. "I didn't think I'd ever miss it, but I do now. I need to get out of this place."

"Good luck." He smiles sardonically.

CHAPTER 2
Welcome to
thePleasureTube

light sensuous sauna	fantasy co-op
lubricious service personnel	foods of the world
aquaplease paradise garden	tactile videon

THE PLEASURE TUBE@

reserve now	fourteen days and nights
a world of your own	twenty-eight to two-eighty credits
orgo-toto	three separate program classes

CONTINUOUS MOVEMENT

LasVenus	suborbital/deep space
LA SoCal	olde earthe/moonloop

TRIP TO THE SUN

risk venture vector	symphonic synesthetic harmonics
the EnergyWest grand prix	megastars in sidereal concert
NoAm biosphere reserve	SoPac tropical reserve

TOTAL HOLOGRAM

tactile reflexive   transcendental sense flight   the world's only

TOTAL HOLOGRAM

our service is pleasure//your pleasure our service

reserve//lie back//relax

tubes daily   thePleasureTube corp.@
l.a. trans-port   a division of EnergyWest

106PLEASURETUBE
//dial from any codex terminal//
106PLEASURETUBE

item 14: If you have only recently learned of thePleasureTube, how did you do so?

☐ nat. videon   ☐ travel agent

☐ automag   ☒ other
                        (enter)

                     leave programmer
                     SciCom rec area
                     SciCom, Guam

item 15: Your PleasureTube credits will come from which account?

☐ prog. vacation   ☐ personal savings

☒ GTR   ☐ gift or employee
                        bonus

item 16: Please enter your beta function code in the boxes provided below:

| 2 | 9 | 2 | F | L | T | V | N | E | N | G | | | | |

our service is pleasure // your pleasure our service

®thePleasureTube corp.

Movement itself has made me feel better—and for the last few minutes more exhilarated than I have been since we danced back into the silvery upper atmosphere with our microweather show a month ago, the tenuous landing of our lame ship. I can't say much for the lower atmosphere of the continent, it is on the brownish side of yellow, but now in descent I can see L.A. through the window rolling from hill to hill, its traffic pattern elegant and intestinal from our altitude, its air light haze beneath its dome. My hand throbs as we lose altitude quickly, the stretched skin of the old scar, hidden in the healing of the new cut, changing cabin pressure.

Werhner is spooked, too—in the month back on Guam he's left his data entirely to others and now just drifts all the time, psychologically and physically. He spends his days diving around the reef—not fishing or collecting shells—just floating around, swimming past the breakers at Utama Bay and coming in slowly only when the light is almost gone. I told him he should come along, but he said no, he was on too high a dosage. He wasn't about to go through what I did, and even if he had, there was no guarantee they would have let him go.

My guess is that he's out there right now, suspended in the blue-green water. I wonder if we're doing such different things after all. That's ironic—all the trouble I went through, those obtuse bastards.

As I pass through X-ray and security a bored Oriental asks to see my papers. When he spots my green card, he waves me through without looking at my ticket. Nor does he open my bag—my one leather bag. I've only brought a few sets of casual clothes—old blue flight clothes, mostly—I intend to relax. One blonde woman, she looks about thirty, has eight bags. When I ask her what she is carrying, her broad face flushes and she laughs; finally she says clothes, mostly, some tennis gear, wig racks, magazines, cosmetics. I wind up helping her guide her luggage on a cart.

I hadn't realized the Tube was so large—this terminal occupies an entire wing of the Trans-Port. Crowded, all kinds of people, some as young as eighteen, others are eighty. I see a number of very attractive women with men, both sexes in jump suits. Some of the women are wearing tight leather skirts and halters; this must be the latest fashion for women trim enough. The blonde I'm walking with is perhaps ten pounds too heavy for the pastel leather outfit she has on; she is attractive, though, in a fleshy way. I wonder if her nervousness is sexual, like mine, or simply the anxiety of travel. Her luggage is new, covered all over with broad rainbows. I like it and tell her so, her face opens with the flattery, and I ask if she'll have some free time tonight on the ship.

She giggles. "I'm paired," she says. "I'm meeting Tonio at my gate, we're almost there."

"Paired?" I say, braking the luggage cart to a stop.

"Aren't you? Not even on your first night? Tonio's an old friend, but everybody..."

"I don't know," I tell her. Then I say: "That should be interesting."

"It's on your ticket," she tells me.

I show her my ticket. My reservation impresses her; I'm going first class on government money. But her forehead wrinkles.

"It doesn't list anyone," she says. "Still," she goes on breathlessly, apparently not knowing what to make of me, "you'll have fun."

A tall, thin man with angular shoulders and a sheaf of black hair is making his way toward us against the stream of people. It must be Tonio—as she sees him she puts her hand on my arm.

"Look," she says, "I've got an idea. Let's do a fantasy co-op some night on the ship."

"What?"

"Just give me your codex number. I'll get in touch."

I recite my codex, she closes her eyes to remember, then guides the cart away.

"My name is Erica," she calls back.

"Rawley Voorst," I say, raising my hand to wave. But she is too quickly submerged in the crowd, disappears. Tonio is up on his toes.

I have to change levels, backtrack through a lounge concourse, then walk a kilometer or so before I arrive at the gate coded on my ticket. Alongside a squinting young man, a tall, gorgeous black girl, whose eyes are so

distinctly green that I can see their color from the end of
the line, is behind a counter punching ticket codes against
space as the young man checks in luggage. Passengers
leave the counter following pastel stripes on the floor. I
loiter in line for ten minutes, shoving my flight bag ahead
with my foot.

Finally the black girl begins punching my ticket into a
terminal. She looks up at me, narrows her eyes, punches it
in again. The green of her eyes is the green of the deep sea
off Guam, jade pale, striking, accentuated by iridescent
eye shadow. She really is lovely, the loveliest woman I've
seen in the terminal. I watch her fingers: thin, long; her
fingernails are a beige two tones lighter than the café au
lait of her skin. She wears a silver name tag bearing the
name Collette.

"There'll be a slight delay in boarding your section,"
she tells me with a practiced smile, suggesting in the same
breath that I wait in the VIP lounge, first door to the right.

I ask her what's wrong.

"We're having an equipment malfunction in your
section. They're replacing a unit."

"What unit?"

"The malfunctioning unit," she says tightly.

When I tell her that she talks exactly like a computer
terminal, I can see a vein jump in her neck, she tells me
that's all she knows. I am annoyed only because until now
there has been no break in my motion—she is more
embarrassed than angry.

"But you don't exactly look like a terminal," I laugh,
"not at all."

She shakes her head and her smile is spontaneous. Her
face is aristocratic, her skin healthy. She has large eyes
and long lashes that are real.

"Next, please," she says, still smiling.

The light through the lounge window/wall is washed,
watery. It seems like night because of the artificial quality
of the light outside, but that may be distortion from the
dome. Nothing to read; I am alone in the lounge. I wonder
if it is because my leave was entered only yesterday that I

am not "paired" for the trip; wonder what that means. Will my company be holograms? I wonder, too, if the blonde woman I met in the terminal will get in touch, will remember my codex. I should have asked her number as well. But then she had a friend.

The lounge is a room larger than the twin studio on Guam, though really just a room. But it's luxurious, especially to a man used to bare floors and cots. Velvet couches, a small kitchen/bar off a divider on the rear wall, paintings on the side walls, one a massive Rubens that astonishes me because it looks real. Mirrors cover part of the ceiling, this entire wall a window overlooking the space shuttles on the tarmac. I fix myself Zubrowka on ice and watch the traffic from a reclining chair. The heel of my hand is bothering me, throbbing with the rhythm of my blood. I hold it to the icy glass of vodka until I feel nothing but the cold.

The girl from the ticket counter comes through the door when my glass is almost empty. "I'm sorry," she says. "I called for staff, but we're running behind. They're still moving the new unit in."

"What unit?" I say to tease her.

"We'll be boarding at the first opportunity."

"Computer," I say again to tease her. But she turns to leave and I have to quickly take it back. "No, I didn't mean that."

She relents and rests her back against the wall next to a painting of two women lost in an embrace. "Look," she says, "you have an hour at least. VIP section is always late, the last to board. There's all that loading—you can't imagine all the things they bring on. You're anomalous for VIP, you know; usually we have managers, administrators, older men or women."

"I had an overload of leave time," I tell her. "They said anything goes."

"Lucky you."

"I suppose. You look a little tired. Is it that busy every day out there?"

"It's getting toward the end of my shift." She smiles

again. She is a high-cheeked woman of extraordinary bearing. The tight cocoa halter she wears outlines the curve of full, dome-shaped breasts, and I wonder if she isn't padded as part of her uniform. Her legs aren't only possible, though—long, finely muscled, sleek above her pearl-colored shoes; she has a dancer's legs.

"Do you mind if I walk around the terminal?"

She pushes herself loosely from the wall, then shakes her head. "No, you'd better not leave. I punched your whole program, your birth date seemed wrong, I thought we'd have to rewrite your ticket. You've been away for a really long time. You should just stay here."

"I'm not a child," I tell her.

"So I've noticed." She smiles. "But there's plenty you don't know." She comes toward me, bends down, and for an instant I think she is going to touch my knee. But what she does is pull up the inlaid top of the elegant, low wooden table I am sitting by. Inside—I laugh when I see it—is an entire computer console, miniaturized, with ivory keys. She punches a few buttons, guitar music fills the room, and the large glass wall becomes slightly darker. My chair reclines and the whole room seems to soften.

"Just relax," she smiles. "It won't be all that long."

I think about the blonde woman I met on the lower level of the terminal and recall a vague, fleeting familiarity about her. Will I see her again? What is it she wants to do? I assume anything goes on this ship, but I had better be discreet. The ticket agent was right; there are some things I don't know.

I do know this, though: this waiting, this lack of motion, magnifies the anxiety which I came all this way to smother and forget. Outside, the daylight is failing and ship lights, lane lights, begin to twinkle and glow. The view from the window brings to mind the array from the Daedalus dome I so often stood watching; the blue-gray shade of the glass is so like the color of the dome when we were cruising that the sight through it is uncanny. And yet we do not move. I slump back into the chair, close my eyes—a lushly comfortable chair whose designer must have had an affection for the small of the back.

In my half sleep I am again at the console of the Daedalus. In the stillness I am again at the lull, an incredible lull so motionless that I can feel the blood coursing through my veins. My mind shunts on, so trained by Taylor's questioning; I recall shutting down and hoping for drift to pick up energy from the front that visually howls on the starboard side of the dome. Nothing shows on the instruments in the lull. My hands sweat. Motionless, I feel queasy, my stomach confused by the sudden end to turbulence. The memory of Werhner's fork dripping sauce, an odor, the odor of curry—there is a shudder in the ship—I turn to grimace at Werhner. He has disappeared. Beyond his station the port hatch to SciCom hangs open like a tongue, through the opening, not the blue-green glow of SciCom computers or pale-blue-uniformed technicians working or the air lock beyond them, but deep space, blue-black space—there is a shock wave—in my body, through the ship. Hurtling at me is a spinning, growing ball of light, the howling sight of a raging sun....

I awake perspiring, startled; instinctively I stroke the heel of my hand. Through the waiting-lounge window the landing lights of a shuttle sever the deep night, sweep toward me, turn away. I sigh and walk off my anxiety, wish we would board and move.

The girl returns, the door hushes closed behind her.

"Ten minutes," she says pleasantly, her voice with a different edge than it had when I first heard her speak. Her hands are at the back of her neck undoing a braid in her hair—she has redone her makeup, I think; her face looks fresher, more natural. As she shakes her hair loose it falls in long curls to her shoulders. "Free at last," she says.

"Time to go home?"

"Time to stop working, anyway." She joins me at the window overlooking the trans-port runways. "You should see home, I live next to a freeway." She, too, looks out over the tarmac and the winking, high-rise city far beyond it. On the tarmac the hulking fuselages of the shuttles wait in trainlike rows. One larger ship, which I had seen attached to a booster, is taxiing toward the far runway whose blue lights stretch away, converging into nothingness.

"You're one of those rare people," she tells my reflection in the window—I can see her looking at me—"who go to the stars." I look directly at her and her vision shifts, she looks out to the night sky. She slowly spreads her arms and stretches them above her head. "To fly," she says, and she turns to me, "to fly like a god."

Her halter has risen and I can see her naked belly, a flat expanse. She closes her eyes and hugs herself. When she opens them I look out at the taxiing shuttle, a little embarrassed.

"Don't you find me attractive?" she asks; she has a kind of nervous glow. She spreads her arms again, and as I watch her she brings them down as a dancer might, her hands coming across her body—they seem to linger for an instant at her breasts.

I tell her, "Yes, of course. Very." I laugh and add, "Collette," only then notice that her name tag is gone.

"You remembered my name," she says, smiling broadly. "You really are rare. I went through your program, everywhere you've been."

She moves even closer to me, or I to her, and I am near enough to see the glistening of moisture on her lips, to sense a weight to her breathing.

"Listen," she says, "we have some time."

I want to look at my watch, my wrist naked. I remember that my instructions were to pack the watch in my luggage. "Time . . . for . . ."

"Here," she says, tugging gently at my arm to draw me against her. She has soft lips, her lipstick is flavored cinnamon.

I am grinning, my mouth has gone dry, her warm body is pressed against mine, and my hands pull flat against the small of her back. "Can we do this?" I wonder, half to myself. "What if . . . ?" My hands are on her bottom, she is silky and firm at once. Her curves are breathtaking, as if beneath my hands her shape conforms to a dream I've never quite had but now want.

"If we're quick we won't get caught," she whispers. "Before you go."

When I kiss her again, her tongue outlines my lips. I can feel her body trembling, no dream but alive. She pushes me away, smiling.

"Wait," she says quietly, unbuttoning her skirt. "I want to show you something." Her skirt falls to the carpet. She wears tiny black panties whose lower edges she traces with the tip of each index finger before she slips them off, saying as she lets them fall on her skirt, she is giggling, "Part of my uniform—they make ticket agents wear satin so we feel sexy. I . . ."

She doesn't let me undress. She straddles me as I lie back on the recliner. Her halter falls open and I see her moving breasts, full and real, her rhythm and mine accelerating, like the whine of the space shuttle thrusting off beyond the darkening window in a blur of light and motion, lifting higher in the blackness of the sky.

Moments later I am waiting for the energy to move again, the quease entirely gone from my stomach. I think Collette is moving my belt in a notch, but then she says, "Welcome to the PleasureTube," and I see that her hands are at my waist, adjusting a safety belt—no, a liftoff rig.

"To the . . . ?" I can feel the jiggle of hydraulics, the entire *lounge* is moving. Lights through the window slip by, some disappear—we are being moved into a ship.

Collette strokes my forehead and offers me a drink that looks like orange juice. "Take some of this," she says.

"I, mmm, don't think I need . . ."

"Take it," she says; "you'll feel better."

The lounge thumps into position, loose equipment rattles, she giggles and kisses me. She puts her tongue between my teeth, then moves away toward her clothing. I want to say thank you, but my mouth is going numb with a feeling that is spreading through my body. I am blacking out even as I feel the pressure of a vast and tidal acceleration.

•　　　•　　　•

I am asleep but then vaguely aware of a sensation in my fingers and palms. I inhale the rich odor of gardenias and come awake enough to make out Collette kneeling beside the recliner, massaging my hands. Through ship noise I can hear Bartók violins—my own favorite from the Daedalus library.

"Time to get up?" I say, though the room is dim, and no light comes through the window. The ship vibrates with the low howl of sustained acceleration.

"No," Collette says. "I'm going to bed. I just wanted to tuck you in."

I rise on an elbow. "What are you doing here? Are you coming along?"

"I'm your service." She grins. "Lie back."

"I'm not sleepy."

"You've passed through five time zones and you surely are sleepy. The computer and I know all your body rhythms. Just listen to me."

"My service?"

"Mmmm. You like to touch, too. I think we're going to enjoy each other. I like you," she says, her hand drifting up, stroking my temple. "The way your hair curls here at your ears."

The lounge has changed—my recliner doubled into a bed, the couches rearranged, draperies along the window/wall. A light illuminates the large painting of pink, fleshy women in an embrace.

"Do I—I mean, is this my cabin?"

Only when she puts her hand on my shoulder to make me lie back do I realize that I am naked. I inhale deeply, and the rich, sweet odor of gardenias fills my lungs.

"Drink this," she says, passing me the orange juice again.

"Where are we going?"

"You'll see tomorrow. Where doesn't matter, does it?"

For the moment I can't think of an answer. I close my eyes as Collette makes me promise to tell her stories from my trip, where the Daedalus expedition went, what we saw on survey. Her asking me, the Bartók, this peculiar motion, tug at my concentration, and for a frightening moment I feel myself on the precipice of my nightmare on the Daedalus, my mind's eye beginning to shape the awesome figure of a howling, whirling sun....

As I struggle for consciousness I breathe an odor of Guam, tropically rich, ripening. Guam: the drowsy questions, the limpid air. Knuth smiling at my requests for leave, not a smile of sympathy, but a smile of collusion with a pattern that will not let me go. I cannot rise past the same numbness I felt weighing on me then.

"The exact position of the thrusters?"

"No readings on any of the mag sensors, Rawley? Let's go over them one by one."

"Don't blame me, Rawley, this is a slow process. This is how it has to be."

"Let's consider analogies, Voorst. What was your personal relationship with each of the other members of the dome crew? How would you describe your feelings toward the Committee Pilot? Let's begin with them."

I feel about them as I feel about you, runs through my mind. *Don't you ever act?*

"Dead in Houston," Taylor says finally to a question about Cooper one day, his voice flat and even, his gold lighter hissing as he pauses to light his pipe. "Cached his drugs." The news of Cooper's suicide slices through my numbness like a razor through my flesh, Cooper perhaps psychotic, I believe, but suicide doesn't seem right; and Taylor had known for two days.

I can feel anxiety rising as a presence within me, my heart is pounding, and Yes, I want to say to Collette, it does matter where, I want to wake....

Then I feel her silky hand slipping across my chest, a satin sheet pulled across my midsection, her lips beginning to nibble at my thighs.

The image of the cold, howling sun, the memories of Cooper howling at Committee Pilot from Damage Control, of Guam, recede from my mind and I am transported. I smile a smile of satisfaction which Collette could only partially translate, as the last music I remember from the lull becomes, not a vivid memory, but simply present Bartók and the piercing sweetness of violins.

"Yes," I whisper, running my hand through the lush softness of her hair, "I like to touch." The tropical odor refines itself, it is hers. Gardenias are everywhere.

CHAPTER 3
Biosphere Reserve

	ITINERARY// FIRST-CLASS PASSAGE//	Prog.	2ndCoord.
DA1	WELCOME AND FLYAWAY	---	I/o-0926
DA2	FLT TO OE//DTRIP//LAYOVER$_{2,3}$	bld	i/f-1021
DA3	BIOS RESERVE//MOVALLEY	bld	i/f-1951
DA4	SYNESTHETIC HARMON//VIDEON SPEC	bld	i/f-cont
DA5	FANT CO-OP//EPICUREAN CONSENSUS	bld	i/f-cont
DA6	ARR LASVENUS//CLUB EROTICA	bld	i/f-0900
DA7	LAYOVER//RISK VENTURE VECT	bld	cont
DA8	RISK FEST$_{2,3}$ //SIDEREAL CONC	bld	cont
DA9	UKIYOE FLYAWAY	bld	I/o-0623
DA10	SENS SEVEN SPEC//MOONLOOP	bld	i/f-cont
DA11	SINS SEVEN SPEC//VIETAHITI	bld	i/f-cont
DA12	AQUAPLEASE//HOLO PREP	bld	i/f-cont
DA13	HOLO PROG//TOTAL HOLO$_4$	bld	i/f-cont
DA14	TRIP TO THE SUN	bl-	i/f-----

CONTINUOUS VIDEON PROGRAMMING
THE PLEASURE TUBE IS AN EXPERIENCE//INDIVIDUAL
   VARIATIONS ARE COMMON AND PRECISE DESTINA-
   TIONS VARY//CONSULT YOUR SERVICE FOR DETAILS
2, INTERSECTION ITIN CLASS 2
3, INTERSECTION ITIN CLASS 3
4, MEDICAL CLEARANCE REQUIRED

OUR SERVICE IS PLEASURE//YOUR PLEASURE OUR SERVICE

LIE BACK // RELAX

thePleasureTube corp.@   106codex

Light in the unit. My body slides, stretching on satin sheets, muscle pulling against muscle in an envelope of warmth—stretch my back and a few cot-twisted vertebrae quietly pop into place, finally straightening out.

Morning light. Through the window/wall the sun is hovering on the arc of an horizon. It looks to be earth a hundred or more kilometers away. The entire window/wall holds a planet's arc in two separating horizons, dark below, bright on a line above. The sun shoots orange-yellow fans through the atmosphere—yellow-brown fans.

"Something bothered you, didn't it?"

I couldn't speak if I wanted to; a thermometer is beneath my tongue.

"You came right up through the drug again. Nightmare?"

A sequence, I think; which? *Key on a color,* Werhner says, *you remember everything.*

The girl—Collette—draws a last drop of blood into a vial. I am in program for tests, final readings to establish my circadian rhythms for the trip, my own day, she tells me. Another way to say proper time.

Remember everything? Or is it a memory at all? Werhner also says that dreams are predictions. The woman frozen in space, the whirlpooling sun: these are not simple memories, they are not sequential points in a time line. My teeth grate the glass of the thermometer, my tongue slides along its side. I remember...yesterday, Collette on my thighs. And now she is wearing a light green satin robe, barefoot. I am still slightly groggy.

Collette finally slides the thermometer from my mouth and gently tugs at the tiny suction electrodes on my wrist, massages the puckered skin. "Anyway," she says, "you've got good figures so far. You're a healthy man, you have healthy appetites, you can pretty much do as you like. You're cleared for total hologram, no restrictions."

I ask her what a total hologram is, exactly. She tells me

it's a holographic projection system whose image is actual, substantial, to the user, not just an optical effect. There is a feedback connection with the user's neurology.

"I'm willing to try anything," I say. Like Werhner's water, the recliner module gives, floats with my weight. When I woke at first light, I remembered no dream, felt only the floating in space, slept again.

"Do you want to talk about it?" Collette asks, adjusting the fall of her robe at her knee.

"About . . . ?"

"What made your EEG go bump in the night."

She sounds like a member of the screening committee back on Guam. What I want is breakfast. "I'm fine," I tell her. "I haven't felt so well in weeks."

"Then how's your appetite for breakfast?"

I laugh at how she anticipates me. "Ravenous," I say.

A sweet juice, purplish and thick, *guava*, Collette suggests. An egg on thick bacon and a scone. The mild bite of a sauce balances the buttery slide of the egg. Melon, cheese, coffee. I ask Collette for another egg, she answers there are only so many eggs in the world, I eat scones and butter, drink glass after glass of guava juice.

Already the cabin seems familiar—perhaps because its spaces analogue starship quarters. This recliner module is set against a side wall, halfway between a dark velvet couch and the window/wall. Like a coffee table, the inlaid table which opens into an ivory-keyed computer and codex terminal sits before the couch.

The rich furnishings are washed now in the atmosphereless spacelight. On the wall opposite the window/wall the fleshy pinks of the Rubens are radiant, and the painting's stark, black frame casts a rhomboid shadow on the wall's soft, textured surface. I notice only now a subtle geometry in the dark brown rug—hexagons with shared lines. The figures are the barest tone lighter—the precise shade of the draperies—and outline a reversed dome. Ghostly, soft, optically active. Off this lounge, or living-room arrangement, the kitchen/bar behind a divider of shelving modules glows with the spun-steel finish of instrumentation and machinery. I can see Collette through the divider, holding a dish in one hand, licking a cream-colored sauce from two fingers of the other.

Werhner, I think, what are you doing? Taylor, what questions are you imagining for me now?

I almost lose myself in the bath: its ceiling and walls are mirrored, a lush green rug is on the floor, and the fixtures are cast in the shape of seashells. The sink is a giant, opening scallop, its surface iridescent, the john a tun shell with its operculum hinged. The shower water has a faint aromatic oil added to it, as rich as cinnamon but lighter. The shower head pulsates, massages as it runs, with a half-dozen different rhythms. I could spend my two weeks standing in that one spot.

Collette is laughing at a chart she is showing me:

MEDEX // CODEX292VOORST // CIRCADIAN RHYTHM
INTERNAL DESYNCH = − 2.7

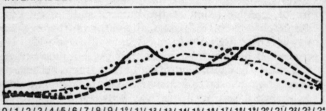

0 / 1 / 2 / 3 / 4 / 5 / 6 / 7 / 8 / 9 / 1⁰/ 1¹/ 1²/ 1³/ 1⁴/ 1⁵/ 1⁶/ 1⁷/ 1⁸/ 1⁹/ 2⁰/ 2¹/ 2²/ 2³/ 2⁴

INDEX
EFF/ACT ━━━━━━━━
SENSU ••••••••••••••
HORM ━ ━ ━ ━ ━ ━ ━ ━
COGNIT ------------

Not at the chart, it turns out, only at the first peak on the red-orange line.

I ask her what it means. She says, "I'll show you in a minute."

I am laughing, too—was I asleep again? Werhner wouldn't believe this. Collette is my luck, she is what's so pleasant here.

I tell her that the smoothness of this ship is uncanny, that speed compresses otherwise undetectable forces to make a kind of weather, a series of fronts, turbulent, there's always pitch and yaw. A smoothness here, as if traveling some other way. I can feel our motion only as a slight vibration, see it in the concentric rings on the surface of my coffee.

"Can you feel it . . . here?" she asks as she takes my right hand and guides it toward her heart, releases my hand at her breast, her nipple stiff under satin.

"Very sexy," I say. "But all I feel is, ummm, a pounding heart."

"Mmmm," she giggles, "that's what it does. That orange line signals an early peak in your hormone level. I can't get over it, you turn *me* on. What a luxury."

Beneath her robe, Collette has the odor of strawberries; the sweet, piquant taste of strawberries is on her shoulder. She slides alongside me—satin on satin sheets. I stroke her lower back, send my hand flat over the firm swell of her bottom. I can feel her muscles tighten and move beneath my hands, her tongue sliding warm on my lips.

She is naked beneath her robe. As I enter her she uses its folds to surround me. The sensation spreads throughout my body, sliding into satin, sliding into her. The perfect smoothness of her skin.

After lunch. We are gliding powerdown in a slow trajectory of apparent descent, perhaps thirty kilometers above a landscape visible through the window/wall. The macroweather is flat, and only a few scattered clouds float over the mountains—the long, vast range of gray mountains that stretch along the horizon. Toward what may be a coast in one direction, the atmosphere there the brownish side of yellow, the surface suggesting an elaborate quilt of cultivation. Directly beneath us the rising topography of foothills—they must be deep green beneath the atmosphere's filtering effect. I hear Collette saying *daytrip* brightly, she is at machinery in the kitchen/bar, tidying up after the cold crab she served. I have been studying the landscape for ten minutes, idling over the last of the Jamaican coffee—Blue Mountain, Collette named it. Have we been continuously suborbital? Daytrip?

"I never saw anything like this. Where are we going?"

"Biosphere reserve. Beautiful, isn't it?"

I watch the foothills, try to sort out the different shades of green. Even in the thickening atmosphere this flight remains velvet-smooth, as if cushioned, its motion translated now into a barely perceptible sway of the heavy draperies pulled back along the window/wall. At the juncture with the ceiling the sun flashes, recedes: slight yaw. I notice for the first time a series of fine lines suspended in the material of the window, lines as fine as human hair. Perhaps that is how the window became a filter earlier today.

Collette comes to the window. She is dressed in her skirt and halter of the day before, cocoa leather, gold PleasureTube insignia—she is pulling the strap of a shoulder bag over her right shoulder.

"You never saw anything like this?"

"Not on the expedition," I tell her. "Nothing quite like this. You can tell those greens are conifer; there's botany down there."

"It's a biosphere reserve. That's where we're going to lay over."

"Do we disembark?"

"For two four-hour trips," she says. "Today and tomorrow. You'll like it here. When we arrive at the terminal, follow the signs to the tramrun. Take the A tram from the terminal, exit at Slot Nine. I'll be waiting for you there. We're due in just an hour; there's really only one way they'll let you go with the ticket."

Collette's hair is pulled up, backlit in a kind of aura. She hands me a green card, the ticket.

"I have to check in," she says. "Is there anything I can do before I go?"

"Do you have a minute?"

"Sure," she says.

I sit her beside me on the large velvet couch and open

the inlaid table setting before it; the console is half-sized only in the button shape of its controls. I switch PowerOn, punch out three sequences in a simple Retrieve/Inquiry code, Uniform Ship Program. Collette is looking out the window; she smells of heather now. I am getting a blur of flashing numbers on the digital readout bar, just a blur.

"All right," I say. "Where did I go wrong?" I have a print light, positive readout function—but I can't get the display to hold.

"Well..." she muses, looking at the console. "You're holding something big. You need more than digital. God, for a Flight Vane Engineer, Voorst, you don't know much." Collette punches BACK/PRINT/FUNCTION, then a bar marked VID.

The window/wall darkens instantly; the landscape blurs, is obliterated. The window/wall becomes a screen, not projected upon, but emanating a huge, dense list of codex numbers followed by program codes, now the brightest field in the cabin, all other lights have dimmed.

"What happened to the wall?" I ask.

"That's the videon. There'll be a big show day four, after we leave the reserve. Then every fourth day."

"The videon." I stare for a moment longer, my eyes adjusting as the smaller figures focus.

"It reads the computer for certain things, visual display."

"You know how to make it work. That's resourceful."

"I also know that's the ship's manifest." Collette smiles. "Looking for someone?"

"Uh..." I start to answer, hesitate. I can't even find my own codex, there are a thousand listed. "Just looking."

"Then look at something that moves." Collette punches in an entry and the screen changes to display a life-size group of people in bright yellow body stockings moving in unison on mats; they are doing stretching exercises—an exercise class?

Blonde woman in the front row.

"Say, Collette..."

Collette looks at me evenly, her eyebrows raised, the

trace of a smile tightening her lips. I have a flash of embarrassment, feel strangely free-floating. One of the women on the screen is Erica. Standing in the front row, doing leg exercises. Standing on one leg, bringing her other foot up to her knee. She has a unique exaggerated pelvic thrust; there is a beatific smile on her face, faint perspiration on her forehead.

Collette is telling me that I am seeing the VID/ACTION sub of her program. "Some people have them made up. Punch codex plus 302, then integrate back to VID."

I am watching Erica pulling her knee to her chest; I am blushing, I think. "How did you know about her?"

"She put in your codex this morning," Collette says, getting up. "Let's just say it's part of my job." She is adjusting the shoulder strap of her sagging leather bag; she is leaving. "Line A, Slot 9," she says with a wry smile. "You can't miss it."

The computer works on Uniform Ship Program for major functions, translates from its own cybernetic language for internal systems into a half-dozen major languages, very well engineered. I find there's no local file under my codex number, then inquire and find that local vane angle confirms touchdown in forty-two minutes. I try to relax by setting up a tennis game through the console. Two sets and I lose interest; an overhand to an unstable backhand is the obvious key.

I punch through Collette's program into her personnel file, find I can retrieve limited access material on Collette by using Werhner's trick, coding the system in a classic Fibonacci Series—1,1,2,3,5,8.... She begins//27 CORETTA KING SCHOOL L.A. SoCal//31 UCAL BERKELEY NoCal P.E. M.S.//SOCIOBIONICS CORP TRAINEE.... I look through with a kind of unfocused intensity, why I am not certain, I am slightly unsettled. No real hint of any SciCom connection, but I am beginning to think I might have seen Collette before, just as I've seen Erica, where? Is it her face? That's what it is, I think, not so much her as the possibility. Strange how that unsettles me.

BIOSPHERE RESERVE

ENTRANCE BY TICKET
ONLY
thePleasureTube corp.
                    permittee
**A LINE
TICKET**

"a pleasuring ground for the benefit and
enjoyment of people" Act 72875-83-4621
NoAm Congress

1/remain on tram, NaturBus, or within pavilion
    parameter.
2/open fires strictly prohibited.
3/retain all dispoz units.
4/return to ship by 1800.
5/passengers must strictly adhere to
    regulations outlined by service personnel.

// Along with Runnell Island in the Melanesian Archipelago, the island of
Dominica between Guadeloupe and Martinique, and the Wadi Howar in
northwest Sudan, this NoAm biosphere reserve preserves an Edenlike
ecosphere off limits to human manipulation // its metabolism is monitored
continuously and anomalies corrected by trained personnel // respect and
enjoy your reserve //

"NoAm's NATURAL PLANT ROOM"

Through the crowded disembarkation chute, into the
rough-hewn wood, post, and beam terminal, most of the
passengers head toward waiting NaturBuses; that
appears to be the third-class program. People are nervous
at being off the ship; even here the air is noticeably
different—once outdoors among the tramrun sheds, there
is a kind of sweet rot to it. On the small A trams there are
only first-class passengers. The tram I board is empty in
the rear, where I sit, except for a heavyset, well-dressed,
European-looking man. Forward a small group laughs at
an older woman's story; she had the wrong luggage, didn't
know until she opened the first case and found a grope
suit. I'll have to find out what a grope suit is.

I sit by a rectangular window and watch our rubber-
tire progress, first uphill, then down through faintly

groomed, quite real, thickening woods. I lay my hand flat on the spun steel of the tram body; it feels queerly unreal, or I do, suddenly moving through these woods under a hazy sun. Insects in the overgrowth, reflections from the guardrail along the tramrun, no breeze. I see a small animal clinging to the lowest branch of a tree as we pass. Squirrel, moving, alive.

Slot 7 is a pavilion where the forward group disembarks. Slot 9, a kilometer beyond, deposits me at a simulated stone walk where Collette is waiting. She's wearing white shorts and a halter top. We follow the walk eighty meters to a small prefab structure, half porch with a large plastic table, plastic/wicker chairs. There is a small brazier in the corner; inside, a cooking unit, a refrigeration unit, cabinets.

The rest house—what Collette calls it—is protected by woods on three sides. We are on a gentle rise on rocky ground. Behind us the land slopes uphill to a series of granite bedrock faces which rise from the ground; around the base of the nearest is apparently the tramrun. Ahead the landscape runs downhill and opens in a widening swath to a meadow, a vast, parklike space, again only barely groomed, perhaps three or four kilometers off. I can just make out a series of pavilions on the meadow's far side, perhaps eight kilometers away.

Since the tram whined away, the air has seemed soundlessly light. The absence of machine hum recalls the beach at Utama Bay on Guam; this kind of stillness is unnerving. I pick out the possible sound of wind in the taller trees, insects, and the faint songs of birds. The sun is a sun of late earth afternoon, bright but hazed over; its light falls into the woods in patches the size of children. In the woods the greenery collides, tumbles over itself. I feel both tranquil here and apprehensive—how can that be?

Collette and I drink champagne and pick at a whole salmon, poached, cold. The salmon is delicate and clean-tasting, the champagne light. She knows of a strawberry patch just downhill, we are going to pick dessert.

● ● ●

The strawberries grow near the edge of the sparser woods to our left, downhill. Small strawberries, but they are exceptional: bright red, tantalizing in texture, ripe, sweet, firm. We eat them out of our hands, propped up against a thick tree, sitting on the soft loam.

"Perfect," I say. "Paradise."

"To me," Collette says, putting strawberries in a ceramic can to take back to the ship, "this is as perfect as a place can be. We'll stop again at a tropical reserve, but there's too much to do there to actually relax. This place... There aren't many people who get the chance to be here, you know. I have a plant room at home, a small one. I wish I had this. It's so peaceful—you're right, perfect."

"Just like my last twenty-four hours," I say. "Everything's seemed... to click into place. Spooky. The first music I heard in the cabin? My space music, Bartók, I wore out a tape of it once. I must have wanted just that breakfast for a year. And a woman like you. It's as if you remember things I've forgotten I really wanted..."

Collette smiles, passes me a strawberry. "You're a pleasure," she says. "There's something about you, it's your tan, the way you look at me. I'd like to do you any time."

I bite into the fruit and feel its juices pique my tongue. Sweet, sticky, almost tart enough to be dry, but sweet nonetheless. "Mmmm. And that blonde woman. Yet... something about her is familiar."

I lean back on my elbows in the softness of the earth, layers of decaying leaves and loam among thinning vines along the shady edge of the woods, at the foot of this tree. "There are moments," I tell her, "when I don't feel very far from the screening committee that kept me on Guam. Taylor and Knuth; then Birnbaum, Lodge. . . . They think I know something I know I don't."

"A *SciCom* screening committee?" Collette asks, sitting up straight.

"Yes."

"Are you in trouble?"

"Am I?" I ask after a moment. "You tell me."

Collette is reading my face, I am trying to read hers, she sets down the half-filled container. "Not that I'm aware of," she says, moving forward onto her knees. "Well, you're not in any trouble with me."

I shrug and suggest that what data there is on me, she's probably seen.

"I saw the program we retrieved," she says, "and I sure can't recall any screening-committee report." Collette pauses. "But I'll guess. Something happened to you on the expedition, didn't it?"

"To the ship," I tell her after a moment. "We blew part of the ship. Three people died—then there was a suicide."

"My God," Collette says. Could she have known? Her expression denies it utterly; she sees my own pain, I think. No, I've never met her before. I want to tell her what happened; I can feel her sympathy.

"We were tracking energy source off the entry horizon of a black hole, near the Crab. We went as far as anyone's gone. Did you know that?"

"No," she says, blushing a little. "The Crab nebula? That's some way. And a black hole? I'm not really sure..."

"A black hole is an old star that's fallen in on itself, collapsed," I tell her. "It's so dense its own light doesn't escape, so dense its gravity attracts light. The physics is still speculation—one theory has it that within a black hole the laws of physics are reversed, and a traveler, say, becomes trapped—trapped in space, and free in time instead. Another theory has it that each is a throat to another universe, another a loop in time—well, that's all on the other side. I don't want to exaggerate. We were tracking well off an edge. Spinning black holes might be a cost-free energy source, that's why we were tracking. That's where it was that we blew."

"Blew? Out there? My God," Collette says, goes silent for a moment. "How lucky you are to be back, alive and back. There's an investigation?"

"The investigation was finished almost four years ago, out on range. But since I've been back, maybe it's just bureaucracy, it's like thick glue in gears on Guam. They don't want me to leave. At *all*. I've filed a dozen reports, answered every question. But still..."

Collette looks away, she picks at grassy weeds growing among the strawberries. "There's truth to that anywhere, nowadays," she says. "My brother used to say that soon enough nothing will happen. Maybe it's already gotten to the point where there are so many administrative strata to go through that nothing happens, nothing changes. That's the way it seems. An investigation can last forever. But look," she says, turning her palms up, tossing grass into a breeze, "right now you're here. You're traveling first class. People wait months for this, people who can afford it. You came right on. Somebody must be looking out for you."

I push my hand at the soil and run my fingers through—dank, spongy, sweet. I did that myself, I think. I rewrote my program at the military office, punched it through while the wormy program clerk was at morning meditation. Technically I have military status. I had such an overload of leave time I went right out. I wonder if SciCom even knows yet; by now there is nothing they can do. I tell Collette just how it was that I got here.

She looks at me for a long moment. "You really entered your *own* leave program?"

"I was only a member of the Committee Pilot, but I flew the ship," I tell her. "So that was by default. Same thing. As far as I'm concerned, they've defaulted ever since I've gotten back to Guam. They write off the suicide, they're encouraging a friend of mine to kill himself, I think, they don't seem to care. Except they do want to keep their hands on me—I've got that pretty clear."

"And why am I assigned to you?" Collette asks slowly, asks herself. "There's security on the ship, you had to clear it, you may not even have known when you were..."

"The blonde woman...?"

Collette stares at me hard. "She's just one of the things that happen here," she says. "They happen all the time—casual pairs, we call them. I can't conceive that it's anything else; I cannot conceive of the possibility."

I sigh and apologize for the question.

"You don't have to apologize," Collette says quietly. "It's all right with me. You can ask questions if you want to, but if you just let things happen here, it works out just as well. Knowing isn't going to make a difference." She pauses, looks at her still hands, at me. "I live by what's inside a program," she continues. "I don't go any further than that. I live by what's inside. Like coming to this place, eating these strawberries, sitting here with you. I like you."

"Thanks," I say, wondering—am I being entirely fair to her?—if that isn't just what she should say, would say, to anyone? I ask Collette if she felt that way—to live only by what's programmed, no matter what—when she was a kid.

"No." Collette smiles, leans back. "I was going to be a volleyball player, an Olympic volleyball player. Then I was going to fly, as a vane analyst, or... Well, I fly. I wound up one day assigned to do this."

"And that's all right?"

Now Collette shrugs. "The flying I like, the food is good, I'm done by someone almost every day. But, well, the truth is, I usually feel like a nurse. First-class passengers run pretty old."

"That puts my self-image back into perspective." I smile.

"You'll survive."

Collette wants to rub my back. She comes around behind me and massages first the nape of my neck as I look toward the light green meadow. I can feel a slight tightness in my muscles only begin to dissolve. I tell Collette I need some exercise.

"Tomorrow we can take a hike if you want to," she says. "There's a trail right near here. Or you can shoot in the game harvest. Did you ever hunt? There are usually so many people."

"A hike," I say, lying down, my face almost in the strawberries. "I don't want to shoot in a crowd. But don't prelog the trip, let's just see."

I meet the European-looking man on the return tram.

His name, he tells me, is Massimo Giroti—white-bearded, Italian, and a UN Governor in SoAm. He describes himself in a thick accent; he is a large man with steely eyes and an elegant handshake, and seems slightly bored. As the tram hums through the twilight, shadowy woods, Massimo tells me that no, he has not always been an administrator; when he was my age he had been an automobile driver on the world circuit, he had been a champion.

I tell him that I have been on a starship and out of touch because of it; yet his name is familiar somehow.

"Perhaps Fiat Massimo," he says. "They have name a car after me. Although it was never Fiat I drive. It was only Ferrari and Lancia. I drive the last Ferrari. But you were on starship? What position did you do?"

I tell him that I was a Flight Vane Engineer.

"Ah, *sorprendente!*" he says, the lines on his face disappearing, his grin wide. "*Piloto*, pilot, you mean. That is like building the curves and driving them at once, you fly the starship! We are *simpático,* my friend."

He shakes my hand again. I laugh and say that control of the ship we are returning to seems more like building the curves and driving them with a car that had marshmallows for wheels.

He laughs at that, he denies it. It turns out he has ridden the Tube before.

"I suppose it depends on the program they run you through," I say. "I've never seen such tight programs for so many people."

"Ah, like everywhere nowadays—but you do not program Giroti," he laughs. "Nor do I think they program you." And then he tells me that a PleasureTube program is unique and interesting for another reason. It must be looked at from some distance, I will see eventually. TheTube is a *process*, he goes on—you don't realize what's happening to you, it builds toward the total hologram. You don't understand thePleasureTube's dynamics until then.

As we pass over the last rise before the cozily glittering terminal, I think of the strawberries. Collette had worn a strawberry scent in the morning—my appetite must have been focused on, intensified by, that scent to precondition my satisfaction in the strawberries we ate. In part the system of this ship proceeds from the appetites it creates and sustains, a kind of loop.

The terminal we enter is as crowded as it was when we left it. Most of the people are third-class passengers who watch with the disdainful awe of the poor as our spun-steel tram hums in. What Collette says—let it happen, what does knowing the system change?—let's say I agree marginally. The knowledge of another system accounts for my being here, accounts for my presence on this class tram as well. Yet another kind of loop, I think, even as the tram quietly clicks to a stop at the very spot from which we had begun.

After a shower under the whirlpool head I join Massimo at a small club on the A level of the ship. The out-cabin facilities of the ship have begun to operate: the club; a spa, Massimo advises, which opens tomorrow morning; a pool; an exercise room; another club; a D-bar. His second trip, Massimo complains about the out-cabin facilities: few, too small, hours irregular. The club is only the size of three or four cabins; tonight is India—three musicians in a dim recess, a triangle of sitar, sirode, drums. The service and the dinner are entirely Indian; we eat *pandoor* fowl as a well-muscled woman dances the "dance for Vishnu" behind a gauze curtain. Backlit, dusky and sensual, after a time she is joined by a man, then the curtain parts and he dances alone.

Massimo is already slightly drunk when the food is served. He's on a high dosage as well—as he came in I saw him put four pills on his tongue to bait the club's stuffy manager; he swallowed the pills conspicuously and with a grin. This trip, as a matter of fact, he is using the hologram against medical advice. We talk about women, he has some outrageous stories about Buenos Aires to tell. By the time we are finished eating he is calling for the Vishnu dancer again, insisting that he's seen her before, fueling the ship. With the gauze curtain gone, the lines of her muscles clearly show—Massimo announces loudly that he will be ready to wrestle after dessert. She glares at him; she is, in fact, attractive; we laugh for a long time—but I rise to leave before the second cup of thick, black coffee, still slightly desynched from Guam. Massimo becomes concerned. He checks the time with the waiter, then he insists, in a drunken, fatherly way, that yes, I must return to my cabin to keep up my strength.

When I return to my cabin, I find an Indian girl in a gauze and silk sarong waiting for me. Collette hasn't returned. A raga is on the audio. The girl—who, I wonder, is she?—weaves, smiling, toward me right at the door, slowly places the palm of her warm hand on my stomach, slides it fingers downward beneath my belt. As I start to speak she opens her other hand to reveal a vial of snowy-white crystals and a tarry black ball, like a soft pebble. "Compliments," she says, "of Governor Giroti." Her accent hints at something other than Indian. When I look closely I see she is Spanish, not Indian, perhaps South American. One of Giroti's women, of course.

"Colombian cocaine, Afghan hashish, both extremely rare. You are not getting your service," she adds. "I need a pipe for the hashish. The woman should be here."

"Collette?"

"Whoever, handsome man. I'd take better care of you. I will."

"I can't complain," I say with a smile.

"You could not only complain, you could have her transferred. She should be here. I need body oil; the recliner should be turned. We need a pipe." She inhales the odor of the hashish, offers it for me to smell.

"I have a small tobacco pipe in my bag," I say. "It'll do."

"Very interesting," the girl says—she is small-boned, dark-eyed; the sarong gives her a doll-like presence. "Just like kiddies playing with daddy's drugs."

I raise my hand, I don't know why, maybe the idea that she is so young—or is it the sneer that has come to her lips, her fleshy, glistening, and sensual lips?

"Slap me if you want to," she whispers. "Slap my bare skin, I'll undress. I want to be your slave."

DA3//I spend the morning working out in the A-deck pool, swimming laps. The spa complex includes a paddle tennis court, an exercise room, a bar, and the Olympic-sized pool itself, ringed by a narrow artificial beach. Its half-dozen butterfly palms are yellow-green, drooping; the sand, I'm not certain it is sand, is dusty, it is a place without life. The pool, small as its deck is, is an obvious place for—casual pairs. Perhaps thirty men and women lie tanning themselves under SunBanks on the far side; the people are oddly private toward one another, most rather old, their flesh doughy, the investors and administrators who Collette told me usually rode first class. On the other hand, there are five extremely attractive women and four men at the thatch bar in the corner, all Oriental. Service, I wonder? I see that one brought a basket of drugs, so I don't think so. I consider asking what they are taking, meeting the extra woman, but I concede to my sluggishness from last night and dive back into the pool instead. I swim twenty-five laps, the water thin and chemetic after the soft salt wash of the Pacific, its dead calm bathlike after the surge and rip of the sea off Guam. I dreamed last night of Cooper, an unsettling dream, saw him crouched over a downhatch ladder in the dome, a wild look in his eyes, his mouth open as if he were howling in pain, but there was only silence and the dome had lost almost all of its light. I see his broad, bearded face again even as I swim, do not shake the vision until I finally leave the water.

Back at my cabin, I cannot resist the whirlpool shower head again. I towel off before the blank window/wall, then punch through the videon and do sit-ups with Erica's exercise class, Collette's and my private joke. Collette has left instructions to meet her at the biosphere rest house where we spent yesterday. I'll be late enough. Yet I frankly wonder where she's been.

Collette is standing outside the screened porch in the early-afternoon sun; evidently she heard the tram. She's tall, has a dancer's body, both more graceful and slimmer than the Vishnu dancer at the club. But she is better filled out than the Spanish girl from last night, an entirely different body under her halter and sleek denim pants. Collette is woman to that girl: her cheekbones are as high as the girl's were shallow. Collette has the slightest scar above her lip, thin, obviously well sutured; it gives a sense of mystery to her face, to the café au lait of her skin. Her hair is drawn back under a silver bandana pulled around her forehead and tied at the nape of her neck; her green eyes are catlike; she has the most gorgeous smile.

"I did the craziest thing," she tells me. "I missed the crew tram last night, called in O.D. I stayed out here last night."

"Alone?" I say.

She nods, she is grinning.

"You'll get paranoid, too," I tell her with a smile.

"Paranoids are survivors." She shrugs. "That's what my brother used to say."

"Where did you sleep?" I ask, then see a set of rumpled sheets on the daybed. I kiss her neck, stop her answer; somehow I've begun to trust her implicitly, anyway. "Is it serious?"

"Cold poached salmon again. Short on champagne. Were you lonely?"

"Not exactly," I admit. Paranoid? I think. What spooks me? It's not her. But now I have the feeling that I've been here before.

Today we take what Collette calls a naturalized path on the mountain rather than the meadow side of the tramrun. At first it meanders steeply uphill along a face from which hulking slabs of granite protrude; the near vegetation is strewn with granite boulders and rubble. The vegetation is sparse, the sun warm. I carry a soft, insulated pack into which Collette has put our late lunch.

The relative proximity of the ship, the fact that I spent

the previous evening, night, and morning among spun-steel surfaces and machine hum, the sensation of these shoes, make me feel again as if we are exploring a planet from a landing site. I tell Collette how I spent my time. I expect her to tease me about the Spanish girl, but either her attention isn't that close or she doesn't care. She is taking in the meadow opening up as we ascend the switchback natural to the face; I can feel the climb opening up my lungs.

We have been gaining distance and elevation on the rest house, the meadow farther beyond has been expanding, the face we are on remains barren. But once we come around the face of the switchback, we are facing a wide, deep draw, a valleylike draw, thick with trees. The trees are evergreen, pine, and fir, and the brush is many-layered, the tree branches umbrellas upon umbrellas. Some of the trees rise a hundred feet or more; their trunks rise from the tiers of brush.

We stop at an outcropping and admire the view—we have it both ways here, the meadow and the draw. We have hiked three kilometers, judging from the distance we have gained on the meadow.

"You went all the way down there?" I say to Collette. "Did you see anything?"

"Just the woods. The sunset. I did my yoga for an hour and a half."

On the far side of the meadow I can see an occasional flash of glass, the single roof of a cone-shaped pavilion just into the trees.

Collette sits on a smooth rock and leans back. "Time to eat," she says. "This is as far as the trail goes."

We sit at the outcropping and eat cold salmon again; the aspic has begun to run. I cannot resist the draw which spreads beneath an escarpment, out of sight of the meadow, the tramrun, the rest of the reserve. I wonder how many people have been into the small valley, I wonder when my next opportunity will come, if at all. Collette says it isn't safe. But when I tell her that I am going, she says she's coming along. We pack the food and leave it where we ate, the insulated carrier propped against a half-hidden signpost: DO NOT PROCEED.

The face we descend is rust-swathed from decomposing pitons hammered in long ago, steep but negotiable hand under hand.

The rock base is thick with brush, litter in fertile soil—the trash is ancient, soft-metal cans overgrown, rotted into fragments. I think we are the first here in some time. We catch our breath at what appears to be a cairn near the base. Collette confirms that it marks the limit of PleasureTube grounds. Then Collette smiles, looks up for a long moment; her smile fades.

"No need to be grim," I say.

"I'm thinking about our being off the reserve. Look at that face. We should have used a rope."

"We made it down, we'll make it up."

"Sometimes I just get depressed," Collette sighs, turning to walk. "I don't even know why I mention it."

The stream bed, I discover, is not entirely dry, as it appears from a distance. The bed is wide enough to disguise a meter-wide stream meandering down its middle—the larger bed is a wash, eroded by heavy rains. We follow its surface slightly uphill and toward a woods. Collette walks alongside me; her wide-soled shoes, the PleasureTube insignia on her halter top, reinforce my initial feeling that we are on a planetary expedition. The unreality of what we are doing, the strangeness of the surroundings yesterday and today after all these years—I have an impulse to go back to the ship, to shower in my cabin's bath, to find a D-bar or club somewhere on the ship with spun-steel walls, artificial light. Both strange and familiar here.

Like deep space.

We hike into thicker woods and follow the stream to a clearing at the base of an outcropping perhaps ten meters high. The stream waterfalls down, misty, and with a peaceful rush of water. As we entered the woods we saw birds, a squirrel, no speakers in the trees, bushes with small red berries and black berries. Collette says she saw a snake or a lizard; it is gone when I turn my head.

The ground on the high bank is soft; I lie down to rest my eyes, fall asleep for a time.

When I awake, Collette is hovering a berry above my mouth. "Yes?" she says, the fruit, her face, a blur.

Yellow-white. I blink into the sun coming through the trees, sink my teeth into the berry. It is soft and sweet, a ripe blackberry. I put my hands on Collette's rib cage, slide them up under her breasts; she lifts her head.

"I'm figuring out the system," I tell her. "No speakers in the trees. Red berries modulate from strawberries; that started yesterday morning with your scent. As far into this draw as we can go. Now we make love."

She slides her legs down, lies next to me after stopping to look at me wryly. I cradle her head in my arm. "What you're talking about is simple short lag," she says. "It gets a lot more complicated than that. Do you know about second stage?"

"What's that?"

"Just a more intense kind of pleasure, pleasure on a different level. I'll give you an example. A game. It's called 'I'll show you yours if you show me mine.' "

"All right," I laugh, "I'll play. Let's see yours."

"No, 'I'll show you yours if *you* show me mine.' That means you show me mine first, Voorst."

I look into her green eyes, her spreading grin.

"I'll let you think about it," she says, smiling, her hand moving over my stomach.

Collette beside me, we hold each other, then doze again for a time.

"Something *is* bothering you," Collette says. We are sitting together as we sat the day before, knees up, looking into the woods. "You know I never logged the hike; nobody knows we're here. Honest. Especially here."

"It isn't that," I tell her, then go silent for a moment. "Let me describe to you a sequence," I finally say. "Or maybe you'll think I need a psychic screen."

"No," she says, "tell me."

"All right. Listen to my...visions—I have visions, nightmares, hallucinations, I don't know exactly what they are. Two especially: one is a woman floating in space, her arms outstretched. The other is a blue-black funnel, diamond points of stars in this kind of whirlpool—it lies in the direction of program—there's a glowing object, a spinning sun, approaching, coming very close, fading at the same time. And I dream about a man, see things from the blow sometimes."

"Happened on the ship?"

"Yes and no. Some are memories, but others aren't memories, exactly; when they occur it's as if I'm experiencing...very vivid memories, say. Or not memories at all. I know they're associated with one another, but I can't figure out how. I don't know if the sequence is real or a hallucination. It's very strange."

"You'd know if they were all from the ship."

"Yes and no again," I tell her. "It was confusing when we blew—Werhner insists on a time distortion, but I don't know. I'd say no, not exactly. The report says all the clocks agreed except one."

Collette looks away for a long moment, into the woods. "What happens to the woman whom you see?"

"Happens? Happened," I say. "She's dead. Motionless, frozen."

Collette turns to me, places her hand on my cheek, and pivots my face so that she is looking into my eyes, I into hers.

"Then don't think of her," she says. "Don't think about any of those things. Think about me instead, think about where we are and what we're going to do here. We can do anything, you know. We're going to have a real time together."

Anyone who knew me well enough, I think, would know of my hallucinations, would know I'd take the faint trail into this draw. Collette didn't. There are some things, I think, that she doesn't know after all, and that alone makes me feel infinitely better. Perhaps her depression had been affecting me. But when I look at her—into her half-sleepy eyes, her wide, liquid smile—she doesn't seem depressed any more, and that makes me feel better, too.

CHAPTER 4
Videon Spectacular

DA4// On the wall-sized screen the holographic dancers fade—Tahitian dancers, men and women in mylar lava-lavas, their dance increasingly more furious and sexual as they move toward one another, almost touching, their bodies glistening, their eyes hypnotic, trancelike—the videon screen flushes in a long burst of deep, glowing red, modulates into a field of blue, then shimmers into a series of vague forms, false color separations. A scene finally appears: a studio set, a panel of three women, two men, in large, white padded chairs placed around a semicircular table.

"What Dr. Buell calls a state of mind, I could reduce to physical contact," the white-haired woman says, pointing to one of the other panel members.

"But no"—this from Dr. Buell—"think of anticipation and satisfaction, think of imagination. There's more than the operation of sensory apparatus in pleasure, and to think of it as...friction, even granting the metaphor...makes a premise of the exclusivity of tactile sense data...."

"Yet pleasure is a state of the body," the white-haired woman insists. "The entire epidermis is a sense organ into whose language all other pleasure eventually translates. Pleasure is a language the body knows."

Holographic titles now stream across the screen:

MAXIMUM MOMENTS//AN ANALYSIS ON THE THEORETICAL LEVEL.

"Dr. Godwin's model is sex-generated, behavioral," a younger woman says, her voice hollow, eerie. "That makes sense to me. Think of the differences in tactile surfaces, the electricity of contact. Think of silk on the skin, for example. When we refine a neurological language for that sensation, transpose it to other sense parallels, transmit this language, language as stimulation, into a body..."

"Total hologram," Buell says. "Where the holographic vision has neurological substance. And yet less than the total hologram—because in the total hologram the mind is active, creating the language as well as receiving it. Thus the only sensible psychiatric conclusion is that pleasure is a state of mind."

"Generated *by* a neurophysical signal," the white-haired woman says, throwing up her hands.

"Think of what you're saying," Buell remarks. "Ultimately it violates the whole notion of pleasure as reward, as something achieved. You're saying in part that pleasure has no aim beyond itself, except to be itself in the body."

"I'm not even certain that reward and achievement are related to pleasure," the white-haired woman says sharply, "pure, *disinterested* pleasure, pleasure which makes the orgiastic moment a moment outside of time.... I say that pleasure must have no goal—it simply *is*, without direction or limitation, without reference to a historical net."

"Outside of time?"

"And so, transcendental sense flight. The first model programs for the Tube...."

The screen fades and cuts to the image of a dark-haired woman sitting on a sofa in an apartment living room, intent on her half-wall videon, sitting tightly cross-legged, swinging one foot from the knee. Her screen shows the somewhat indistinct image of a young man in blue coveralls staring into the camera, his hands loosely in his lap. The image holds for a full minute. The young man moves only ever so slightly, beginning to smile. A sound from within the apartment.

"Look, Kenneth, the oddest thing...."

She is answered by the shutting of an interior door, the word "What?" then the sentence "I can get what I want across the line—I've got to go, anyway." The sound of a firmly shutting heavy door.

She is half rising after the sound, she says, "Kenneth?" leaves the sofa, then turns quickly as if she has sensed the subtle change in light. The videon screen shows the same mauve background, but now the chair is empty. She stands, flushed.

After a moment the doorbell rings. She sighs, strides to the door.

It is a young man in blue coveralls—the same young man, now he's stretching.

She says, "What do you want?"

He answers slowly, a curl to his lips, "I've been watching you."

"You?" She touches, merely touches, one of the straps of his coveralls; it falls from his shoulder. He begins undressing her—they eventually sink together onto the sofa, arms snaked in thighs, then thighs in thighs. Still shot.

The screen fades again and cuts to tethered women, tethered men, the setting for some kind of game....

Call it videon overload, call it saturation, the long series of programs induces in me a kind of waking sleep, there's a numbness in my forehead, my eyes. Collette tells me that average daily videon time is more than four hours. I suspect the average viewer is better conditioned than I am. Not that the programming isn't spectacular: holographic sunrises of the world, Japanese geishas singing, old footage of bullfights in Madrid, Balinese dancing...these narrative interludes, panels, training, and explanations.

It seems as if I have been on theTube forever. The recliner has become familiar, this cabin, the videon itself, with its vivid colors and holographic capabilities, as ordinary as an idle terminal or the back of my hand. The idea of my being here, the surprise of the trip, are diminished—and yet when I calculate that I am well into my fourth day on the ship, and I try to remember what has happened, it seems I've been here no time at all, that the four days have passed with unaccountable swiftness: time frozen and accelerated at once.

LASVENUS VENTURES//PLAN YOUR MINIWEEK NOW

NEW BREAKFAST OPTIONS//LASVENUS ONLY

Figs and Prosciutto
Fettuccine Alfredo
Celery Grissini
Espresso

Rhubarb Compote
Kedgeree with Curry Sauce
Toast Marmalade

Prunes in Madeira
Sauteed Calf's Liver
Bacon
Boiled New Potatoes
Toasted Rolls
Marmalade

Red Caviar and Sour Cream
   Omelets
Crisp Hot Rolls, Butter
Cream Cheese
Strawberry Preserves

THREE-DAY RACING PACKAGE//
                //Two Liter Two Hundred
                //The EnergyWest Grand Prix

LASVENUS VENTURES
   //NEW OPTIONS EVERY HOUR//

PRERESERVATION
FOR FIRST-CLASS
PASSAGE

   //PLAN YOUR MINIWEEK NOW
   //DAYS 6-9, THEPLEASURE TUBE

   //Consult your service for details

The screen cuts again, to a woman seated before a table set with a half-dozen wine bottles. Title: TASTE TUNING//THE EXPERIENCE OF WINE. Voice-over: Stay *tuned*. Cuts to: a group of dancers, megastars. I find myself thinking of Knuth, the intense little man from Guam—how I'd like to put him in the wine woman's lap.

I try to contact Giroti, but he is blocked off, we are all blocked off, privatized today. Lunch does not come until it is quite late, but the lunch is crepes, which Collette prepares—light, sweet, delicious—followed by pears and Brie.

I convince Collette that I need some relief from the programming, and she sets up the videon for a MoonGame Co-op—an immensely complicated spinoff from sedentary tennis, played against the computer and other passengers. She is still explaining the rules when the ship jolts.

I feel through the floor the metallic thud, the shudder; I see the draperies sway. We restabilize immediately. I look up at Collette, my heart pounding. The light seems brighter.

"Moving an adjacent unit," she tells me. "Nothing to worry about."

"Tricky business."

"They don't make many mistakes." She grins.

Yet before I can get my defense fully organized on the wall screen, she is pulling my channel, the screen flushes. . . .

"Sorry, you have to see this," she tells me. For a brief moment, still feeling the shudder, I am alarmed about the ship, I am conscious of my breathing, concentrate on steady inhalations, prepare to rise and . . .

Collette wasn't kidding—the screen and audio don't display Damage Control, they display a VisEd whose subject is the total hologram.

"Where brain-wave anticipation is immediately translated into full spectrum sensation," a pleasant black man says soothingly.

He is describing a loop.

"Where, best of all, *you* are in control," adds a black woman so similar that she might be his sister. They are identically dressed in bright, burnt-orange body stockings, seated together on a lush sofa in an elegant cabin.

"*Some*times," he laughs, they laugh together.

"In the comfort of your cabin—chemical, electrical, visual, audio, tactile—all systems—full spectrum sensation responds to your deepest needs, an ecstasy beyond compare...."

"The only such system in the cosmos is on this ship," she reminds the camera. "A hologram that's more than a hologram, controlled by you, automatically, unconsciously, instantaneously...."

"Orgi*a*stically," the young man adds. "In a way you've never experienced before, including *direct* electrical and chemical stimulation of the hypothalamic center of ecstasy. You are in control."

"Or out of it," the woman laughs, her teeth sparkling white, her leg rising as she runs her hand from her knee down the back of her thigh.

The screen dissolves into moving geometric figures—or parts of figures, shifting, a kaleidoscopic effect. The figures are vaguely genital. The sound of a beat—an exaggerated heartbeat.

The couple begin to describe dosages and instrumentation. I wonder if what they say is true. Collette says that it is. They speak of direct electrical stimulation of the orgasm center of the brain.

"That's dangerous," I say.

"Which is why there's medical clearance," Collette tells me.

"Mmmm. It seems to me that arrangement could, it *could*, kill you."

"Some people it does." She shrugs. "Maybe that's why it's the only one, I mean, the circuits and apparatus are only on this kind of ship. Mostly it's heart attack; it happens."

"What prevents it?"

"Scanning. And limiting circuits for blood pressure, pulse rate. But it's a freewill choice; there's the risk, part of it is the risk."

I run my hand along the brown velvet arm of the sofa and ask her if she's tried it, what it's like.

"Twice," she tells me. "It's scary, but...I felt as if I

were . . . toasted; it was incredible and frightening, too, I felt obliterated. I was sick for a week. But God. I couldn't begin to do it justice."

"Though if people die . . ."

"You know," she says thoughtfully, "they say the deaths have something to do with population control. The managers don't care, they say it's up to Medex. It happens more than they say it does. I think you have to be really healthy, your dosages have to be right, and the scanning . . . That's what's important. Then it's not a problem, it's just . . . a special kind of trauma. You never want to come back." She grins. "It's so incredible, your mind is filled with the most exciting things, they seem to grow in there and pile up, and *then* you feel them in every cell of your body . . . ."

"Where imagination is immediately translated into full spectrum sensation," the black man is saying again on the screen.

"Not for *everyone* . . . ." His twin smiles. "But . . ."

"But riding the PleasureTube without a trip to the sun is like climbing a mountain and not reaching its peak."

"Like leaping from a cliff and never reaching the sea," the woman says.

"Twenty units for twenty-four hours," the man says. "Thirty-five units for two days. The option that is extra but extraordinary. Come with us to the sun."

"Come with me." The woman shows her teeth, she touches them with her tongue. "Come with me to the sun."

What follows is a preview to the hologram, the videon spectacular itself. Collette feeds me two capsules while the screen shows a test pattern. I sit watching; slowly the pattern—dome geometry, hexagons—is becoming holographic, shimmers, then my head, the top of my head, takes off. The images recombine and expand into vivid, electric swaths of pure color. . . . Intense, lush sounds surround me and something happens to the air: the odor of crushed grapes. I do not know, this has happened in moments, where my consciousness ends and hallucinations begin. In the end—I do not leave the cabin, I am certain, but I feel I have expended enormous amounts of energy—I finally close my eyes and count visions, I lose consciousness, fall asleep.

Awake, I chew cola nuts which Collette slices finely—plum-sized, white and washed red nuts, tart and effervescent on the tongue—she stabilizes my metabolism with another two capsules. Now I am bored, though oddly enough I feel well rested. The videon is showing the most recent WorldBowl clips split-screen. They are playing NewBall now, the game that has replaced almost all others. Sixty players, two soccer balls, fifteen referees—each side of the screen is following one of the balls, the violence is considerable—men kicking at the ball carrier, grabbing at receivers, satellite fights between offense men and defense men. The goal I watch seems to come on a fluke. A powerful kick grazes off a Red NoEast defense man; it was headed out of bounds. NoEast is running away with the game nonetheless; they lead at the half 9–3.

Collette asks me if I will try the hologram. I say of course. I have decided to look into the tolerances myself—enter control that way at the input and see what I can take. Each thing seems worth trying, if only once, if only to see. I wonder if I will ever be here or any place like this again.

Collette tells me that it is possible to pair on the hologram, that the effect is synergistic, but she has never tried it.

"Do you want to?"

She nods slowly, grins. "With a flier? Yes indeed," she says.

For a long moment we both sit there, oddly embarrassed, I think, staring at the WorldBowl violence. A Yellow SoCal player has just been kicked in the mouth, blood running through the fingers he holds up to his face. The camera is following him in close-up as he walks, hunched, toward the sidelines; no foul is being called.

"But this," I say. "Well, I can take only so much of this."

"Yes," Collette says. "It's too much."

We sit in silence for a while again. Now Yellow is driving behind a wedge, but they don't have the weight to punch through a bearish Red defense.

"Yes," Collette says, shutting down the audio. "I want to. The time I've spent with you has been good. That's an understatement—I mean, it's somewhere under the truth, the truth is a larger thing. That speaks well for the truth," she finally concludes, grinning at her logic.

"I didn't think you were so interested in the truth," I tell her with a smile.

"Not in the same way you are. Maybe that's what I like about you. I mean, it speaks well for you," she says, her grin really spreading.

Collette wants to show me something, something we are not programmed to see until eight in the evening. She says I have to leave the room, so I indulge myself in a long, relaxing shower. I feel deeply satisfied already; I cannot imagine more. What I do have to imagine, the hologram, does not interest me now. It will be something to tell Werhner about, but what he would not understand pleases me even more—Collette's openness, her warmth. I wish I could show her some skill of mine, some ability—to take a ship, perhaps, through a dazzling array of weather. I want to do something of that sort so badly it aches inside me—or is it my vanity? I find myself studying my shape before the mirror. No middle sag. I laugh. I left earth eighty years ago, earth time. Young forever.

What Collette has to show me is yet another transformation of the videon, different from anything we've seen before: the screen displays full-sized the interior of another cabin; this can't be a shipwide program. Its occupants are familiar.

The naked back of a tall, thin man, his buttocks pinched together, standing facing a recliner, the roundish, flushed face of—by God, it is—Erica, she is unmistakable—soft, wide mouth, blonde hair in thick curls down to her neck. She is seated on the recliner, just behind him. Cards lie on a small cubic table before her, she flips a card over, something happens with Tonio—impossible to tell precisely what, his back is to us, but I can see his leg muscles tense.

"Tape?" I say.

"Live."

I look at Collette; she is watching intently with a smile. I look back again, look at Collette.

"Do they know? Good God," I say, "doesn't this make you feel—I mean, aren't we invading their privacy?"

"No," she laughs. "If we were on another kind of ship—but not here. We're free here. We can do anything."

I watch, Erica's hands are up, Tonio leans over. "You're right." I grin. "I feel free here. I've never felt so free before. It's amazing."

What I can't do justice to is the next stage in the transformation. After we watch for a time, Collette becomes anxious about something. I am aroused, but she will not let me touch her. "It's better to wait," she says. Yet she is anxious.

Wait for what?

She punches up the console inlaid in the table—Erica and Tonio turn toward us as if on signal, and—*the screen tracks apart from its middle*; the cabin doubles; Erica and Tonio stand before us, not holographically, but in their perfumed, perspiring flesh. The fantasy co-op: a moving wall. My disorientation is given another turn, Collette is hugging Erica, they know one another.

Erica turns out to be Tonio's service, Tonio a videon producer; he's anxious to know how I liked the day's show! I'm anxious to get my hands on Erica. I do. We all do, and on one another. This goes on through dinner.

Whenever dinner is. Tonio is directing Collette in a masturbation sequence he is videotaping; he says she inspires him. Erica and I are in the kitchen/bar, Erica has begun to microwave coquilles Saint-Jacques, I had to help her set the unit. She has located a steel can of whipping cream and has laid a line of it around my midsection; she licks it slowly, holding my legs and pressing her large breasts against my thighs—the effect is extraordinary. I can watch Collette through the divider. Erica is a fleshy woman, moans with me in her mouth, Tonio's "Now lean farther, Collette" behind her.

The window/wall is a mirror and Tonio has Collette alongside it moving her hands over her body, leaning back, leaning down, leaning back as she moves in time to Jamaican music. She is leaning down as Erica and I come in with the food—Tonio is masturbating. I cannot resist entering Collette from behind. After a minute we tumble to the rug and Erica is somehow beneath Collette and Collette begins licking Erica's breasts, running circles around the nipples, taking them full into her mouth. Finally I roll from Collette and as Tonio enters her I enter Erica from above. By the time we finish, the scallops need reheating, but they are delicious, the wine has gone flat, but Collette, gorgeous woman, has found some champagne.

It is much later. We have all taken waferlike dosages of D-Pharmacon. I am on the recliner with Erica, Tonio is fixing a snack.

Collette comes to the recliner. "Room for me?" she says.

Erica shifts over, slips away to Tonio.

Collette takes my face in her warm hands and kisses me with a wide mouth and a flashing tongue. "You luscious man, you," she whispers. "Mountain climber. Why don't you just program yourself on a continuous circuit here, ride with me all the time?"

"And what if I get bored?" I say.

Collette kisses me again. "Do I bore you?"

I laugh.

"No," she says, "you're right. We ought to go alpine climbing together, to the Andes."

"Or sign on for the next research ship, fly to the stars. You could be my aide."

"What a dream," she giggles. "I thought of something else I like about you. You don't hold your breath. Watch Tonio, he does. You don't, you just breathe when it happens. You know how to fly."

"That's something I've missed, flying. This ship rides like a barge."

"What's it really like?"

"Like this," I say, cupping her breast in my hand. "Like this," I say, kissing her nipple, sliding my hand up her thigh.

When I wake the next morning, Erica is preparing breakfast in the kitchen/bar, has an accident with the range, that's what wakes me.

"I wish Collette were here," I hear her saying. "She knows how to run this mother-fucking thing."

I look around the cabin, stretch, and yawn. I see Tonio isn't here, either; the cabin, my cabin, has been tidied up— the videon again a window/wall, now showing suborbital flight, though we are still quite a distance from the planet. "She'll be back," I say.

"No, she won't," I think I hear.

"What?"

"She won't be back," Erica says very clearly; now she is leaning around the divider. "She's been transferred."

"*What?*"

"*Transferred.* They came for her last night. You were out like a stone; she was, too, really. Well, nobody wanted to wake you."

"Tonio?" I say.

"No, no," Erica is saying, she's almost laughing. "Tonio's switched to male service for LasVenus. No, I'm going to take care of you."

She brings the tray and sets it down on the coffee table, strokes my chest. "Your *coun* is a love root, my *couillon* its flower," she says. Apropos of what? "Wait and you'll see," she tells me. "Eat."

"How can she be transferred? That isn't the understanding I had."

"It happens," Erica mutters through a fistful of pills she is taking one at a time. "I think she may have gotten herself in a little bit of trouble, but it can't be serious. Not where to, but *whom* to, and how should I know?" She is downing pills one after the other, she must have five more left in her hand.

I ask her why the drugs.

"We're on a downangle already, I just know it. I can't stand landing or taking off."

The coffee boils over in the kitchen, Erica lurches up. "Goddammit."

"Can you find out?"

"*What?*"

"Where she went, whom she was transferred to."

"You know, you'd better watch your step," Erica says from the kitchen/bar. "One of the security men last night said there was a tracer out on you."

I feel blood rush to my neck, my heart beginning to pound.

"Whom to, Erica?" She says nothing. "If you don't tell me, I'm going to find out for myself."

"Shit," she says. "Look at this mess. I'm on your side, lover, but you're not going to get anywhere on this one. Steiner," she says. "Steiner, Eva B. *That's* who."

I reach Giroti on audio—he has been awake for hours, he encourages me to pack all of my clothes. The next three days we will spend at LasVenus, he wants to show me something he's had flown in.

I tell him my service has been transferred, I want her back. Is there anything he can do?

"Ahhh," he says. "Did she do something special? Tell me about it."

"I'm not sure that's it, Massimo, it's more complicated."

"A man as young as you, don't get attached," he tells me. "You must be part Italian."

"I want to find out why," I tell him. "And I want her back. Is there a way I can make an inquiry?"

"Ahhh, passion, to be so young. In the circuits of the ship—well, a man like you can find out almost anything. But to get her back... No, if I were you I'd give it some serious thinking. Since it wasn't your request, it was handled from the outside. That's very unusual."

"Then you know nothing about it?"

"Nooo, I heard nothing. You didn't mention this, my friend."

It could have been his woman, I think. Massimo and I will talk later, after disembarkation. At the moment I need to make a computer search before we land; the landing could change everything. I ask one more question.

"Who runs the ship, Massimo? I mean, what organization?"

"The corporation," Massimo says. "Which is controlled by EnergyWest. Which is controlled by NoAm Congress. From that you could say SciCom, but with SciCom, who knows?"

"SciCom? Did you say SciCom?"

"Ah, but who knows with them, whether they run anything or not?"

"SciCom."

"Rawley, my friend, good luck. Until we see one another—LasVenus, ah, *fantástico. Ciao,* my friend, *ciao.* Drink to poor Italy."

"Patching in."

"This is traffic. How did you ..."

"Do you have an open line?"

"Iden, please." Another voice crackles: "He can use 363." First voice: "I'll need an authorization figure, or do you want this through control? I can give you a circuit in the console dome."

"No, patch me through this terminal, identify as deadheading. What you can do instead of an authorization figure is give me a line through Guam SciCom."

"That's like Sunday at the zoo—uh, look, use 363, it'll be open. How long do you want it?"

"Indef. Let's say a ten-day parameter."

"It's yours. I'll just vacate. That's a big ship—you've got a downangle, LasVenus arrival in less than an hour. Look, when you touch down, you're going to have to loop the channel through ground."

"Affirmative. And in the meantime, how about a sixty-second display on PT/coord. 1427-82, location map LASVENUS, then sixty more, personnel write on Steiner, Eva B., codex 1819-79, passenger PT class one."

"Eva Steiner? The EnergyWest VP, a Director, that one?"

"Eva B."

"Roger and out. Traffic series 300."

PART II:

SCHWARZCHILD SOLUTION
[=df special solution to general
relativity which describes the
distance between event horizon
and naked singularity.]

CHAPTER 5
Welcome to
Las Venus

    I sit at the oblong window of this pale green cushiony room, my head throbbing. I am watching the ships being serviced on concrete pads and the light traffic on the trans-port runways. Shuttles sail in on the long glide path on seagull wings past this thick, tinted glass; I watch yet another offload then towed to a pad for dismemberment into units by the cranes. Behind me the wall screen displays the single readout I have been able to punch through. Even with my sign key, every query I make comes to the same thing, the computer's wink for computation and the identical display I have been sitting with for more than two hours. The pale green figures pain my eyes. I can't shake a strange feeling that I've sat here before, waiting, just this way, waiting.

LasVenus DataBase Information Service//
Current DataBase Information//

Voorst, Rawley//

MAP ONE OF THREE

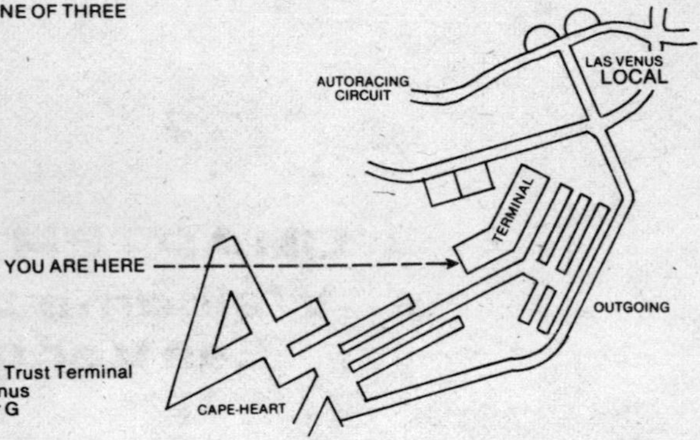

AUTORACING
CIRCUIT

LAS VENUS
LOCAL

TERMINAL

YOU ARE HERE ⟶

OUTGOING

Huges Trust Terminal
LasVenus
Sector G

CAPE-HEART

MAP TWO OF THREE

OUTGOING

LV.

YOU ARE HERE ⟶

TRANS SERVICE

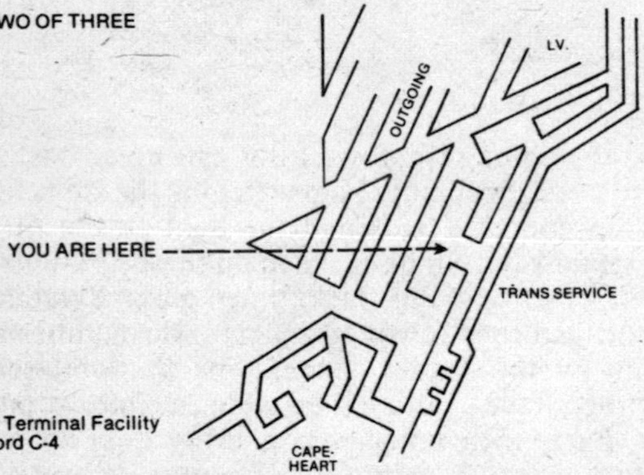

VIP Terminal Facility
Coord C-4

CAPE-
HEART

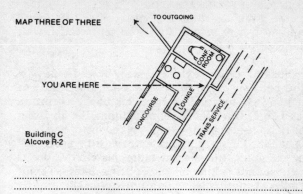

MAP THREE OF THREE

TO OUTGOING

CONF ROOM

YOU ARE HERE

CONCOURSE

LOUNGE

TRANS SERVICE

Building C
Alcove R-2

your local residence is------------------------------- SectorGold
Casa del Sol
202//Suite 3

your local program
     instructs you to----- YOU ARE RESTRICTED
                       PLEASE REMAIN WHERE YOU ARE
                       PLEASE REMAIN WHERE YOU ARE
                       PLEASE REMAIN WHERE YOU ARE

Program LasVenus DataBase//"We serve your need to know"//
thePleasureTube corp.

    And so I sit staring in the other direction, wondering
what part of my headache I owe to this morning, what
part to last night, watching one ship in particular, which
could only be our ship. Massive, dull silver, wings barely
wings in retraction, its fuselage apart in sections now,
sections from which units protrude for service, the area a
forest of cranes and hydraulics. How similar and much
simpler by comparison the Daedalus was—an even larger
ship, but one whose mass was formed by the circular

clarity of a single propulsion system, one hull to these three, each dome a dragonfly's eye—and how much simpler it was to fly straight out.

Something nibbles at the edge of my mind, that sense of having been here before. I want to get in touch with Werhner, I know that is my right.

The shock of seeing Taylor clears my head. In the past week I've been surprised more than once, but I had not prepared myself to see him here, his bushy eyebrows rising as I enter this cold conference room, the air sweet with the odor of his pipe tobacco. My chemistry had been shifting back to Guam, and this settles it. Sitting at the far edge of the long, transparent table, his elbows on its surface, his hands resting on amber SciCom files, Taylor nods, smiles at another man I only now notice standing by the other door. He is someone I have never seen, a brown-haired man with a farmer's build. Taylor rises from his chair and points the stem of his pipe at a seat midway down the table, says to me, "That's quite a chase you led us on."

I feel my palms becoming clammy and the atmosphere acquiring the weight of Guam between Tayor and myself. Taylor *here*; yet this is just like Guam, him standing up as he sits me down, the mechanics of his practiced insecurity. I sit, shifting my feet apart on the rug. I know where my center is, anyhow; I lean back in the chair.

"It'd be a chase only if I were running," I suggest. "I had the right to leave time under military procedure and I exercised it."

"That's under review," replies Taylor, packing his pipe with a blunt finger. "For the moment, you're coming back with me to Pacific SciCom. The sooner we start back the better. Where are your things? Your ticket will say. Show it to Mancek, he'll get them for you." Taylor looks at me as he relights his pipe, his gold lighter tight in his hand, hissing.

"I'm not going anywhere with you," I say evenly, "unless you have a criminal arrest warrant and he's got status to serve it. In that case, I want to see a local attorney."

"No, now, I..." Taylor murmurs, the faint smile that had shaped his thick lips fading.

"Then show me the orders you have. I'd like to see the authority flow on this one."

"I *make* the orders," Taylor says, setting his lighter down, his face reddening.

"Not for me you don't," I say evenly. "I have military status and I'm exercising my leave time."

"That's a technicality, Voorst."

"I'm staying here," I say.

"For the life of me," Taylor sighs, "I can't find out why the military office let you go. I'll concede the technical grounds of your presence here, but we've lost a week already. Let's get on with it." Taylor's bushy eyebrows come together, he punches something through a table console and calls Mancek over. "SectorGold. Casa del...Christ, Voorst, what are you doing with a local residence in SectorGold? I'm in Green, what are you doing in SectorGold?"

It is a nice moment. Taylor sucks on his pipe, glaring at the screen.

"I was with a woman," I say. "She was taken away from me. What do you know about that?"

"...well, I'm in Green," Taylor says, expelling a breath. "Christ, Voorst." He looks at me and his expression twists another way. "That black girl, West Indian? She was working for us."

"She *was*?" I ask, my heart sinking. "She was working for you?"

"I'm not saying," Taylor tells me, beginning to drum his fingers on the table, "that she was doing a very good job. Look, Voorst, SciCom takes precedence over military, let's not press it. They obviously resent that fact, they're always splitting hairs over authority flows. We don't like to abuse our prerogative."

"Well, you have been," I say, thinking, She lied—straight-faced lied.

"I'm going to insist on your cooperation. This is an important enough project, a project everyone, even the military, eventually benefits from. . . ."

"Would you say Cooper benefited?" I ask, my anger rising. "I'm fed up. You ask questions you have no right to ask; my personal belongings have been searched. Maybe you benefit from that, but I don't see what you've done for anyone's welfare. Cooper was a little odd, but he was no suicidal psychotic."

"We had no control over that. He did it himself, Voorst."

"Whose care was he under, Taylor? I've felt different since I left Guam, you know that? I'm not so tired any more. Cooper's whole boring report identified the cause of the accident as an impact event, unknown interstellar material. Why do you need another report? We had that from the beginning. You can find it in every tape from the mission. I've told you time and time again that squares with my recollection, and Werhner's, and Tamashiro's, and Levsky's. And Cooper's, right? But Cooper's not alive to defend his report."

"You jump to conclusions, Voorst. Your conclusions color everything you say. You're a walking example of Heisenberg's Effect, I've observed that, though for your sake I haven't put it on record. Let me remind you that we draw the conclusions. Of course there was an impact event. What I'm concerned about is why there was impact."

Then Werhner's right, I think, it's SciCom itself, not the dome crew, that should be investigated. Which Taylor must know as well as I do. "It's my conclusions about what you're doing that bother you," I say, "not my conclusions about what happened. Look, have you ever actually finished a debriefing? Or does the crew finally die of old age?"

Taylor tells Mancek to get my things from the local residence, to which they've been transferred. I think how I might have been going there with Collette; sigh.

"Don't touch my bag," I say to them both, "or you're

going to deal with military police. It may be only a technicality, but I'm staying here."

"Voorst, you don't want to do that," Taylor says angrily, his forehead tightening. My bluff hand—and thinking of it that way, I raise the stakes.

"Don't tell me what I want. Release my program or you're going to have to restrain me from using that alarm console outside. I'm serious, Taylor, I mean what I say. It's already serious enough for me."

There is another long moment of silence. Taylor glares at me but then leans back. "You really want to stay here," he sighs. "I can countermand your status, Voorst, I can have that done." Forward again over the console, Taylor looks at his wristwatch, punches through a program, scowls. "Well, it's going to take three more days. So Monday. In three days' time I can wallpaper you with authorizations."

Taylor looks at me blackly. He has said it himself; three days' time. I look him straight in the eye; we both know I am not going with him until Monday.

"And I'll file an appeal to sustain leave," I say.

"Good luck," Taylor says flatly, whacking his cold pipe against the ceramic ashtray. "You're too arrogant, Voorst. You have no respect for us."

"Maybe because Daedalus SciCom doesn't know its ass from a wall screen," I say as I rise to leave.

In the pastel room, Taylor is telling me that he is going to see to it that I won't fly again, not even out of the service, until he and I are through, not if it takes until the end of his career. Blood rushes to my neck—no bureaucrat can cashier flight crew, what an ugly thing to say—my anger is palpable to me, a thickening of my blood. I slam the door behind me with both hands, as if I want to throw it in his face.

At one time—it was when Maxine was sleeping in my cabin on the Daedalus, and I realized she was seeing Cooper all along—I told myself I wouldn't let a woman make me feel this way again. Now the woman is Collette, and I am again depressed by the sticky gloom, the heart-thumping mud of betrayal. Seeing Maxine with Cooper—well, they say the first cut is the deepest. I'm not sure. There might be another explanation for the way Collette's behaved toward me, but I shouldn't delude myself. I'm certain now that she lied to me about where she was the night she was gone, lied through her soft lips. I know she was in touch with SciCom at least from the third night.

Erica meets me at a D-bar in the trans-port and I am finally able to leave the terminal. It is already midafternoon. On our way to the local residence LasVenus sprawls before us from the elevated freeway, bright in the three o'clock sun. The city, Erica tells me, is a layover for sections of theTube and a separate resort complex, the largest of its kind. I am almost too low to appreciate the spectacle. Glittering casinos, a floating Hong Kong nightclub on an artificial lake, three domed stadiums, emerge miragelike in the distance, along with sports and racing circuits, in a high-rise clutter whose buildings shine like mica sheets under the bright haze of the sun. The centerpiece of LasVenus is a massive new club with a forty-acre garden on its roof, complete with artificial weather—occasional summer storms with lightning streak across its sky, thunder rolls in as if from a distance, rain pours into its ponds. From our distance driving in I can only see the Tower as a beige, transparent high-rise. The shimmering movement of its sides, Erica explains, comes from its elevators; the first twenty floors, which shimmer more than the rest, house an administrative core. In the other direction must lie the ongoing city of permanent residents—rows of drab, blocklike buildings stretch into the desert.

How can I sort out my feelings? It seems useless to try. I miss Collette even as I think, The bitch, the manipulating bitch. Massimo is probably right about these women. And yet . . .

```
EXIT 33A

SECTORGOLD / / / / / / / / / / / / / / / / / / / / / / /

  TOWERCLUB AND CASINO / / / / / / /
  CLUB EROTICA / / / / / / / / / / / / / / /
  VANWECK ERLEN SEXUARIUM / / / / / /

ALL LOCAL RES GOLD/CASA SERIES
```

We take the exit, offramp through a greenbelt
separating sectors, cross over a wide, banked track for
land-vehicle racing. From the overpass I glimpse two
Formula E's, flywheel-propulsion racing machines I've
only seen on the videon. Toadlike, awkward in shape,
their power is tremendous. I remember hearing they don't
handle well as I watch the lead car lumber into a curve.
The oddest thing is the high whistle of their passing.

Our taxi swoops beneath pedestrian level for a
kilometer, then ascends for a slow drive down a boulevard
lined with shiny, artificial trees and pastel buildings which
flash above like gems set in gems. Erica is telling me about
shows she wants to see as we drive on. It is the overall
effect that I am still trying to absorb. The size still
impresses me, not only the size of this district, but of the
other LasVenus. I cannot have seen the end of the
residence blocks stretching into the desert.

"We'll have to play it by ear. I'm sorry," Erica says.
"You're entirely desynched from the program. We could
stop somewhere if you like."

"Why not," I say.

We wind up at a place in the Tower Complex called the
Club Erotica, a big, shimmering bar of several levels, with
men and women suspended on small stages, outrageously
dressed, some completely naked, some in intimate
heterosexual and homosexual pairs. Erica and I sit at a

long walnut bar, talk for a while. I feel preoccupied. I am looking for someone in the mirrors, I realize, looking among the scattered blacks. I am embarrassed, angry, and humiliated at the same time.

The suite is laid out like the cabin unit on the Tube, a couch/recliner, a window/wall, a kitchen/bar. But here space is tripled and the furniture is larger: a huge, tiered sofa; a white, circular dining table. In place of a shower, there is a lavish bath with a sunken marble tub, the bath illuminated by thin mauve neon tubes which skirt the mirrored walls. From a balcony beyond the sliding window/wall I can see the whole of Sector Gold and beyond its freeway border the vast rows of drab, identical residence blocks of the other city. Even from this elevation they fade into the brownish haze of late afternoon without visible end.

When I key into the computer, a message jumps up right into video, a short tape loop waiting for me from Massimo Giroti. He asks me to meet him tomorrow, about noon, at an address which reads like a warehouse number. He doesn't say why, fades out with a grin. Working for a while at the small console which lifts from a coffee table, I discover that outside communication is not well developed here, and when I look through my bag for the routing book I decided to take along, I have the feeling someone's been through my things again. Why, I wonder, is the LasVenus page smudged? Even with the routings and the traffic channel I secured just before we landed, I cannot raise Werhner on a live line—one routing I try lists Werhner as off station, the other as on station but unavailable for outside calls. I think they both amount to the same thing. A little later, I decide, I will compose a message, key in, and route it as a teletype, not to Guam's SciCom base at Agana, but rather to the maintenance station at Utama Bay, where Werhner dives. A debugging rider will make it disappear if someone listens in.

I doze on the couch, and when I fall hard asleep

something wakes me—as if the darkness of sleep carried with it something monstrous, something unformed, a nightmare. I recall the darkness, but I don't remember a single detail of whatever it was that woke me until I am seeing it all—Cooper's tight lips, his narrowed eyes as he tells me, Let her go, and Maxine's flushed face, her vacant, embarrassed smile, her watery eyes. Erica is in the bath. Now I am angry, I want to throw that door at Taylor. The thought of Collette makes me sigh audibly.

```
channel 393//
sign key 0202/Voorst//

telex medium//

route:   SoCal Center
         Honolulu
         Midway
         Guam Utama Sta. (des.)
debugging rider:  erase if intercept

ATTN:   WERHNER SCHOLE

QUERY: DO YOU KNOW ANY INFORMATION ANOMA-
LIES OUR DAEDALUS MISSION? EXCEPT FOR THE MISS-
ING, AM NOT AWARE OF ONE IN COOPER'S REPORT. BUT
SEE WHAT YOU CAN FIND: CHECK WHAT SCICOM IS
HOLDING IN ITS BANKS, COMPARE WITH C'S REPORT,
WOULD YOU? THE CIRCUS HAS COME TO TOWN, HAD A
TALK WITH TAYLOR, REPEAT, TAYLOR HERE. SEE WHAT
YOU CAN FIND.

RAWLEY
```

Once I punch that through I begin getting nervous, my palms sweating—I am always nervous when I compose one of these:

```
channel        393//
sign key       0202/Voorst//

telex medium//
```

```
route:    local
          local
          Military Flight HQ
```

ATTN: MILITARY CMDR, FLIGHT

APPEAL SCICOM ORIG. RECLASSIFICATION TO GUAM SCICOM, EFFECTIVE 10-24.

APPEAL BASIS: ACCUMULATED LEAVE TIME.

S/Voorst, Rawley//Flt Vane Eng. Class 2//codex 292//sign key 0202//

"Too many drugs," Erica is saying from the kitchen/ bar; she is taking one capsule as we settle in before dinner. She is telling me about an older woman she saw while waiting for me. The woman staggered out of a D-bar down the way and fell at the cement curbing of a ramp, fracturing her skull.

"And in a SectorGold street," she goes on. "I say that's not her fault, she should have been better taken care of. The thing is not to take so many. I happen to be a moderate person. I mean, I don't believe in the drugs themselves, just what they open up inside you, it has to be there already. Do you know what I mean? God, she wouldn't have known if somebody was *do*ing her from the way she was walking. I saw it a block away."

When Erica comes to the couch, she is stirring Viennese coffee with cinnamon sticks, still talking. She is wearing the tight silver halter she wore when I first saw her in the L.A. trans-port, still slightly flushed from the bath, sweet-smelling.

As she settles next to me I point out that she took a handful of pills this morning—a handful. At the console I have begun retrieving some of the coded information I've assembled on Eva Steiner, beginning with a map array from LasVenus DataBase. We both watch it click into place on the smoky bronze window/wall:

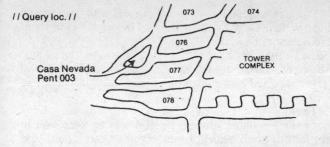

// Query loc. //

"But that's when I'm flying," Erica says. "I only do that many when I'm terrified. Taking off. Landing. Cruising. My stomach goes up to here," she says, pointing to the level of her breasts. "My nipples go crazy. I think it's all in my mind. I mean, I have to concentrate on getting the ship up, keeping it up. Which suits me for another kind of work, I guess," she giggles. "But otherwise, I'm very careful. I'm like a monk about what I put in my mouth." She giggles again. "Though we could try a little D-Pharmacon for kicks tonight." She focuses on the map, then asks what I'm looking at.

"A local residence," I say. Then, using Werhner's trick, I retrieve the personnel file I saw but didn't closely study before—the listing on Eva Steiner. The data on the screen describes a busy executive, but something is confusing. I can't determine whether she is an executive in security for EnergyWest, or whether she is given special security facilities for her EnergyWest work. The second, I think—or are they both blinds, covers for something else? She had originally been trained as a nuclear engineer, and seems to fly regularly on the ship.

"My God," Erica says when she realizes what she is seeing. "What are you doing reading that, how did you *retrieve* that? Eva Steiner—she's a *Director*, look, I told you about her. Oh, Rawley, lover, you ought to just forget it, you're going to get into trouble. What are you going to do?"

"I'm not sure," I say, switching off and letting the window/wall clear to show the city beyond. "Don't you have a report to make?"

Erica raises her hands. "Not me," she says, then sighs. "All right, look, *I* told you about her. I'll tell you everything else I know. This hairy man with glasses talked to me..."

"Taylor."

"That's his name. But all he said was to keep you in sight and in good health. Lover, I'm on your side. I told him that's exactly what I'd do, that's what I'm supposed to do. That's all. I think they treated Collette pretty rottenly, I told him that, too. I saw the way they took her. I don't know what this is all about, except that with people like Eva Steiner, you might get into trouble, so between you and me... I've been in trouble myself. It's not worth it."

I ask Erica what kind of trouble she's been in.

"They caught me getting off in L.A. six months ago with a suitcase full of brandy and ampules," she says, flushing with embarrassment. "I'm still on probation."

I punch up Erica's file, run through the security sheet; what she says is true. Courvoisier, Five Star, twenty-four bottles. I could use some right now. "You know," I say, half to myself, settling back on the sofa, "all I wanted to do when I came here was to get away."

"Honestly, I didn't know you were being screened till this morning," Erica says quietly. "I can't tell you what Collette's up to, but I know what I am. I mean, why am I here with you? That's what I told that man. This is the *Pleasure* Tube. I have a job to do, and look, I should be taking better care of you."

I look into Erica's slightly glazed blue eyes and laugh.

She laughs, too, pushes back her blonde hair, and sidles near me on the couch. "Well, actually, it doesn't seem much like work today," she says, putting her hands around my neck, then trailing one hand across my shoulder. "You have a nice body." She grins, moving her hips so that her skirt rides up her thighs, still moving her hips. Her other hand has slid down my spine and I can feel my back loosen up. "It's whatever you want, you know.

Don't forget that. You're your own worst enemy if you forget that. Anything. Anything you want."

Her breast cupped in my hand, a nipple in relief on the lamé halter, I feel a kind of sad detachment even as my sexuality responds to the touch and the soft weight of her. I ask myself what I have to regret—and as if in answer, Erica's head falls back, her eyes open wide and their pupils roll back as her mouth hangs open in heavy, self-absorbed breathing. Her legs come up across my lap and she opens her thighs. How overripe, how voluptuous, how enormously sexy she is, I think. And how enormously empty and alone I feel at this moment.

I roll her from me, rise, and ask her to help me strip for a bath.

We go to the Tower Complex to do a little gambling before dinner—risk ventures, Erica calls it. We pass through the viny, damp jungle lobby of a hunting game, the pornographic lobby of a population game—stills of couples having sex flash on the ceilings and walls; their juxtaposition with the formal, ornate chandeliers makes me laugh. We bypass the command center lobby of a game called WorldWarInfinity, curious as I am to know what's involved. At the moment I have an aversion to uniforms, and there are enough costume generals, both male and female, at the entrance to a bunker mock-up to make me instinctively turn away from the place itself. The game, it turns out, occupies the entire three-floor sector of the complex.

Erica says she enjoys the lavish display here in SectorGold but personally finds it more exciting in the other sectors, where popular games have at stake first-class tickets for the winners, while the losers drop a class. For the losers in the third-class martial arts competition, along with the beating comes a mandatory service assignment for two flights—without the good pay.

I mean to know where I am at all times, but soon enough, in the maze of corridors, intertower ramps, moving sidewalks, different scenes, and bright lights, I lose sense of where we are. There's something appealing about the traditional gaming rooms; perhaps it is the familiarity of their atmosphere. Finally we begin to gamble, spend a while at a green velvet table in a hushed, mahogany inlay room playing baccarat with couples dressed for the evening. The game quickens my pulse, and it is satisfying to come out a few hundred ahead, a quarter unit, after an hour.

We are looking for a D-bar when we come across StarFlightVenture on the seventieth floor. The hallways of the entire floor are designed to look like hatch passageways, and behind each thick glass door is a computer-linked starship console. The ship is of the newer Eagle class; I toyed with one on Guam and found it almost a duplicate of the Daedalus. Ah, I think, a setup, a piece of cake. All I need to do is shake the bank. I sign up for a unit with a sparrowlike, small woman at the control desk.

The game turns out to be work, but the work is worth about two thousand an hour. I stand just as I had on the Daedalus, at the three-meter-wide central console cluttered with monitors, vane keys, thruster links, and microweather sequence units; a dome ceiling follows the flight. Erica's pretty excited when I stop just over three thousand ahead. I'm a little swept away by my luck—over half the money, according to my own calculations, I owe to luck—and when the money's presented at the control desk, she does a little dance of ecstasy when I give it to her. Then she calls upstairs to the roof garden from the desk attendant's phone, asks for "something very nice, we aren't counting the small change tonight. The very best," and says that tonight an option dinner is on her.

"Turns out there's something for everyone here after all," I tell her with a grin.

We eat at one of the smaller, though the most expensive, of the rooftop restaurants of the Tower Complex, teahouses in the garden of a temple. The garden is sculptured, its air rich with the exotic odors of jasmine and ginger. We are bathed and clothed in kimonos, wrapped with obis, and taken by the hand by geishas to our separate teahouse on a knoll from which the stage of the Tower Shell is visible a half kilometer away, in the Moorish garden. And we see some artificial weather, a misty, thirty-second thunderstorm just as we finish our first round of warm sake.

Erica is flushed with pleasure, eating oysters. The last time she ate oysters, she tells me, was at her second wedding, when she was married to a Japanese linguist in New York. This brings it all back, she says.

Earlier, as my back was being scrubbed by a young, tittering Japanese girl, I had genuinely relaxed for the second time today, but again the comfort doesn't last any longer than the money I won. What a day. The more spectacular, the more dreamlike, LasVenus has become, the angrier a part of me feels—anger at myself, at what this trip has become, at SciCom most of all. It's so easy to lie back and let it happen here. Erica is rambling on, telling me about her love affairs. The memory of her second husband and a half liter of sake lead to a train of thought which makes her conclude that men have disappointed her over the years. Her first marriage, she tells me, was to a psychologist. Perhaps that accounts for the sheer quantity of her talk; she really has been talking incessantly. What, I wonder, can I do? I know very well from the maps I pulled this afternoon that Eva Steiner is probably less than a kilometer away, Collette in her vicinity; there's been someone at her suite all day, but I can't get a live line through.

After sashimi, tempura, Kobe beef, greens the like of which I've never seen, I suggest that we walk back to our suite. Erica has stuffed herself, and she tries to beg off with a painful moan. I tell her a little exercise is just what she needs, let's walk.

After only a few blocks, Erica is dogging it; she complains that she's already taken one long walk today, fetching me at the trans-port. I ask her if she'd like to take a cab—hoping she will; what I have in mind does depend on her wanting to go away.

"God knows," she sighs. "Please?"

We cross an interbuilding ramp, descend a set of elevators to transportation level.

"I'll walk," I say as she slides into the back seat of a taxi.

"To each his own. I think you're crazy."

I laugh. I am a little drunk.

She blows me a kiss as the cab drives away.

And so I go alone to the dark-glassed, curve-sided high-rise that contains Eva Steiner's penthouse. In cross section the building is a cloverleaf. I enter the main door—security in the lobby is satisfied only to see my green card, the class identifier—and I'm in before I can wonder about it. I find C leaf on the building plan, look up and think eighty floors up, a little drunkenly looking up, trying to picture Eva Steiner in my mind. According to her personnel readout she is 5'2" and dark, not the blonde bulk I had first imagined when I heard her name.

The doors of an express elevator open and I lift up the first sixty flights like a launch, the place close, the rug-covered walls smelling new. Then local elevator service takes me to seventy-eight and the small, elegant, and empty transfer lobby for the penthouse elevators. I signal for the penthouse lift without hesitation—there are two cameras in the hall above the French mirrors—the quicker the better, I think. It arrives in an instant, I begin to step in even as its doors begin to open—then step back toward the Louis XIV furniture; to my surprise the elevator is occupied.

A brawny, uniformed woman with short hair stares sharply at me, then slaps the inside STOP button of the machine.

"What do you want?"

"I'm here to, uh, check some of your secondary circuits," I say. "Sorry, we've got some out on the lower floors."

"That's not possible. Go away."

"Hold on," I begin.

But already the doors are closing and she disappears. The elevator no longer responds.

Alone in the lobby, I use my stiff green card to slip the

lock of the service-stairway door. I climb the dim stairway up its one flight and wind up in a small area facing a freight elevator—it doesn't respond, either. I am standing absorbed in thought when a shaft of light floods the stairway from below.

The same uniformed woman orders me to come down.

When in my embarrassment I reach the doorway where she is standing, she shoves something into my chest, a tubular metal frame—she has a rifle jammed in my ribs, she's as strong as a man.

"Hey," I say, backing up against the doorframe. It seems important to me at least to stay in sight of the lobby, the service stairway is too much like a dark alley, I can't get over her strength.

"That's twice," she says. "The third time you try to penetrate this security barrier, somebody's going to shoot."

"Closed party, huh?" I try to say with a smile.

She glares at me, perspiration in the hair on her upper lip, eases the weapon back, and I turn to walk slowly away. Then the back of my skull explodes, white like a huge wave broken just behind me, sense falling forward, see in the instant before my palms cushion against the carpet, looking back, rolling, the butt of her weapon raised like a sledge.

I am up, seething, as she pulls it back, a malicious smile on her face. "Get out," she mutters. "I mean what I say."

While Erica sleeps, her black satin robe collapsed beside me on the couch, I sort through my flight bag, folding my shirts, my blue flight suit, my old leather trousers. I've turned numb, my head throbs. Sitting on the edge of the couch, I take out the small package of photographs that had just been processed when I was leaving Guam. Most are from Utama Bay, photographs of Werhner with arms spread on the beach, the reef from the hills above, the Magellan statue, the base. One photograph of me before our shoebox, dingy cottage; I can almost see the heat of the dusty flat of the base rising beyond it. But I had begun the cassette of film months ago, and at its end, the sequence reversed in my looking, are the three photographs I had quickly put aside when I had first seen them as I waited for the flight out of the military terminal at Agana on Guam. Cooper, whose voice still rings in my ears, grins behind his beard in two, and in the third he is standing in the background, behind the three women who tended the program console, worry lines creasing his face. I stare at the photograph, stare at Cooper there still alive, wish the photograph could speak. Where *was* he in the ship then, at the blow? I vaguely recall seeing him, so he wasn't in the program wing—obviously, since it was the small program pontoon that was seared off at its hatch. Though why wasn't he where he belonged when we blew? That never seemed to matter on the way back—and, I think with a sigh, doesn't matter very much now.

I shuffle aimlessly through the photographs of the vivid, bright green and yellow hills above Utama Bay, the soft blue of the Pacific; Magellan's statue, a memorial to his landing at Utama Bay, is before my eyes. I think of his circumnavigation, the first loop, of the two unknown Portuguese sailors, the only two to survive the trip, Magellan dead in the Philippines. Those two Portuguese sailors, unknown: the first men to circumnavigate the earth and know in their bones how going straight out, sailing dead away, leads you back to where you began. Magellan's face is blank, his gray stone eyes without pupils. I consider what a vast ocean the Pacific, uncharted, was to those frail wooden ships, sailing straight out. How impossible, how simple, it seems.

It happens at night, in memory, dream, and darkness. When I come awake, my own perspiration cools the sheets, but my skin is burning. I remember this: a woman floating in space, then a funnel of light, deep blue light, into which I am falling, and it brightens, brightens into white as I fall faster and faster, and it is as if my bones explode, my body one with the vision of white light, a howling sun, a whirling sun.

I rise from the bed, stand naked on the small balcony,

and watch the constellations of lights from the city, a dull thumping at the back of my head, the night air a cool ache over my body.

DA6// The taxi lurches to a stop in the bright midday sun. "This is it," the young driver says, pointing. "That warehouse, next to the grandstand."

Erica steps out the opposite door, and I'm wondering just how discreet I have to be with her. We are on an industrial road off SectorBlue, but close to the automobile track. I can hear the whine of Formula E.

I try the door at the nondescript metal hangar whose address Massimo gave me. It is locked. I lead Erica into the grandstand to look over the side of the building—and the racing circuit opens up as we climb into the seating tier, a broad green expanse, a patch of woods, the track weaving out into the sector and back again. The seating tier angles along an S curve in the track, looks obliquely into the trackside of the warehouse: open hangar doors. Not a warehouse after all, but a cavernous garage whose business end is a series of busy pits, wide tires stacked four high, sleek cars. I decide to leave Erica in the third row, tell her she doesn't have to stay if she doesn't want to, then slip down through an unlocked gate to trackside.

Massimo, a big man, is easy enough to spot on the near side of the garage. At first glance I think he's organized a café, but there he is behind canopies and tables, between two blood-red cars of immaculate presence. They are antiques, elegant cars without a blister of corrosion on their lacquer-smooth surfaces. The cars obviously aren't Formula E, their design is so much older; one is a racer and the other a coupe. Massimo is talking with two technicians in red jump suits, his flushed face almost matching the color of the cars.

He grins when he sees me, opens his arms in greeting, then they open more broadly to the cars. Of course. They are the surprise he predicted the day before yesterday, what he'd had flown in.

"These come from Milano," he says expansively, "only for these days." The larger of the machines, he says, is the only surviving Ferrari Bianco del Guidici. It is low, combustion-powered by a V-16 slung between fat rear tires and topped by mirror-shiny exhaust stacks. The car radiates speed and quality, gives me a strange elation that seems to please Massimo as much as it pleases me. In this world of the videon, there is something familiar about the Ferrari, a world which seems more like home.

"And other," he says, showing me the smaller but equally striking two-seater coupe, "is Lancia. Not the power, but with Lancia—ah, with Lancia you are making love with young Neapolitan woman," he laughs. Massimo shows me the Lancia's unique strut suspension, and we look under its hood as he describes its antiskid braking console. More than a coupe, it has run at Le Mans. He describes the Lancia's ability to slide as a lover might describe the curves of his woman. The sculptured surface is so mirror-smooth that the Lancia reflects itself reflected in the Ferrari, translated through the Ferrari and transposed again into the parabolas and loops of its sleek lines. The technicians are sloping off the Ferrari's tune; it takes another ten minutes for its thunderous rumble to meet the test of Massimo's ear.

We wind up sipping Campari and waiting for lunch under a trackside canopy, my head finally coming right. I guess I hope Erica will just get bored and leave, though when I check she seems to be enjoying the show. Giroti's pit is just at the beginning of the S curve, and from our folding chairs we can watch the new Formula E's, looping the track in practice for the EnergyWest Grand Prix, whistle toward us, braking furiously, enter the chute, then chatter away. Massimo explains that, Formula E aside, with what his mechanics have been able to do, the Ferrari can hold its own on a track as tight and curvy as this one. His Bianco, as a matter of fact, held the standing lap record at Monza until a mere ten years ago.

Massimo wants to hear about Collette, he wants the story from its beginning. "With all sexy detail. Do not spare an old man." He smiles. I begin telling him, and we soon get sidetracked in SciCom's interest in me. So I tell him what I know about that, too, grateful that he's willing to listen. In the shade of the canopy, eating a Roman squid salad, I relate my interview with Taylor yesterday, my confusion about Collette as well as my confusion about why they want me back on Guam.

He's amused by my feelings for Collette, fascinated by our first meeting in what I had thought was the VIP lounge of the L.A. trans-port. A wonderful story; he smiles. He thinks Collette is probably not a malicious woman, but that I was a madman to trust her. The key, he tells me, to seeing her again, if that's what I really want, is SciCom's interest in her, which hinges back again on their deepest interest in me. So we loop even further back and I begin another story, the one which begins more than four years ago, out on range with the Daedalus.

I tell him how SciCom left us flying, for all practical purposes, blind; how the Committee Pilot, unable to decide on anything but the most general direction of our survey, left the tangent angle of event-horizon approach to the dome crew's day-by-day response to prevailing macroweather. I tell him how we nervously sat out the lull, the circumstances I recall at the blow, the three who died, Maxine included.

"This is at black hole," he says. "*Fantástico.*"

"Well off," I tell him. "Theoretically, had we been near the event horizon, or blown there... well, I wouldn't be telling the story. Of course we took precautions, we had a safety factor of more than ten. It's only speculation, but do you know what the physicists say?"

"Yes, I know black hole. *Prego*, this is what *I*, Giroti, say—a star described by a poet, *poeta romántico*—where a traveler can lose his freedom in space and become trapped forever—where the traveler is given freedom in time instead. Amazing possibility."

"We came as close as anyone has," I tell him. "It was a pretty hairy trip—it's still hairy." I explain how Cooper, who had written up our report, became separated from us at recovery in the Pacific and later died, how the rest of us have been kept on Guam for a pointless month. Massimo is charmed by the way I managed to slip away, and we drink a toast to that day—for what it's worth now, I think.

In the end, given the circumstances, he doesn't think that Collette is a SciCom employee assigned to watch me from the beginning of the trip; rather, someone they've used, who used me in turn.

"But who can finally tell?" he wonders. "Only this woman knows, if she would tell you. If you could trust her."

When I tell him that I've tried to get in touch with Collette by trying to get in touch with Eva Steiner, and that there is a barrier around that woman, whether it's private sex or security, I don't know—he lifts his hands palms upward and sighs.

"Both," he says. "And then we come back to SciCom. After I talk with you I remember this woman's name. She is well known. This woman is like a man, she walk like a man, she wear clothes like a man. She is Director of EnergyWest—but that is like saying SciCom, they are together like a hand which slide into fitted glove. Perhaps they are using her, I think, using the strangeness of this woman to see that you don't talk with Collette. This is a circle we are making, now I see. I tell you I have seen things with SciCom which frighten me—things like this. I will give example how it works. We have plutonium plant in Brazil with terrible discharge for a week—one week, I tell you. The river entirely dead, the people downstream sick, for a hundred kilometers, some die. Why is this? SciCom data overrides discharge controls, everyone knows this is so. But investigation goes on for six years now. I give you another example. In Argentina, two thousand cattle die from a wrong inoculation; it is SciCom instructions again. That investigation is lasting eight years, this is joke to me, but it is not joke to SciCom. For yourself, they cannot question your competence, since you have flown your ship back. But if *they* have made a mistake, they will never take responsibility. They never admit mistake. You know what my agriculture man says in Argentina? 'Until they have other explanation, they have only investigation.'"

"My navigator thinks they're trying to set us up. I don't know," I say, rubbing my chin. "I would really like to talk to the woman."

"*Non pensarci piu*," Massimo says, waving a fly from its loop around the salad. "Forget this one—you will see, there are others. And in this place? The man who wrote your ship's report, dead—ahhh. For your sake, I do not think it best you see this woman they take from you. Perhaps you will have luck with appeal—then, maybe. Almost always these people in SciCom are harmless, *castrati*—no, like men who play with themselves, *masturbati*. But if you catch them—ahhh. They do have . . . power," Massimo says quietly, his hands flat on the table. "They protect themselves, like Mafiosi. They do what they want."

A white Formula E whistles past as I lean toward Massimo; a shiver runs down my spine. For an instant I see Cooper's face in Massimo's, they share the same broad nose, the same thick hair. "You're afraid of them, too?" I ask, thinking of my run-in with security last night. "Do you think Werhner's right? He thinks that Cooper's death . . ."

"All right." Massimo nods, smiling to himself. "I exaggerate. A marr dead—this frightens me. But yes, I exaggerate. This is only my advice, to leave them alone— what can you do, a pilot? Ah, Rawley, let us not think on these things for now, let us forget them for a time."

"I've been . . ." I start to say, then notice Massimo is looking at the cars.

"You think you can handle Lancia?"

My pulse quickens, I tell Massimo I'd like to try.

"Well, come, I am going to run Ferrari. We shall see if perhaps you can drive, too."

The pleasant coolness of its leather upholstery aside, my immediate impression of the Lancia is that its steering is too tight and its suspension very stiff; I can feel every bump in the track, the car seems jittery. But as I learn the course, its straights, banks, and S's, I pick up speed and with a rising howl I enter a tunnel of motion and the machine itself seems to smooth the ride. The cockpit becomes comfortable in the moving air, and the car begins to feel the way hand-cut clothing feels—close, comfortable, another skin—seems more like flying than the days in theTube. The sunny track is a good, long ride—over ten kilometers—on a banked, twisting surface like an idealized freeway through the city. I roar past separate grandstands in different sectors, through a tunnel of high-rises, down a straight through a greenbelt with a murderous, decreasing radius hairpin at its end, accelerate up into a set of elevated S's whose edges raise the hair on the back of my neck the first time through. In the curves the Lancia resists braking, it wants the line, it propels itself through a corner with its own fine calculus of speed, weight, and cohesion into a beautiful slide.

The Formula E drivers practicing the course for the EnergyWest Grand Prix make for fast traffic. Massimo laps me twice, then I hang on his tail to catch the pull of his slipstream and sail with him through the turns, feeling the G's accumulate, feeling the car adjust to sustain them just on the line. He shows me some very nice driving, takes us both past two Formula E cars in the tight S's by finding and holding a deeper line of descent at a higher entrance speed. I learn something in ten laps, the tranquility of Massimo's driving. Despite our speed, his driving seems unhurried, an exercise in simple grace.

We pull into the pits, talk about the track, then switch machines. The balance and the instinct for the line are the same for the Ferrari, but what a powerful racing machine. When I'd floor the accelerator in the Lancia, the car would dig in, push me back into the seat, and go; in the Ferrari in any gear the wide rear tires burn blue, and I am slapped back into the seat as acceleration forces my breath. Until I get its feel, the Ferrari is too slippery for me; once I make speed I lose it completely in an embarrassingly long slide out of the wide S's near Massimo's pit. Then finally it comes on the roller coaster of the final turns. I get the feel of the car, or it gets the feel of me, and I'm able to bear down the straights almost with the Formula E's and slip past the slower ones in the S's and hairpin.

When we are finally flagged off the track to

accommodate Formula E time trials, Massimo is pleased. A hundred meters from the exit gate of the tight S's, he was still nose ahead of a Formula E whose driver, he tells me, looked at him and checked his gauges, then nearly lost it on the next embankment—where Massimo was able to slip under him again.

"How can those cars have a soul," he asks as we wash at the mechanic's sink, "if driver can know how he is driving only by watching numbers?" He tells me that when he was racing, he would practice with the tachometer of his Ferrari taped over. That kept his mechanics awake nights, he laughs. He was with his Ferrari like this, he says, snaking one finger around the other.

"But now"—Massimo smiles—"I prefer Lancia. She forgives, like a woman she forgives. At my age, a man need forgiving, yes?"

I laugh and tell him I'll count having driven the Ferrari among the genuine pleasures of my life.

"Ah, yes," Massimo says. "This is like hologram, everything comes true. I think you are right for that car, reckless enough to run too fast into a turn to begin with. How old are you—I mean, you tell me proper time."

"Thirty-five."

Massimo nods; his age exactly when he drove the first Ferrari Bianco.

"What's the right age for Formula E?"

"Fifteen," he says with a sneer, his eyebrows raised in irony. "The car has two gears—two gears!"

Before I leave we sit under the canopy again for a time, and I ask Massimo if he can do something for me.

"Of course," Massimo answers with a wry smile.

"I'd like to meet Eva Steiner," I say. "Just to talk. You never know. You're a UN Governor—is there something you could do?"

Massimo fills his wine glass, fills mine, then lifts his and drinks. "Worse than myself," he says with a grin. "I've told you about Eva Steiner. And you could not get a single live line to her? Rawley, I don't know."

"Will you try?" I ask. "This isn't SciCom, just one woman."

"Well, I will see. *Domani*," he says. "Tomorrow. We will talk more then. And do more driving. Agreed?"

When I look for Erica, I check the time and realize that half my stay in LasVenus is gone already. I have one tomorrow left—two, if I can count a morning a day. I find Erica almost in the top row of the grandstand seats. She has a sunburn and has had, she tells me, a very nice sleep.

After a relaxing hour in the aquaplease whirlpools, Erica and I have dinner again at the temple garden, the Japanese restaurant on the roof of the Tower Complex. I haven't done justice to the rooftop—we are tucked in a small corner where the temple rises on an artificial hill beyond carp ponds, the night sky is beyond, the impression is one of a mountaintop. In the other direction, the Japanese garden shades into an orchid grove, which melts into a tropical garden of ferns, fan palms, royal palms, MacArthur palms, butterfly palms, queen palms. Today I notice people milling around in English, French, Dutch, gardens, other restaurants and clubs, of course, and a central Moorish garden with its show. We can take part in gaming and risk ventures through a plug-in console that is now on our low table; it seems people are arranging to meet one another through the consoles as well. Erica is absorbed in a complicated, penny-ante card game through it—bureaucrat's bridge, she mutters. Different strains of music float through the air, in our cubicle the Bartók I program. Directly above us, the sky is being used as a holographic projection screen for cloud displays to complement the artificial weather. Between weather displays, the clouds are dreamlike, suggestive, shaped into stories both fantastic and erotic—it would be pleasure enough to lie back and watch.

This whole affair—not only LasVenus, but theTube as well—is easy enough to understand in terms of technology, but harder and harder for me to comprehend after what I saw today walking back from the track with Erica to Casa del Sol, a walk that consumed an hour. I kept along the perimeter; the other city is separated from this resort by highway, mostly, or by high fencing in two rows with a bleak no man's land of fifty meters between. On the other side the housing was crowded, steamy—there is no dome here as there is over L.A.—and the city seemed to stretch away interminably. A population problem exists there; the contrast with LasVenus resort is immense. The air even in SectorGold has a kind of acid smell to it at street level, masked by gardenia and jasmine here so far above.

I am getting my bearings here, yet time seems to be slipping away too quickly for me to make use of my temporary stability. In the end I find Werhner still impossible to raise, Eva Steiner locked into a private world whose surfaces seem without seams.

I find myself sitting on the edge of my low chair, not following what Erica is saying about the plot of a narrative cloudshow, evidently an erotic version of a popular daytime serial. Erica, it turns out, has been married four times in all, each marriage more a disaster than the last, at least from the way she tells the story through dinner.

Finally I suggest we go—my appetite is back, but I have to move to work off this nervous energy. Erica ate too much, I think, she moans painfully at the idea of getting up, her sunburn is bothering her, too. It doesn't make any sense to do something stupid again, I suppose, and I think that if I walked home alone again, I might. And so we go down to the lobby to look for a cab.

"Rawley Voorst."

We are passing leather couches in the lobby near the activities screens when I hear my name. I see the older man, Mancek, first, before I see Taylor himself, rising from one of the couches by the bright show-program screen.

"Enjoying yourself?" I ask halfheartedly.

"Quite a place." Taylor smiles. "Quite a place, don't

you think? They have everything here."

"Everything," I say. "Including people following you around."

"Don't be so hostile, Voorst. The Tower Complex is open to anyone who can afford it," Taylor says calmly. "We're just looking around. I thought I'd let you know we were waiting. Won't be long."

Taylor is looking at Erica; her tight dress is tighter still after dinner. His thick lips are slightly parted, he's leering, if you ask me; his eyes wander from her breasts to her belly to her breasts, straining under the silver lamé. When he asks what we've been doing, he asks her.

"Look," Erica says, "I told you yesterday I'm assigned to him and not to you. We're doing just fine."

Taylor's face reddens, he looks as if he wants to say something, but his lips tighten and he doesn't. Behind him, in the sleek lobby, the rainbow-hued screen displays show programs: two women dancing with one another; behind them the same, increasingly sexual movements are being followed by a dozen pairs of men:

SIDEREAL CONCERT/SIDEREAL CONCERT/CONCERT
DUNES/DUNES/DUNES/DUNES/DUNES/DUNES/DUNES/DUNES
SHOWTIMES// 10/12/2/4/6/8/10   10/12/2/4/6/8/10

As we climb into a small, elegant cab I thank Erica for the way she behaved.

She shrugs, adjusting her skirt under her thighs, letting her hand slip over to my leg. "I don't blame you for not trusting me," she says, "but I meant what I said. I'm on your side, Rawley. I like you, that's all—and so long as you don't complain about how I treat you, there's nothing they can do to me. There's something with him, anyway—did you see the way he looked at me? He's got about as much tact as a truck. What a creep."

"You would have liked the debriefing," I said sardonically. "He was the one who told me that a guy I knew pretty well from the ship—a big, healthy, part-Indian guy named Cooper—killed himself. Told me with a kind of grin."

"He could work for Service Control," she sighs. "Same

type. I can just see my next assignment, some dried-up old cheapskate who doesn't need an hour's sleep for two weeks."

"Well, thanks again," I say, kissing her on the cheek and drawing her closer to me in the lush darkness of gold sector local transport.

CHAPTER 6
Risk Venture Vector

What I will always owe Erica is this massage. Her hands are strong and confident as she flexes the contours of my neck muscles, straightens something in my back I didn't even know was out of place, cures my headache for good. But I feel a little depressed this morning after, awake again in the middle of the night—I feel as if it's a morning after, that says enough.

Silk sheets again. I don't know if I'm going to be able to sleep on a cot after this. I'd settle instead for my old bunk on the Daedalus, or even a freighter's gravity hammock. Here I have silk sheets and a triple-sized recliner that adjusts to my weight like a lover. I remember the first morning of this trip waking on silk sheets, opening my eyes, and the odor of Collette, so pleased that she hadn't disappeared in my sleep.

Erica is telling me that Tonio is guest-producing a videon special from the Moorish garden tonight. He called this morning to invite us both to the sound stage for the secondary shots he will be setting up all afternoon— says, moreover, that he's dropping the male service he picked up in coming here.

"Go if you want to," I say. "I'm going to do a little more driving."

Erica is pleased that I don't mind. "Just promise you won't get into any trouble," she says, her hands slipping upward on my neck to ease the base of my skull.

"Well, I could lose it in the S's like I did yesterday," I say.

"Keep your *head* down. Drive carefully, will you? I do feel responsible for your health, special instructions or no. Promise?"

The seating tier adjacent to Giroti's pits is virtually empty again today, except for a young, stylish camera crew in the top row and a middle-aged couple who seem to be curious about taping. We are on the very edge of SectorBlue, I think; from the plastic-backed seats of the tier the S's stretch away to the right along the green swath of infield, toward one of the stadiums. When I turn to the gate, the pits obliquely to the left, the line of cars seem like patients in a trauma center linked to electronics consoles and plastic tubes among the stacked tires.

Once through the chain link, I see that Massimo is with someone, a shorter man, I judge automatically from the soft black leather suit; then when I get closer, I realize from the turning profile the someone is a woman—straight forehead, angular chin, fiftyish. They are talking and I stop ten meters away, wave hello to Massimo's mechanic. The woman with Massimo has her hair short-cropped, she is aiming some sort of pointer at the Ferrari's cockpit.

Massimo sees me, calls "*Ciao*, Raoul-lay," his hand comes up in the air to wave me over to the Ferrari. Halfway the engine starts up with a rumble, then a mean crack of revolutions. The smell of nitro exhaust slices through the thick odors of oil and rubber.

The woman seems transfixed by the car—she doesn't even notice my joining them. She hugs herself to the sound of the engine—Massimo has the oddest look on his face; his eyebrows are raised nervously and his cheeks are reddening as if he wants to shout something but knows he won't be heard above the engine.

It shuts down quickly at the wave of his hand.

"Director Steiner," he says to the woman, then turns to me. I can see the smile on his face. He started talking too loud, his voice drops dramatically: "Allow me to introduce a friend, Rawley Voorst. He is pilot and driver. Rawley—Eva Steiner."

Massimo looks at me through his polite laugh, I look at the woman again—her gray eyes take me in without recognition or interest. She nods, then moves next to the Ferrari, putting out her hand. "Feel the heat," she says to herself; "there is nothing like this, nothing."

Of course. Her hair is black, but it's been dyed black. In every other way she fits the description of her personnel readout, though I don't think I would have recognized her. She has a small, straight nose, thin lips. Something's not right about her eyes. There is a glaze to them, or a sheen. Drugs, I think. D-Pharmacon. I look at Massimo, he looks as uncomfortable in her presence as I've become, his smile seems as uncertain as mine.

"Director Steiner is a great admirer of all Formula cars—and she has hydroplane, think of that, Rawley," Massimo says, trying to start a conversation, but Eva Steiner is absorbed in the cars—the feel of their metal, their leather interiors, the sound of their engines. She acts as if I'm not there, barely Giroti, and I think he shuts the Ferrari cockpit from her approach for just that reason.

"It was really kind of you to let me come," she says to Massimo. "I should have shipped in my own Formula E—my delicious Formula E. But even that's not quite the same. There's something wonderfully cruel about the Ferrari, don't you think? You should have it painted black—everything black."

Massimo's forehead creases in annoyance. "My country, Director Steiner, you see..." Before he can even begin to explain racing colors, she has moved around to the rear of the car, where she squats down and rubs her hand across the surface of the wide rear tires.

"Very good," she says, stroking.

Massimo is livid. "Would you like to drive the car, Director Steiner? Perhaps then you can get what you came for. Take it on the track, I don't care. Perhaps you can even drive it."

"Can I drive it," she says flatly, rising and flexing her

back. "Yes, I can drive it. I've driven Formula E in competition." Then she smiles thinly. "You really are a darling man, Governor Giroti, don't be upset by a . . . fantasy. I would love to drive it." It is a pointer that she has—or something like one, a thin black cylinder about a half-meter long—and her hand has been gripping it so tightly that her knuckles are white.

Then she relaxes; and I can see Massimo relax, too.

In a few minutes Eva Steiner is checked out in the blood-red Bianco, takes some stimulants, and moves loudly onto the track. My hearing is numbed by the noise and for a minute we can't quite talk.

"I'm sorry I get angry," Massimo begins sheepishly. "I do not like that woman."

"I don't, either. But look, I appreciate your getting her here."

"I find out last night she has a passion for such things," Massimo says. "I tell you she has hydroplane also, can you imagine? She is worse than they say—in this place, yes, she can do these things."

At the rising whistle I look out toward the track and follow a wedged Formula E skittering through the S's.

"But as you say, what a woman this is," Massimo begins in a tone that sounds strange. "Skin the color of life."

"Of death, you mean," I say, turning to see what he is talking about, seeing that he is looking over to the seating tier. Three women dressed in charcoal suits are being seated by an older man dressed in the same style.

"No, not Steiner." Massimo is laughing, beginning really to laugh, "Rawley . . ." he says.

In profile she is unmistakable—perfect forehead, aquiline nose, full lips that pout a little, skin the color of *café latta.*

The woman is Collette.

She is staring ahead, oddly inert; when she looks our way from twenty meters distance, her face is slack. She meets my gaze with a blank stare and a faint movement of her lips; doesn't really seem to know who I am.

"Yes, yet it is true, they all look, for this time of day, Rawley, *troppo imbalsamara*—what you say, embalmed."

She doesn't seem to know quite who I am even as I point my index finger at her and gently pull the trigger of an imaginary pistol. I hear the low whine and rumble of the Ferrari, look to see the bright red car pounding too high toward us in the S's. Eva Steiner is visible for an instant, fighting the wheel. She skids along the fence dangerously high, makes it down for the first turn, but the Ferrari is pointed sideways, and she has to let the car slide itself up and out into the far curve, almost to a stop, a dead stop, before she is downshifted and fishtailing into the straight, hard after a Formula E that had blown by her in the second turn.

"*Porca madonna,*" Massimo says in disgust. "She thinks she is driving Formula E. My car!"

When I saunter over to the gate, the older man with Collette and the other two women comes over and puts his fingers through the steel links, keeping the gate between us.

"We're just fine," he says. He is older, but he isn't as old as Eva Steiner. His combed black hair is thinning and his complexion is pasty, his eyes watery. "We're all taken care of."

"I didn't ask," I say. Collette and the other two women are staring ahead at the track. "What are their names?"

"Private party." He smiles. "That's just the way it is."

"Oh, I'm just looking." I smile back amiably. "I see they're all dressed the same way. Attractive, really attractive."

"They're all named Max, actually," he tells me with a smile, moving aside a little to show the women off.

"Max?"

"That's what Eva calls them," he says, putting himself in my way again, the nervousness returning to his smile.

An irony compounds itself; Max is what we used to call Maxine. Up in the stands the film crew has a telephoto trained on the chute to the S's, I hear the Ferrari, turn to see. Eva Steiner is too high again. She loses a tenth coming in, two tenths in the way she sets up for the next curve, she still doesn't quite have the feel of the car.

Collette never takes her eyes off the track—but it doesn't look as if she's following any of the cars, either. Or maybe it's me; when she seems to start to turn my way, I avoid her. She knew all along, I think, she knew all along. Collette looks like heaven in a waiting room of hell.

When the rumbling Bianco del Guidici eases into the pits, Eva Steiner is peeved, her face wet with perspiration, her makeup smeared. She grants the Ferrari its balance but claims the car is too light, says so even as she is climbing from the cockpit.

"I prefer Formula E," she states once her helmet is off and she drinks some ice water—she scoffs at her lap times, the last few of which weren't that bad. "It is a matter of power over style. I prefer the power of Formula E to this relic."

I think Massimo, who has been looking with worry at the Ferrari, has had about enough from Eva Steiner. I can smell the car now—the sharp, overripe odor of nitrogasoline, the heat of it. There is a long, embarrassed silence, Massimo is simply refusing to speak, looking past Eva Steiner's smile and mocking eyes.

"I could beat you in the Ferrari," I say evenly. "I don't think it's the car."

The space between us for a moment turns electric. Eva Steiner raises her eyebrows, Massimo falls a step back and looks at me with surprise. Eva Steiner says she considers my remark a challenge; her nostrils flare slightly as she says that.

"I don't know." I shrug, thinking, Push this woman, not knowing quite where this is going to go. "I don't have much time for games."

"Men only say that when they're not very good at ... games," she snaps. "I think, with the Governor here as a witness, you're obliged to prove what you say or retract it. Apologize."

"I don't see I have to do either," I say, rubbing the back of my neck.

Now Massimo's jaw has gone slack, he is looking at me in wonder—and I'm wondering again what I'm going to say next. If anything is going to happen, it had better be soon.

"Not interested," she sneers. "Not much of a man, either."

"Well, what's at stake here?" I say. "Let's get this straight. If you'd like to race, fine—that's about a twenty-five-second handicap I've offered you, each lap. But there had damned well better be something on the line. I don't race for kicks."

"Ah, *straordinario, fantástico*!" Massimo exclaims. "I forget I am in LasVenus, yes—there is something in the air of this place!"

"Perhaps you'll wind up as one of my slaves," Eva Steiner scowls at me.

"Or you one of mine," I answer even as I am trying to be certain I've heard what she's said.

The silence of our circle is filled with the noises from pit crew and track, but it is a silence that is charged and palpable. Eva Steiner is appraising me, looking me over from my forehead to my flight shoes, looking straight into my eyes with a slight squint to her own. "I didn't know you were so inclined," she says slowly, her pale lips curling into a thin smile.

I say nothing, only raise my eyebrows slightly to suggest that she hasn't begun to guess the range of my inclinations.

"Very well," she says, reddening slightly. "I can have a decent car here in two hours. Governor Giroti, I would be pleased if you'd act as our witness. The young man has named the stakes. The loser will become the winner's slave for a day—until theTube lifts off. Those are my terms. We'll race one lap from a flying start. Acceptable?" she asks. "You've named the stakes," she says without really waiting for my answer, verging on anger. "We'll see who can drive."

● ● ●

"It is because of this place—do you know we are between two large fault lines in the earth? There is something in the seismicity of this place," Massimo says after the woman and her service leave abruptly. "The risks men take here are exceptional. I have seen it, that's why I come. The air here smells of ozone from burning dreams."

Technicians are pulling the hood on the Ferrari in the cool shade of the metal and concrete building; there is an odor here, the odor of the heated engine, the burning smell is familiar. It takes me back somewhere, pulls me inexorably; yes, I think—the odor of seared cables, of metal too hot to touch, of the last time I saw Maxine. Now to think of Maxine is to think of Collette.

"How far can Steiner go?" I ask. "Let's say if I can't catch her. I figure she does have fifteen seconds, maybe seventeen. What can she do to me if I can't make those up?"

Massimo shrugs. "Who can tell? This is why I wonder if I should have stopped you. The flying start is bad for you, good for her. As for your wager? She is Tube passenger, she cannot be controlled; you see how it is. So I think you know what it means to make this wager with such a woman. Her slave for a day—enough. But to take that risk—this is beautiful, it is passion—for a woman, Rawley..."

"Well, I'm in it for a while now," I say. I tell Massimo I'd like to take the Ferrari out for a few laps. It's amazing how my head has cleared.

Later, I determine the optimum fuel load for the Ferrari on the full-sized terminal in the air-conditioned office/console room, separated from the pits by a glass wall. Since we'll be racing only one lap, I will be able to save eighty kilos in gasoline weight, I realize. I plug that figure into a formula and find I will pick up ten or eleven seconds over a full tank. I'm going to need those ten seconds. I know I will lose almost that much time to the more powerful Formula E in the first long straight following the initial S's, and I'll be too far behind by the back straight to use the pull from her slipstream—so I'll have to count on being close enough at the final turns to win.

Mulling over the formula, I punch up channel 393 and do a double take at the screen when I realize there is traffic for me—something from Guam through a debugging rider.

Something from Werhner. I set the printer to relieve debug, the message is holding as a blur, waiting for the proper decoding signal—I key in and watch it appear quickly, letter by letter, on the screen:

```
channel 393/ /IN IN IN IN IN IN IN IN IN IN IN IN
sign key 0208//Schole

telex medium//

route:   Guam Utama Sta.
         Midway
         Honolulu
         SoCal Center
         LasVenus Local (des.)
debugging rider:   erase if intercept//only 393

ATTN:  RAWLEY VOORST

ACKNOWLEDGE QUERY 7-8. SO NOW YOU THINK I WAS
RIGHT, YOU SKEPTIC.

YOUR SUGGESTION TO CHECK WHAT SCICOM IS ACTU-
ALLY HOLDING LEADS TO INTERESTING RESULTS,
FRIEND.

TWO GROSS ANOMALIES—MESSY BOOKKEEPING OR A
BLIND.

FIRST// THERE IS NO OUTGOING DATA ENCODED
UNDER DAEDALUS TITLE IN GUAM DATABASE—OTHER
THAN THE DATA IN COOPER'S REPORT. SECOND//DATA
CONFORMING TO FLIGHT PLAN, EXCEPT FOR DATES,
ENCODED IN PAIR WITH INCOMING DATA, SHIP TITLE
ICARUS, TOUCHED DOWN FOUR YEARS AGO.

LOOKS LIKE A BLIND? I WILL TRY AND SORT OUT THIS
SPAGHETTI.
```

YOU GOT ME OUT OF THE WATER. I'M FOR SEEING THIS
THROUGH, ADVISE YOUR END. ESTIMATE HERE TWO
DAYS FOR SEARCH PROGRAM.

WERHNER.

My blood pressure is up, adrenalin into my system for
the fifth or sixth time today, my right hand is throbbing.
Down from my palm the two scars describe a lazy figure
eight lying on its side across a descending lifeline; the dull
pain is a kind of stiffness to the heel of my hand, I feel it at
each heartbeat. Beyond the thick glass wall of the office,
mechanics seem to swim over the Ferrari, the two
Formula E cars up on hydraulics beyond it as if floating in
a vivid dream. There is a light change in the glass and the
scene looks unreal to me.

channel 393//BREAK BREAK BREAK BREAK BREAK

routing: Pre 1
           debugging rider Pre 1

ATTN: WERHNER SCHOLE

TAYLOR HERE FORCING MY TRANSFER GUAM MONDAY.
APPEAL TO MILITARY DOESN'T LOOK GOOD. I WILL TRY
TO CHART ONE LINE FROM HERE, PERHAPS WE CAN GET A
FIX IF YOUR DATA CHARTS.

CROSS-CHECK ICARUS PERSONNEL AGAINST SERVICE
RECORDS, OMEGA SYSTEM AGAINST DATE OF MANUFAC-
TURE, ETC. THIS ONE REALLY LOOKS LIKE A BLIND.

COULD USE YOUR BRINE-SOAKED SKIN, I MAY BE IN FOR A
FEW WELTS. WAIT UNTIL YOU HEAR ABOUT THIS ONE.
MAKES VIVIAN FROM PROGRAM LOOK LIKE FABLED
JEANNIE D.—REMEMBER HER?

RAWLEY

I clear the terminal and sit with the fuel formula I have
written on a pad, the cold-white dancing in my vision.
Vivian, the lady with the whip, and fabled Jeannie D., the
milk-white English girl—I wonder again if Werhner

remembers Jeannie D. from the other leave in Hong Kong.

CLEAR TRACK/ /CLEAR TRACK/ /CLEAR TRACK/ /CLEAR TRACK/ /

RISK VENTURE VECTOR/ /RISK VENTURE VECTOR/ /RISK VENTURE
VECTOR/ /RISK VENTURE VECTOR/ /RISK VENTURE VECTOR/ / / /
TWO PARTICIPANT ONE LAP RACE AFTER FLYING START/ /
TWO PARTICIPANT ONE LAP RACE AFTER FLYING START/ / / /
SPECTATOR WAGERS CONCOURSE NINE/ /SPECTATOR WAGERS
CONCOURSE NINE/ /SPECTATOR WAGERS CONCOURSE NINE/ /
CLEAR TRACK/ /CLEAR TRACK/ /CLEAR TRACK/ /CLEAR TRACK

"All system go? Ready?"

"*Sí.*"

"*Buona fortuna.*"

"*Grazie,*" I say to Massimo.

My knees are rubbery, but that will pass once we're moving—sucked into the Ferrari, that's how it feels, my legs extended, the seat cradled around me, belts snug. Massimo signals the starting cart, a thunder cracks the air just behind my head, the cockpit is lowering, and I secure the releases with both hands, lean back into the headrest. Alongside me on both sides the bulbous fuel tanks. This is driving a bomb, I think; what it would be like to crawl out of here. Not a car to crawl from, but to race in; what an idea, just what Massimo would say, *cosi simpático.*

I ease the tight gearbox into its high first, let out the clutch and the Ferrari staggers into the sunlight. Massimo has for us ten minutes of empty track, his contribution at an enormous price. Eva Steiner's Formula E is angled on the first bank of the S's, ass end up for the roll to start. I roll to a stop just at the end of the pits and work the choppy engine. As it warms it smooths from velvet to silk; higher on the track I watch the black, squat flywheel car shimmer in the heat, Eva Steiner absolutely motionless within, glaring at me.

Massimo walks past with the white starting flags, gives me a high sign. I signal ready, thumbs up. Eva Steiner begins to creep down the track when he raises the flags—we will roll through a lap together and then take the flying start from this point, race to this point again for a finish.

I think of Collette for an instant—then I get angry as hell.

A flag points at each of us and we go.

In a moment I am traveling through the blurred tunnel of rapid motion, hard on the right rear tire of Eva Steiner's broad, squat machine, the eerie high whistle of her engine audible through the bone-shaking roar of the Ferrari's V-16 and the whine of its gears. Once out of the S's, we boom into the straight alongside one another and she picks it up. Halfway through the greenbelt she pushes the pace of the prerace lap almost to the Ferrari's top end. She is pushing it in the pickup lap, why, I wonder—for a startled moment I think we might have actually begun the race.

But no. I ignore the line for the decreasing radius hairpin and position myself at her right rear tire again—she's passed me—she's in the high chute faster than she's prepared for, judging by the way her rear end is chattering, almost a skid. Ah, the speed she made in the straight was meant to spook me, but she wasn't ready for my being so close, it's spooked her instead.

Coming out, I squeeze into second and roll to the inside, blow by the wallowing Formula E.

For the rest of the lap—through the short straight, the elevated S's, the back straight, and reentry turns—we run at a smooth and even hundred, she wants me alongside and I accede. Without turning I can see in the periphery of my vision her helmet turned toward me. Coming into the flying start the tunnel of motion surrounds us both, I concentrate on my breathing, take it down from fifth to slow us both, I know this is annoying her. She does seem shaken by her mistake—but she can afford a mistake and still take the lap we are about to run.

A hundred meters from Massimo, who's energetically waving the flags, I brake hard, pop behind, and switch sides, jam the throttle. As we cross Massimo's lap line and the race begins I am above Steiner on the track. She's lost me until she looks for her own line in the S's—but that's where I am, up on her right, the Ferrari doesn't belong up here and the wheel fights the track. But the Formula E has to slow, and I drop in front of it.

My mirror shows her inches behind—and I tap the brakes. The Ferrari weaves and her pass is disabled; I downshift, downshift, tap the brakes again, take us out of the S's in what seems like slow motion, is slow motion, down to forty. We begin the run at the straight, but this time she is far below her torque range. I have the Ferrari's sweet spot in third, then fourth, and before she can catch me I've picked up a few seconds, then move up behind to get sucked into her slipstream, the hairpin ahead.

We are both sliding too much in this turn, its radius decreasing, becoming sharper and sharper, I bang my hand and jam a shift, the wheel is pulling fiercely. Still, I get below and out again, the Ferrari so flawlessly smooth as I get on it that the blur of acceleration makes me feel as if I am flying over the track, flying toward the elevated S's.

I almost lose control—wind, a gust of wind?—my mind registered nothing, had to have been blank—the Ferrari breaks loose, I feel a stab of panic drifting up to the Formula E, passing but then behind in its slipstream inches behind the black car, the Ferrari straightens out and Eva pulls the two of us tail to nose into the approaching curves.

Ice grips my heart—for an instant out of control, had I not been caught by the Formula E's slipstream, who knows, I don't remember just why I broke loose—but now, surfing through the elevated S's, the car is in full communication with the paving, responds perfectly, tracks its line as a sailboat in perfect trim sails itself. My breathing settles back to something like normal. Inches behind the Formula E, these turns so wide my advantage is to use her greater speed by riding her vacuum, I gain seconds this way and I ride close, the inch between us a static moment amid the smear we scream through, so close that she cannot shake me until two hundred meters into the back straight. She begins to pull away meter by meter, the distance between us increasing more and more rapidly when I lose the vacuum from her tail. But I think she is too late, the straight won't be long enough for her to get what she needs for the last rights and lefts that will finish the race.

By turn eight, three to go, I am back at her right rear wheel, up on the high side of the track, teasing her line and watching her rear end chatter and slip. I can take it down to the Ferrari's proper line and get by, but I wait, want her higher still, push her through the next two turns.

I know I've won; I tell myself, Easy, now, as we perch up for the last left, shift down a gear and right into the center of the sweet spot of maximum torque as I aim the nose for the lowest line I can imagine and slip by her, through the chute and thrown out by its massive G's propelled dead center on the track, booming toward the checkered flag, Eva Steiner a length or more behind—like tick-tack-toe, lady, and I had the first move—cross the line, I am exhilarated, high out of my mind, float through a victory lap on the sunbathed track, barely make *that* on the gas I've got remaining.

I guzzle from a split of Asti Spumanti, accepting Massimo's congratulations, I am radiant. What driverly moves in the final turns, Massimo tells me, not a mistake. Why did I drift up in the first straight? Reckless but somehow right, since I gained time. What a triumph for the Ferrari, he laughs expansively, *trionfo, vittoria.*

This is genuine pleasure, I tell him, impossible to program, dazzling to grasp.

Pulling into the pits, I saw Collette in the first row of the grandstand, wide-eyed and carriage erect as I have not seen her since our first meeting.

Helped from the cockpit of the black Formula E, Eva Steiner is ashen, a pallor to her face visible under the sweat-smeared grime.

"Si raccoglie quel che si semina," Massimo says.

"Which means?"

"How you say? If you dig the pit, you will fall into the pit."

She pulls her racing helmet from her head, swings it by its chin strap, arches, and slams it into the car—then lets the helmet fall clattering to the concrete floor.

"You drove well, Eva," Massimo says kindly.

She takes a long breath and glares at him, at me. "I'm *mortified*, of course," she says to me. "But you're reckless. I didn't see that in you, but you're reckless, you're dangerous, now I can see that in your eyes. You nearly killed us both in the first straight."

I slosh some wine in my mouth and watch her expression. I still don't know what happened there, and it seems inconsequential; something happened, yes, the Ferrari was out of control, but from that error I locked into her slipstream and perhaps won the race because of it.

The skin surrounding her gray eyes is creased with fatigue, but her head is erect and her lips tight. "I might have won with my own car," she says bitterly. "I could have pulled far enough away from you. Such a race isn't worth my life." She is motioning toward the chain-link gate, to the pasty, older man looking after the women of her entourage.

"Campari?" Massimo offers. "Eva, you drove well, you have no need to be ashamed. Rawley has run the lap in 202. 202!! That is faster than my own best time."

"Perhaps you will allow me to make some arrangements," she says to me. "I'm not so sure I feel bound by our agreement. You're a dangerous man, I can see it in your eyes, I don't trust you. You tried to kill me in the straight."

"Now, Eva," Massimo says, "such things can be in a race, do not misunderstand—"

"*Prego*," I say, interrupting him, I talk to Eva Steiner. "I never did like your game. You're about as interesting a prize as a lovesick Doberman. Tell your man to bring those women over here. Maybe we can reach a compromise."

● ● ●

An anger rises in my blood as I stand before Collette, look from her body to her face. Her hair is tucked under a vaguely military hat the same charcoal as the severe suit she wears; she looks severe, but passion and fright bleed through the glaze of her green eyes. Her lips—her lips are in almost an inviting smile, full and glossy, they compress as I squint every so slightly at her. When I ask her to turn and she does, she ends up facing me but not looking at me now, her lips tightly drawn, her face paling. Her whole bearing, the scent of her, the warm familiarity of her face so close to mine, make my heart skip a beat. I exhale nervously and turn away.

"This one," I say. I've gone slightly out of breath and look to Massimo, whose thick features are flushed, whose suppressed grin begins to move my own.

In the end I listen to Eva Steiner nervously asking that what happened this afternoon, our agreement, the race and its outcome, be kept confidential. What she does on theTube as a passenger is a private matter, she says—this affair might be a disaster for her on the outside, it would be a humiliation.

She is relieved when I tell her I wasn't thinking of filing any codex numbers to make official Collette's transfer, manages a thin smile when she suggests that there are ways in which we might enjoy one another after all. "It is your recklessness," she says. "I didn't know. If I had, I wouldn't have raced you. There are other games we might have played," she goes on, her smile actually widening.

What a strange thing for her to say—to a pilot whose last eight years have depended on control in the face of default, on total attention to the operation of a flight to return a lame ship. She is a small and insecure woman, finally—at least that's what shows in her when I tell her I don't think she'd enjoy what I have in mind, and I laugh.

"Yet we might see one another again after all," she says before she leaves. I send Collette over to the canopied trackside table where Massimo and I had lunch; *la fortuna mei*, Massimo keeps saying. He is going out in the Ferrari to better my lap time "as act of love," he laughs. In which case, he says, still laughing, maybe it is he who should see Eva Steiner again.

"It is the magic of this place," he tells me. "Everywhere else is like Rome now—so many people, barely the food, there is no joy in life. This place. Ah, if all the world could be so."

An Italian steward is adjusting a sun screen as I sit across from Collette, cappuccino for her and pastries between us. She won't look up, but I can see that her eyes have become wet, and the long, thin fingers of her right hand tremble as she takes her coffee.

"Well, you sure do look familiar," I say. "But I'm not sure I know who you are. Max, is it?"

She looks up, hurt, her breasts are heaving. "My name's Collette," she says. "Service codex 782, service codex." She's gorgeous, the bitch. Her face is flushed, her head is uncovered now and her hair blown back, her lips are shiny.

"Look here, Max," I say, "tell me about SciCom retirement pay. Is it as good as they say it is?"

"My name is Collette," she pleads, biting her lip. "My codex is a service codex, a service codex."

I tell her that she talks exactly like a computer terminal. I mean to make her smile, but her eyes close and her face pinches up and she begins to cry, tears slipping down her high, flushed cheeks, her breath coming in sobs, a napkin in front of her nose. For a minute it seems she wants to bury herself in its fabric. Her shoulders shake, her breath becomes a gasp, and she turns her face down toward her knee—too much for me to bear. I sigh, move my chair over next to hers, and put my hand on her shoulder, try to calm her down.

"I'd like to hear the story," I say. "You can still talk to me."

"Please don't make me talk about that woman. Please don't send me back to her."

"I don't see that anybody deserves her," I say, half to myself. "I just thought we could talk about the time we spent together. I'd just like to know the truth, Collette."

"Oh, Rawley, I have so much to say to you. I should

never have lied to you in the first place. God, how stupid. And that woman, too, she's part of it. Service Control transferred me to her for discipline. They knew we went off the grounds when we went hiking—they were watching us, Rawley, I didn't know what to do."

I lean back in the chair—well, I fall back, too, trying to comprehend. This is new—watching us; I think: That pavilion. A blue-white Formula E approaches through the near turn, the rising and falling whistle of its passing bringing a chill down my spine.

"I didn't know if the man I saw was really you this morning," she says. "It was like a dream. We had just been woken, and the drugs . . ." Collette drinks half her coffee at once, puts the cup down, and looks at me tearfully. "I didn't think I'd ever see you again," she says, her breasts heaving with a deep breath. "Oh, Rawley, you drove so well."

There is such a look to her face that I can do nothing but lean closer and kiss her warm, damp lips—and so taste the salt of her tears. "Thanks," I say. "Erica said you didn't leave, they . . . took you away. Whichever, I felt pretty bad to find you gone."

"Oh, this job," she says, squeezing the napkin in her fist. "How I hate this job. That woman and her games—God, what a pain in the ass being a *slave*—every time something like this happens, I say to myself . . ."

I give Collette my napkin to wipe her face. Her lower lip is quivering as she tries to laugh at what she's said; her makeup is smeared. I don't quite know what to think. Everything's become so complicated in the last two days, and Collette—well, what has she been through? What, exactly? I can't take my eyes off her.

"I need to know how you're involved with SciCom," I say. "I need to know what they're after."

"I want to tell you, Rawley. I want to tell you everything. Can we talk here? God, how I wish I'd told you the truth. I lied to you and then . . . Do you know why I lied to you? I lied to protect this *job*, this lousy job, this ugly *job*. How stupid I am. You trusted me and I fell for you. I had already lied, and the things you told me about yourself that afternoon . . . meant you really trusted me. I felt so bad. But I didn't tell them anything. I said we talked about sex, we spent the whole time talking about sex. God, it was awful."

"Told whom?"

"I was straight with you until I was missing that night, believe me. I swear to you, Rawley. Do you remember? The third night, at the rest house? There was a signal from Service Control for me to remain, you left . . . and these two men came in an electric cart and took me across the meadow. They questioned me and questioned me and told me I had to report on you. They weren't just interested in that, either. There was one with bushy hair and glasses, he's as bad as Eva Steiner, he's . . ."

"Taylor," I say. "Taylor was at the biosphere reserve."

"That's right," she says. "Taylor. And the other one's name was Mancek. They had just come in, I think they had just found out where you were, because they wanted to know what we had been doing since Thursday. I don't think they knew where you had gone from Guam."

But they knew exactly where I was then, I think, yet didn't approach me.

I stare at the track at the sound of Massimo's passing, see the Ferrari as a red blur. What do they want? I told Collette about my hallucinations, my nightmares, that second afternoon. They are a personal key to something, I'm certain of that—the horror of the experience, I think, though that doesn't seem right. Is that what they want? Do they want to destroy me with the horror of the blow? Is that what they did with Cooper, was that his psychotic episode? My visions aren't horrible, only having them is. . . . It's spooky, not right.

"And then after the fantasy co-op. It was about four A.M. I didn't betray you, Rawley. I made up some stories, and that's when they knew I was lying. I told them we never left the grounds on the day we had. They knew we had hiked off. They turned me over to Service Control. He told them to 'see that I'm taken care of,' that's what Taylor said. The next thing I knew, there was Eva Steiner. . . ."

I bite my lip and look around, look up into the stands and see the videotape crew still at work, shooting across the track, some people in the stands. It is becoming like the ship again, life on the Daedalus, my life consumed by problems of navigation and confrontations with SciCom, looking for a way to go but not drifting—*as I have been*, I think, as I have been since we touched down in the Pacific a little more than a month ago.

"How do I know you're telling the truth?"

"Please," Collette says. "Please don't be like them. I am telling you the truth. Rawley, they're going to try to take you back to Guam. I thought they *had*."

"You don't say," I mutter.

"Oh, Rawley, please, I'm telling you everything I know. Believe me, in the end I wanted to protect you. Please let me stay with you. I'll do anything you want me to. Even if I only have a day—you'll see. I just want to be with you again. I want to sleep in your bed. Maybe there's a way we can spend the rest of the trip together. In more time I can show you. I love you. When I thought I'd never see you again, I kept saying to myself, 'Oh, shit, Collette, you dummy, oh, shit, you did it so wrong....'"

I take her smooth hand and move the gold bracelet at her wrist, feel the warmth of her skin, she's feverish. "I saw the same men two days ago," I tell her. "I've filed an appeal, but they've set up orders that ship me back to Guam tomorrow morning. They're pulling me back."

"God, how I hate this world," Collette says in a shaky voice, looking away. Then she sobs.

I squeeze her hand and there is a distant siren, then a siren close at hand. Yellow lights begin to flash along the track, the scattered crowd is climbing the grandstand to see something in the distance, I rise, I can see it from where I stand—a column of dirty black smoke mushrooming from the far side of the course. Massimo's pit crew is up and phoning, his car lapped a few minutes ago, he is still on the track. Nothing's come by under the yellow—and now the track lights flash red and stay red as the fire-crew alarm moans a kilometer away and sirens whine and scream from all directions.

I see the Lancia coupe still in the shade, the chief mechanic begins telling me to go, I am going, anyway. I clamber into the cockpit and fire up the engine, rap it to a purr. Collette is standing where I left her, tall and erect, her dancer's body motionless, her hand over her mouth. I sigh; it still makes me angry to see her. I motion her in.

There are cars scattered, stopped here and there on the course under the flashing red warning lights. I weave the Lancia through the turns cautiously in second and third, watching for Massimo's Guidici. A red and white ambulance moves a half kilometer ahead, full speed, the wail of its siren blending with the sirens farther off.

We pass down the main straight. The pits are filled with cars, jump-suited mechanics, spectators. The crowd in the grandstand is up, watching the distance. The black smoke rises off to the west, not far off to the west now, a narrow column near the ground fanning into a growing cloud.

We swing through a wide left. Ahead is the shorter straight, the chute of its exit hairpin blocked by a welter of emergency vehicles, more than fifty people milling on the track, the brake lights of the ambulance flash red. Beyond is wreckage. I cannot see Massimo's car; every racer on the infield border is squat Formula E.

The smoke is deeply black, dense, rising slowly in its own weight. Chemicals ooze over the road surface at the inner edge of the crowd down from the crown of the track. I slide the Lancia, barely moving, through on the infield edge, on the infield. There is a single, burning car on end against the concrete outer wall of the curve, the wall itself is smeared black for a distance, the flames are orange-red, searing, the car itself invisible in its compact fireball, the acrid smoke wafts around—and *whump*, there is a minor explosion. I think, Fuel, combustion, Massimo, while a piece of crumpled sheet metal catches the periphery of my vision. Clambering out of the cockpit, I see scattered fragments on the infield. Blood-red. Ferrari.

I push my way through the crowd, spectators have somehow gotten onto the track, the car is still burning, upended and burning with orange-red flames, the heat is palpable and intense. Chemicals now plume toward the track wall in arcs, the fireball abating, but the smoke for a minute becomes a dense gray fog in which we are all consumed.

The car falls to its side, its cockpit creased, charred metal unmistakably the Ferrari—its frame folded on its driver's side—the flames begin to settle under the load of foam. I have searched the crowd with a sinking heart for Massimo, don't want to look at the wreckage, but do, and focus, and see: the mangled sleeve of a jump suit protruding from the wrenched metal, limp as if empty. Metal crushed like wadded paper. I have to turn away.

"Who is it?" Collette is asking. "Rawley, is it that man?"

I stumble past and she turns from the fire, I feel myself gagging from the sharp odor, look into the blank reflective faces of vehicle crews, see in their faces the strange mixture of satisfaction and awe in the face of destruction so complete.

I have walked down the track. Higher toward the wall at the chute to the turn there are two wide black swaths smeared on the concrete. Someone is moving toward me through the thin edge of the crowd, a technician rolling an instrument along the road surface with fierce attention. The technician wears thin-rimmed glasses, steps carefully, absorbed in following the dead center of the lower swath along the banked surface, the ticks of his instrument just audible through the welter of other noise.

"Skid?" I yell to him, my voice uncontrollably cracking. "A hundred meters of skid?"

"More than that," he yells back without looking up. "Don't look like near enough, wasn't near enough. That machine was at two hundred when it hit."

At the *hairpin*, I am thinking, the decreasing radius hairpin, the slowest curve on the track.

A hundred meters away the wreckage is still smoldering; ash and acrid smoke hang in the air. The site is encircled by red flashing lights, yellow lights, blue lights, while eerie figures in silver flameproof suits approach behind their own chemical clouds, making a way for a white van backing perpendicularly up the track to the Ferrari.

I look down at my feet. Squat down, look closely in a numb daze at the wide, distinct tire marks on the road surface—rubber seared onto concrete, welded. I see only waste at first, then for an instant I am frighteningly disoriented. The rubber fragments vulcanized into oozing tar masses gather on the wreckage side of the texture of the concrete; I feel reversed on the track.

No, I think, this is not exactly a skid.

I try to follow the line with my eyes: it weaves twice, then disappears at the thin edge of the crowd. I look beyond at the wreckage from a higher point of the track.

The flames have abated, but not the smoke. Two of the men in fireproof suits are bringing the body out while the other two ease the creased cockpit with long rods as tall as they are used as levers. The body: limbs hang loose, the flameproof driving suit is streaked with char. For one wild moment I am thinking, *Survived, survived,* but before I can even move, the ambulance attendants have opened a large dark bag, a body bag. Massimo is laid within, his lifeless body sealed by one of the white-suited figure's long pull of a cord.

Collette is kneeling on the infield edge of the track, up from her heels as if in prayer. Her body shakes and she sways, shudders. Her hands at her stomach, she leans forward and vomits, not once but again and again and again, shuddering and swaying, again and again and again.

"Better? Better now?" I am wiping Collette's forehead with linen from the ambulance, soothing her and cooling her face with the wet cloth. Her hair has gone stringy, lipstick gone, we are both of us sweating from the sun and our states at the grass of the infield—she is sitting now, quietly sobbing, her face warm, slightly puffy.

"This goddamned *place,*" Collette sobs in sudden anger. "I hate this place, I hate this place."

Her dark clothes are in disarray, she lifts her knees and sobs into her hands. She has long passed the point of caring about herself, her naked legs glistening brown in the sun.

"You've been through enough," I say. "Come."

"Oh, Rawley," she sobs.

"Lean on me," I say. I want to walk her away, but she seems not to want to move. I hold her warm body next to mine—she is pressed against me and clings, I can feel her breasts pressed against me, I can feel her heart beating heavily.

"I'm through," she says. "I'm going to quit. I don't care what they make me do, this is my last trip. I can't take it any more, I just can't *take* it. Rawley, I've seen too much of this. I don't want to ever see people destroying themselves again. Never again."

I wonder. I think about getting on as a commercial pilot somewhere—SoAm, Africa. A different future. Not like this, I've had enough of this, this place, my life since Guam.

Collette is turning hysterical now, her chest is shuddering with sobs. I hold her tightly, as if to make my strength her own. The smoldering, steaming wreckage, white wisps of chemical fumes, fill me with a sinister chill, anger. Collette is shaking against me. "Oh, God, oh, Jesus Jesus God, woman," she says to herself, "does it have to be this way?"

I help her up and toward the Lancia, walk her slowly a few steps, and she wants to walk on her own, then leans on me. She is a tall woman, her shoulders only a flat hand lower than mine—my arm around her, she naturally turns into me. Beyond her distress her womanhood bleeds into her walk, her hip rhythm against mine, her breasts palpable through my thin shirt. Her breathing is regular now, the wreckage behind us. Rich liquid red in the hazy sun, the Lancia makes me think of her and Massimo at once, the feel of her warm body, his blood burned black on the legs of his driving suit.

I could go, I think. I could stash the Lancia, be on the road at first light tomorrow morning and through the perimeter before Taylor was ever awake, long before the office end-processing my appeal could act.

I wonder what's out there. My impulse is to run south. The location maps I've seen show wide access through the perimeter west of the trans-port, heavy traffic to the adjoining city; once through, just trust my sense of direction and hope for Mexico. I remember stories of a dried-up Rio Grande, a border like Swiss cheese—it excites me wondering what it's like out there.

At the car I kiss Collette to comfort her, and myself, I suppose; once our lips touch, the kiss becomes deeper, longer, a loss into one another. She whispers that she wants me, more than anything she wants me.

We make love in a private lounge in the warehouse, lock ourselves in. We hold each other, have sex with a passion that can only come from such close pain. We quietly shower together, and afterward, sitting in the silence of the room, I tell Collette of my idea to bolt from LasVenus once I'm ordered back to Guam tomorrow morning—to stash the Lancia tonight and to take it through the perimeter before Taylor even knows I'm packed.

As I tell her, her expression changes from loss to determination, and a brightness comes into her eyes. She takes a deep breath. "I'm coming along," she says. "If you'll let me, if you want me, I'm coming along."

In the middle of the night I wake from a deep sleep, shivering and sweating at once. I've seen something. The vision of the woman suspended in space, arms spread as if crucified, her features indistinguishable, but the void beyond as vividly present as the sink I lean over now, its presence palpable and vast, cold and endless.

I look up into the mirror, the blood has gone from my face. The mirror reflects the mirrored wall behind me, the back of my head, and I watch the mirror in horror as the room in the room in the room becomes a corridor of infinite regress.

I sink to my knees, shaking, my hands slipping on the

cold rim of the sink. I fight to catch my breath, suck in a draft of chemical air, and vomit into the john.

DA8//5:42:19 . . . 20 . . . 21 . . . 22—the digits blink from my chronometer as I adjust its strap on my wrist, its grasp the pull of a familiar hand; I have not worn the Seiko since Guam. I awoke twenty minutes ago at first light, Erica facing the window/wall with her back to me, her arm cantered over her face, one knee up and her foot hanging over the edge of the recliner. Collette lies toward me, the flat of her hand on my chest, her breathing almost inaudible, twisted toward me so we lie thigh against thigh—yet her touch is as light as the thin blanket's. Her lips are vaguely pursed in sleep, and as I kiss her, her eyes come open and she slowly, languidly, smiles, then moves against me; the two of us are naked under the satin sheet. We make slow and quiet love without waking Erica, who tosses once, moves with a muffled grunt when we leave the recliner, who lies there still sprawled on her stomach deep in her rest. I feel good now—so much better in general, I think, since I've decided to go. Collette moves toward the kitchen, she wants to put together a basket of chicken, fruit, cheese, wine, and the rest, enough for a few days.

Erica doesn't know our plans. I agree with Collette that Erica might try to cover for us if she did know. We will tell her that we are going to spend the early morning watching the Grand Prix and boarding the Tube for today's late-morning liftoff from there.

The sun is rising and I go out to the small balcony to look beyond the city as Collette wakes her. The air is still and the haze light as the sun shows a liquid and brilliant line on the rough horizon, its enormous mass tucked behind a range of mountains, the line rising into a dome above them with the incipient thrust of a launch. The atmosphere is shifting from gray to spectral and vivid red. This is the farthest I have been able to see. The city in its low urban fog stretches far into what looks to be scrubby low hills rising to foothills to a mountain range in the east, forming a north-south line of ridge. To the southeast, roadways are obscured in the steel-gray fog, but the land looks ripe for a road laid flat through opening desert country.

Collette is wearing a pale green bandana, a pale green blouse, and dark shorts, a walking snapshot from a picnic. I tell her to pack some stimulants in case we need them. She already has.

```
channel 393//IN IN IN IN IN IN IN IN IN IN IN IN IN
sign key 0208//SCHOLE

telex medium//

route:  Guam Utama Sta.
        Midway
        Honolulu
        SoCal Center
        LasVenus Local (des.)
debugging rider: erase if intercept//only 393

ATTN:  .RAWLEY VOORST

FIRST//ICARUS ENCODING IS CLEARLY A BLIND.
SECOND//SOMETHING IS BREAKING HERE. I THINK
SOMETHING HAS CRACKED.

ALL SCICOM SCREENING TEAMS IN CONFERENCE UNDER
SECURITY, NOT MILITARY SECURITY BUT SCICOM'S. YOU
REMEMBER THOSE NAZIS.

BASE CONFINEMENT FOR ALL DAEDALUS CONSOLE
PERSONNEL LIFTED BUT NO RUMORS FROM PERSONNEL
OFFICE OF LEAVES. SAW KNUTH, HE SAYS ALL FUTURE
INTERVIEWS RESCHEDULED.

OF COURSE I REMEMBER JEANNIE D.

WERHNER
```

"What do you think it means?"

"I don't know," I tell Collette. "Makes me nervous. I'd like to know before we take off. But I don't think we have a choice about waiting. Wait another hour, maybe." I honestly don't know what to do. I know we'll have to pass a gate on the way out, I have tried to put running it out of my mind. I tell Collette she could always stay.

"For what?" she says. "Stay for what?"

They are just opening the Administrative Center at the Tower when I run up, deep in the bowels of Personnel Section, Military Concourse, Flight Assignment, Force 8A—sleepy uniformed clerks unlocking doors and files, switching on machines, arranging their desks. A minute ago I had a terrible scare: down in the lobby I'm certain I saw Mancek, his shoulders slumped with fatigue, I'm certain he didn't see me. I don't want to be here long—I'll have to disappear until something comes through the line. I wonder if I can talk one of the clerks into a discreet call up to the roof garden, perhaps—I don't want Mancek to see me here. I'm more certain the information about the appeal will have to sit and process here before Taylor sees it.

I have to fill out a tedious form for an inquiry; the yawning clerk who leans over the counter on his elbows to watch me is only eighteen or nineteen. This is taking too long. I look into his slightly glazed, innocent eyes and wonder about an approach. Not money but a favor; he looks decent enough, pink-faced and earnest, to respond.

"Mmmm," he says as I turn the form around to him. "Appeal. Already filed. You need to enter your local residence . . . here. And sign line three."

He laughs at my birth date and says I must have been out on a long one, laughs again. I ask him if he can do a personal favor for me—I need to know the appeal result before SciCom does, it's a problem with my commanding officer, he's going to be pissed when he finds out about this and I want to talk to him in case it's denied.

The boy scratches his head, says, "Hold on. I think we had some stuff come through in the last hour—you know, time lag from the East. I bet nobody's even picked it up yet."

He is gone for a minute that seems like forever: 07:33:13 . . . 14 . . . 15. Clerks move papers across their desks in slow motion, I move out of sight of the door,

watch the clerk through another wide doorway in the next
room reading down a yellow teletype sheet he is picking
up from the floor behind the printer.

He saunters back, still looking sleepy. The counter is
cold under my hand.

"Voorst. Rawley? Codex 02-292. I mean, Captain, sir.
Captain Voorst."

I look at him and the door at the same time.

"Wanna see for yourself? This is supposed to go
through channels, but I don't see any harm in your
looking at it, got a local rider."

He hands me the tear sheet:

sign category//002
message category//MILITARY ORDERS//MILITARY ORDERS

SUBJECT//LEAVE STATUS, VOORST, RAWLEY, SIGN KEY 0202, FLT
    VANE ENG CLASS TWO, RANK CAPTAIN

COPIES TO//LOCAL FLIGHT ASSIGNMENT, LASVENUS
            FLT ASSIGNMENT CENTER, HOUSTON
            LOCAL SCICOM OFFICE, LASVENUS
            SCICOM HQ, GUAM BASE

ORIGINATING OFFICE//FLIGHT PERSONNEL ASSIGNMENT, WASH-
    INGTON

ORDERS FOLLOW ORDERS FOLLOW ORDERS FOLLOW ORDERS

APPEAL OF REASSIGNMENT FROM LEAVE TO GUAM SCICOM
    STATUS:
APPROVED APPROVED APPROVED APPROVED APPROVED APPROVED

DECISION BASIS//ACCUMULATED LEAVE TIME

ADVISORY//GUAM SCICOM, PERSONNEL OFFICE
            PREDICTIVE ATTACHED FOR INFORMATIONAL PUR-
            POSES:

            VOORST, RAWLEY, TO REMAIN ON LEAVE FOR THIRTY-
            DAY PERIOD BEGINNING 7-10 ENDING 8-09. ELIGIBILITY
            FOR LEAVE EXTENSIONS TOTALING 120 DAYS FLT
            CREW HNDBK 17.442 REV. #2332.

ORDERS END////LOCAL RIDER FOLLOWS LOCAL RIDER FOLLOWS

**********ADD ADD ADD ADD ADD ADD ADD ADD ADD ADD ADD ADD

**********LOCAL RIDER LOCAL RIDER LOCAL RIDER LOCAL RIDER

COPIES TO//VOORST, RAWLEY
LASVENUS SERVICE CONTROL
ALL CODEX PERSONNEL OFF.

ORIGINATING OFFICE//PROGRAM OFFICE, CENTRAL
THEPLEASURETUBE, LASVENUS

VOORST, RAWLEY, RESTORED TO CLASS ONE PRIVILEGES THE-
PLEASURETUBE FLIGHT 8 LIFTOFF 1100 7-18//SERVICE RESTORED
EFF. 0900 7-18.

QUESTIONS CONTACT CENTRAL OFFICE//////////////////////////////

YOUR PLEASURE IS OUR SERVICE//OUR SERVICE IS YOUR PLEA-
SURE

I scan back through the appeal result, can barely
believe my eyes:

APPROVED   APPROVED   APPROVED   APPROVED   APPROVED

PART III:

NAKED SINGULARITY [=df
product of tidally infinite forces
manifest within collapsar;
condition of irreducibility.]

CHAPTER 7
Moonloop

Through the window/wall I see the latticework cradle move away, the wisps of preignition float up from beneath the ship.

"He wasn't angry, then?"

"No, Taylor was. You should have seen him, talking with his teeth clenched. It was Mancek, the one who looks like a farmer, who didn't say anything; he seemed to enjoy the news in a funny way. I still don't know what to make of it, exactly. Wish I'd hear from Werhner. Something in me isn't going to relax until I find out what's going on at Agana."

"Just be thankful for good news." Collette grins, adjusting the last buckle of my liftoff rig, patting my stomach. "The next few days will take your mind off beige uniforms, you'll see." She kisses me with wet, big lips.

"What service," I tease her. I've been teasing her because she's still on the job after all.

She laughs along with me. "Today we celebrate," she says. "I've got a surprise for you once we're in orbit. And then I've already got the whole day planned. Notice anything different?"

I look around the bright cabin, the familiar brown couch, the deep brown rug with its faint hexagonal pattern. Collette's sagging leather flight bag is stacked alongside the divider to the kitchen/bar; the other velvet lounging chair is reclined as her liftoff rig. "What do you mean?" I ask. The light from the LasVenus trans-port illuminates the Rubens behind her to a glow, warms the soft brown walls. Now I notice a halo around the painting, a rainbow halo.

"Just a drug." She grins, easing into the lounging chair, strapping in. "We're going to be high until tomorrow, higher than we are. Consider that an invitation to a party."

A thunderous shake wallows through the ship, modulates into a sustained roar. The dusty LasVenus pads begin to slip away, low hills and desert form on the horizon to the sound of fine tinkling of equipment in the unit. A gravity grows in my blood, intensifies in the flesh of my forehead, chest, groin—the continent begins to shape itself, receding, and at the very center of the growing weight itself I begin to feel the sweet freedom of flight.

	RESIDUAL ITINERARY, RE.//		
	FIRST-CLASS PASSAGE//	Prog.	2ndCoord.
DA8/	//UKIYOE FLYAWAY	bld	1/o-1100
DA9	MOONLOOP//SENS SEVEN SPEC	.bld	i/f-cont
DA10	VIETAHITI	bld	i/f-cont
DA11	SINS SEVEN SPEC//AQUAPLEASE	bld	i/f-cont
DA12	HOLO PROG//MICROSSAGE	bld	i/f-cont
DA13	TOTAL HOLOGRAM//TRIP TO		
	THE SUN	bld	i/f-cont
DA14	TRIP TO THE SUN$_4$	bl-	i/f------

CONTINUOUS VIDEON PROGRAMMING

THEPLEASURETUBE IS AN EXPERIENCE//INDIVIDUAL VARIATIONS
ARE COMMON AND PRECISE DESTINATIONS VARY//
CONSULT YOUR SERVICE FOR DETAILS
4, MEDICAL CLEARANCE REQUIRED

VIETAHITI VENTURES//PLAN YOUR LONGDAY NOW
//SOPAC TROPICAL RESERVE
//AQUAPLEASE SPECTACULAR

NEW FIRST-CLASS OPTIONS EVERY HOUR//CONSULT YOUR SER-
VICE FOR DETAILS

Our service is pleasure//Your pleasure our service
@ thePleasureTube corp.

The recliner doubled, the window/wall a spectacular
view of deep space, Collette and I are playing shamelessly.
I had a few moments of real depression when we came on,
thinking of Massimo, how he would have appreciated the
luck I've had using my military status, it's the only thing
that ever used to work, how he would have enjoyed
another launch. But Collette's been making me forget. I
am on my stomach now, she is massaging my back after
we've made love while the ship has been in preorbit
maneuvers. Her fingers are working into the tight base of
my skull.

"Let's see," she says. "If you understood these curves,
you'd understand why you have back trouble. First, your
spine curves in for seven vertebrae," she says, tracing
them with her stiff fingers. "This one's your neck bump.
Then your spine curves out, along the ribs, then in again
at the lower back. And finally out again at the pelvis," she
continues, giving my butt a slap. "Twenty-four moving
parts, the discs like little waterbeds between them. Your
trouble might be spondylolythesis. Mmmm. Let me
recommend treatment."

I laugh. "That word. Look, I barely know you," I say to
Collette. "Watch what you say."

She laughs, too, a quiet, low, sultry laugh. "I've known
you forever, known these curves, these places," she tells
me, now running her hands up my sides, running them up
along my bare muscles to hold me under my arms. Then
she puts weight on my lower back, leans with the ship.

I laugh again, this time at myself, turn on my side, and
trace a line on her body, from her chin down through her
breasts to the flat surface of her stomach. I stop at her
navel, touch it playfully. Sweet God, there is something so
familiar about her now, the counterpart in a woman to
some habits of mine, to a sense of touch and odor that I

am only half aware of. "I feel I've known you," I say, poking my finger into her navel, "right from the start."

When we reach stable orbit, Collette tells me to put on my robe and come along. She leads me down the carpeted, spun-steel passageway to Tonio's cabin, a cabin identical to mine except for the Japanese painting on the wall and its pale yellow furnishings. Tonio's produced something for us to see, is busy with a console when we arrive. I offer my help—feel a little odd, still lazily euphoric from the drug—and recall he's used male service in LasVenus, odd to be back into this. Tonio's scent strikes me as feminine; so does his pale yellow pullover. I'm not sure what to think. Erica, arranging canapés and pouring warm sake with a ruddy glow, gives a satisfied wink to my puzzled look; I'm not sure I understand. Then when I ask about the Japanese painting on his wall— startlingly pornographic, a woman, legs fully spread, entangled with a standing man, which Tonio identifies as a classic of the eighteenth-century Ukiyoe school—Erica giggles. "Ask Tonio," she says. "That works." So they're lovers again.

Once he has the programming straight, we first sit through a continuation of the Videon 33 discussion Collette and I watched on the first leg of the trip; his tape must follow. The subject has shifted to the role of fantasy in the programming on theTube; the same physicians lounge in plush white chairs. Given the last three days of my life, it's hard for me to concentrate at first, but I listen. It brings me back to this whole world of pleasure I've returned to.

On the wall screen, a white-haired older man goes through a long analysis of model programs. Simple tactile-stimulation sequences yield diminishing returns, he says. In the end, the fantasy-fulfillment program is one of the richest models, which leads him to speculate that the locus of pleasure itself lies in the imagination.

The woman with the hollow voice disagrees. She says that pleasure is independent, absolute; she can prove that by putting any man or any woman into a grope suit, any time. She says that fantasy-fulfillment programs are provided only to keep the passengers sane.

"A wholly independent pleasure event, one entirely disconnected from a subject's imaginative life, is a kind of mental short circuit," she continues, leaning back. "If you introduce a series of disconnected pleasure events to a subject, the result is invariably dementia paranoides. The Tube structures fantasy and fulfillment in its programs to induce a kind of antiparanoia instead, a feeling that the world serves the subject's motives and neurology in a *soothing* fashion. But pleasure? The pure experience of pleasure? It has a character that is independent, absolute. It remains one of our closest experiences *of* the absolute, though we cannot finally disengage it from a neurological signal. Whether that signal's source is tactile stimulation or a surgical implant, it clearly comes from outside the imagination."

"You've ignored the loop," the white-haired physician points out, shaking his head. "For the true connoisseur of pleasure, we know very well that only the most suggestive, the most . . . imagination-producing, signal will do—the lightest touch, the most delicate flower, the most subtle scents. Think of the Japanese. . . ."

"I don't quite . . ." Erica begins to say. I am becoming nervous, remembering now the character of this place and thinking of Massimo and his blood-red Ferrari, but the screen fades through false color separations and reassembles to show a young woman, perhaps a scholar, looking at a series of paintings in a museum, Japanese paintings in the style of Tonio's. Both Collette and Erica say "Ah!" at the same time, and I notice what they notice: the first painting is precisely the one on Tonio's wall. Then Erica says, "Aha!" and in one of the paintings, in all of the paintings, the figures are beginning to move.

Tonio's done an ingenious job of producing: a little story follows, the woman scholar's fantasy. But I lose its thread, obsessed with something familiar about the half-dozen Japanese who act out the erotic scenes. I watch one couple move to climax before it comes to me. They are the Orientals I saw lounging at the ship's pool on the first leg of the trip. Amazing—and their flexibility is amazing. In the loose abandonment of limbs, they all seem so flexible I wonder about their bones.

In the end, the woman scholar pulls her hair back up into a bun and puts her drab dress on again. She writes in her notebook that she's discovered something about the truth of art. I look to Collette and Erica, not certain what we are now going to do. Tonio answers the question by saying that he and Erica are programmed for the VanWeck Sexuarium—tells us to make ourselves comfortable. Erica seems embarrassed, answers my look with a shrug.

"Which painting did you like best?" Collette is asking me.

I open my eyes. I have been dozing on the couch after Collette and I have made love; I wonder if it's time we returned to my cabin. The light is dim; now I see she's wearing a black and red kimono. "Mmmm," I say, "...third from the left." There's a sexy look in her green eyes. I stir, think, Well, I'm not desynched from this part of her program, here she comes again.

"Surprise," Collette says, stepping aside. The sight of another woman sends me awake. The other woman is Japanese, she's from the third painting, dressed in a gold brocaded kimono. She looks at me sharply with wide almond eyes, tilts her head, and giggles, her hand over her mouth.

channel 393//IN IN IN IN IN IN IN IN IN IN IN IN IN
sign key 0208//SCHOLE

telex medium

route: Guam Agana
         Midway
         Honolulu
         SoCal Center
         LasVenus Local
         thePleasureTube flt. 8 (trace)
debugging rider: erase if intercept/only 393

ATTN: RAWLEY VOORST

TRIED LIVE LINE WITHOUT SUCCESS, WILL TRY AGAIN AT
1800 TOMORROW. FRIGHTENED DOWN TO HALF DOSE.
FEEL LIKE WE'VE JUST LANDED.

DEBRIEFING SUSPENDED 48 HOURS. REPEAT: DEBRIEF-
ING SUSPENDED 48 HOURS. CREW RELEASED SCICOM
AUTHORITY TWO-DAY LEAVES.

BUT LISTEN TO THIS: DID ROUTINE CHECK AND COO-
PER'S NAME NOT ON DEATH LIST. REPEAT: COOPER'S
NAME NOT ON DEATH LIST. AND NO RECORD OF
INTERNMENT. LAST GUAM PROGRAM ENTRIES SHOW
INTERVIEW, THEN EVACUATION TO HOUSTON, THEN
"APPARENT SUICIDE." FINAL INTERVIEW GUAM IS ONLY
ONE NOT IN TRANSCRIPT, MISSING TRANSCRIPT: ONLY
KNOW INTERVIEWER WAS WOMAN. I TELL YOU MY DATA
SHOWS COOPER MAY STILL BE ALIVE SOMEWHERE.
KNUTH SAYS IMPOSSIBLE, BUT COOPER'S NAME IS NOT
ON DEATH LIST.

MORE LATER IF I FIND SOMETHING. GETTING OUT OF
HERE, LEAVING NOW HONG KONG.

WERHNER

I read the message again, my eyes racing through the
words, my feelings shifting from relief to a crawling
sensation. God, I don't know what to think. I feel
vindicated; at the same time there is a hollow itch in my
chest, an overwhelming, crawling sensation at my
sternum. Cooper's name not on a death list?

I am confused and relieved at the same time. In the
middle of my tumbling thoughts I find myself wishing
Massimo were alive, that I could talk to him. The thought
of his death makes me sigh audibly again; I've wondered if
he was the one who saw to my appeal and didn't tell me,
that would be his way.

"Cooper," I say to myself.

"Who is he, Rawley?"

I see Cooper in my mind, chewing on his mustache,
forehead drawn tight, mulling over figures on his
clipboard, looking up, his eyes for an instant meeting
mine, looking away, his lips becoming motionless as he

stares out a low porthole in the dome, something else on his mind. "He's the one Taylor told me committed suicide in Houston, the program man who wrote up our report," I tell Collette. "I . . . don't like to think about Cooper. He did me over with a woman once. That got straightened out, but after that we avoided one another. They said he came in experiencing a gross psychotic episode—I tried to see him, but they shipped him almost straight to Houston. I thought he might know what was missing, what SciCom was after."

"Does this make sense to you?" she asks; I can see my worry flooding onto her. "Do you know what's going on?"

I clear the screen, obliterate the message and leave a blue-gray ground, start to unbutton my shirt; the crawling sensation is becoming unbearable. "Says the debriefing is suspended for forty-eight hours," I say, scratching my chest. "Let's call that good news. My leave was approved, Werhner's probably in Hong Kong already. It looks to me," I say deliberately, "as if I'm in the clear. I don't see that anything can happen here."

"What about . . . that program officer?" Collette asks, close to me, moving my hand and putting her own in its place.

"I don't know, I just don't know," I say. Strange how quickly my relief at the approval of my appeal has passed; strange, the news about Cooper. Werhner might be wrong, I think, Cooper is not alive until one of us sees him. The last interview is puzzling—could he have told them something different from the report?

As if in response to the questions I have, a winking light appears on the console—incoming traffic.

My heart jumps; from her expression Collette feels it. I am thinking, Well, my leave is good, at least for the next few days, anticipating Werhner. I punch up the screen, reset the code channel. No, it doesn't take, the traffic is local. I let the message come through.

The screen displays the tape of a very Swedish couple inviting Rawley Voorst and friend to a dinner party in the suite of Director Eva Steiner. As the woman speaks she slowly opens the silky black robe she is wearing. Beneath it she is wearing some sort of harness, she is writhing at her midsection—the man is tugging at the harness from behind as the woman goes through the menu in her heavily accented, sultry voice. "Come," she says finally. Then she snaps her robe shut, stands stock-still, perspiring, saying, "Come. Come."

I shut down the wall screen, clear to the view, and realize I've started to perspire myself. "Eva Steiner," I mutter. "Jesus Christ."

"She makes *you* nervous?" Collette responds. "God." Collette asks what I'm going to do about the invitation.

"Ignore it," I say flatly. "Just ignore it."

"Look," Collette says after a minute, "let's go somewhere to relax, to the pool. Let's go swimming, spend the rest of the day there."

Very late. The hours since Werhner's message have been so blessedly uneventful, my paranoia has collapsed of its own weight into heavy, jangled nerves. I adjust the screen to display the program/information channel, time it to run for a few minutes along with the lights, then move from the couch to the recliner, where Collette lies waiting for me under satin sheets.

On the screen a woman's face is almost transparent, silvery, superimposed on the image of a receding earth. "For night owls," she says, her voice soothing:

> "thePleasureTube offers a variety of stimulating options. Martial arts competition continues in third class. In second class, couples can reestablish their pleasure bond with a hologram production that chases symptoms of sensory overload away, leaving you as fresh as the day you boarded. In first class, all the clubs are open, and there's something new: a quick-cure plastic surgery that erases wrinkles and makes that new face you. A special

> Vietahiti options tape, BaliHi in the new
> Pacific, runs every two—"

The screen flashes on a beach just as the timer switches
it off, the lights go. I sit in the darkness alongside Collette.

"Vietahiti?" I say, sliding down with Collette.
"Tropical reserve?"

"Mmmm. We'll be there for a day, the day after
tomorrow."

I close my eyes. I think of beaches, think of Utama Bay
and the soft bulk of the ocean. I remember Werhner
standing, staring out to sea in gray weather, the sea gray,
the sky gray, the horizon impossible to distinguish in the
distance. *There are other possibilities,* he said. *You're
right not to think of them.*

I touch Collette, run my hand up her back, circle the
nape of her neck, feel her pulse in the soft hollow above
her shoulder. At least we've been left alone, at least I've
shaken Taylor. No nightmares tonight, I tell myself,
curling up against her, my body warm against hers, no
nightmares tonight.

DA9// In my dream state I see Werhner vividly,
straight, sandy hair, biting his lower lip as he punches a
sequence through the console. I can hear voices. I feel my
body shift on satin, feel a change in my weight as I sense a
massive relocation. In my half sleep I'm not sure what's
going on—a vivid memory of the Daedalus in the
movement of this ship, in the metallic voices of dome
control—I hear thruster corrections and vane angles
traded between the bridge and propulsion, think this is
not a liftoff but a course correction, a course change,
vaguely think we launched yesterday, yes, remember the
moving paintings. But there's something else.

I *can* hear voices. As I open my eyes I am as sluggishly
alert as a man coming up from underwater. I struggle to
rise on the recliner, come awake, the sight of the cabin is
a relief, though I don't feel quite all here. Collette is at the
foot in a white satin robe, her hair falling loose on her
shoulders. Behind her is the window/wall's display of the

earth's moon, it is moving onto the screen with the underwater motion of large bodies in deep space, it fills the screen. We are near enough to see the nested craters rising like islands in flat seas, near enough to distinguish volcanic masses from fields of thrown rubble.

Of course. Moonloop, day nine of the program. Through the fantasy co-op yesterday and overnight we have reached the tangent point for our orbit around the moon. The audio is traffic from the Tube's own dome, fixing the tangent angle. I am blinking awake to the sight of the full moon; we are close enough to see the large base at Tranquility, a gold-gray mass with a dull sheen punctuated by the amber double loops of SciCom's insignia. What a vision—the huge, bright circle of the moon, blue-black deep space beyond, strange and familiar at once.

"Mornin', lover," Collette says as I sit up. "We have an orbit correction. Thought you'd like to watch."

She runs her hand lightly over my thigh as she moves from the foot of the recliner toward me, moves her body, warm and soft, against mine. I look at the moon, the huge, luminous ball we are approaching, identify the vast seas: oceanus procellarum, mare nectaris, mare serenetatis. I realize with a start that it is not the vision which distracts me, not the way I came awake, but one of the voices which crackles through the cabin—yes, that's it, the voice from propulsion sounds almost like Cooper's. Its inflection, a slow American drawl, is smooth behind the static,

and I can almost imagine Cooper speaking, his large frame leaning over the program table, his headset almost lost in his wild black hair and bushy beard. But the voice is definitely older, its roughness a deepening from age, another body.

Initial on number three.

Comin' right along.

Mark.

Roger. Mark one.

"Lover, are you all right?"

The confusion is not unpleasant, but that voice like Cooper's shakes me, makes me wonder where I am, gives

me the sensation of floating free without a point of
reference. I wonder what he told SciCom before he died,
what he said in that last Guam interview; now I'm
wondering if he's alive.

"You don't look well," Collette   *Clean burn.*
says. "I've got something to tell
you, Rawley. But it had better   *Number three,*
wait. What's wrong?"   *number three.*

I ask Collette if she minds my switching off the audio.
She says no, it doesn't matter; starts to rise. I put my hand
on her shoulder, get off the recliner, lean over, and hit the
toggle on the small console myself. The crackling and the
voices disappear. Soft music in the unit, the tape has
looped back to Bartók. I settle back on the recliner,
concentrate on the music, and my mind mercifully shifts
to the first time I heard this music on this ship.

I look into Collette's liquid green eyes.

She seems a little shaken herself. She slides one hand
across my chest, the other around to the back of my neck,
and sidles up half behind me. I sigh and feel the relief of it,
the light pressure, the sexy warmth of her touch. The
weight of her breasts moves across my back, settles as she
sighs.

The moon's bright image is still on the window/wall,
and in its silvery light I turn to her, watch her full lips part
as she lies back. She is stroking my chest with long, thin
fingers, her nail polish as silver as the moon. Tracing
patterns with her fingertips, her touch is now so light she
barely bristles the ends of the hair; the sensation is
extraordinary.

"Better?" she asks. She takes my hand and moves it
beneath her breasts, presses upward into its firm weight.

"Mmmm," I say. "Let's imagine we took the Lancia.
We're about three hundred kilometers south of LasVenus, alone in the desert, we haven't seen another vehicle
for an hour. We've made it."

"Nice thought," she murmurs. "Nice to think of it here.
Well, at least we're together."

Why, I begin to wonder, does she say that? But I am

lost already. I sink to her, my hand drifting to the
undulating firmness of her thighs, her mons, as she rises to
meet me.

As she pours the coffee, aromatic and brown-black,
Collette's hand is slightly wobbly on the handle of the
silver pot and she avoids my eye. Now I ask her what it is.

"I wish I didn't have to tell you this," she says quietly,
sitting on the edge of the recliner; I am on the couch.
"Rawley, that man, Taylor, he's on the ship. Erica came
in and woke me at five A.M. She said an early day-
briefing, that's what she'd been told. But it was him, he
wanted to talk to both of us. I saw him, Rawley, on this
ship."

I moan. Tantalized by Werhner's last message from
Agana Base, growing smug over my appeal, I have kept
Taylor out of my mind. For the life of me I can't figure out
what's going on—and at the same time wonder about the
voice like Cooper's, wonder if the similarity was a
hallucination on my part, triggered by the strange data
Werhner reported yesterday, or now if Taylor might have
had something to do with my hearing it.

"I hope he didn't give you too bad a time," I say finally.
"I guess I really should have expected him to board the
ship. But I didn't think he'd bother you. They don't give
up," I sigh. Then after a moment I ask Collette if there was
anything in particular Taylor wanted to know.

She shrugs, puts one knee over the other as she leans
forward. She is still wearing her white satin robe, she's
barefoot, but now the robe seems to droop. "The same
thing. Are you talking about the flight you were on, are
you saying anything about your debriefing. I think he's
worried about you, maybe whether you'll put him on
report. He asked me if you were doing anything outside
the program."

"The debriefing's suspended," I say. "He doesn't have
the right."

Collette nods, tight-lipped; there is an exhaustion in
her green eyes. "He made me wish we had taken off in that

beautiful car, just run from LasVenus. But what's the use?"

"Taylor," I say with a kind of nervous scorn. "What if you did go through with a resignation now, what if you did quit?"

"Now that we're in flight, they'd, well . . . It's what we talked about before. They'd put me in third class and make me pay. I suppose I could stay here with you. But they'd send you someone else, another woman."

Despite my growing depression I can't resist taking advantage of the look on Collette's face, a hangdog disgust at both third class and the idea of another woman living in the cabin. "How do you know I'd mind?" I ask with a smile.

"What?" she says, putting both feet on the floor and stiffening her back. "I have to put up with him, and now I have to put up with you? What are you going to do, Rawley, run off with all of us when we get back to L.A.? You're going to need a bigger car. You bastard."

"No," I grin, "just you. There'll only be room for you."

"You bastard," she says after a moment. "You did me last night and you did the Japanese girl yesterday afternoon. Are you trying to set a record?"

"The Japanese girl was your surprise," I remind her. She begins to glare at me. Since yesterday, there's been a new electricity between us—her presence, the looks she gives me with her jade-green eyes, make me a little weak-kneed. And we seem to say less, communicate in glances that require no explanation. She is giving me one of her looks now—close-mouthed, haughty, her eyes wide and menacing.

"All right," I say, "you just hang on. We won't be on this trip forever. And I'll talk to Taylor. I'll talk to him myself."

She actually smiles.

I rise and kiss her on the cheek, then begin helping her clear away the breakfast china. I want to get the console clear, to get started.

As Collette finishes in the kitchen, I punch a query through:

```
SEARCH PROGRAM SEARCH PROGRAM SEARCH

QUERY LOC.//
COL. R. TAYLOR//
SCICOM OFF./GUAM STA. REF.//

CABIN #/PT FLT 8//
CABIN LOC: ENTER ENTER ENTER ENTER ENTER

RETRIEVE   RETRIEVE   RETRIEVE   RETRIEVE

###############################################

RESET RESET RESET RESET RESET RESET RESET
```

Taylor's presence doesn't register on the ship's roster; he must be under another name. I pull the list of names of passengers who boarded for the first time in LasVenus, think at first there can't be many, but sixty-four names show up. In the end I try Werhner's trick for limited-access material, but there's no record of Taylor's presence on any of the classified rosters. Now it's Taylor locked into a private world to which I cannot find a seam, there's no way for me to get to him short of searching the ship.

I start seething, decide to trace through to Guam. But now I find not a single line clear. Agana is apparently under a blackout, not even routine military or SciCom traffic getting through, not even a weather report coming out. Incredible, I think, how stupid. I should have put Collette in that goddamned car and taken off.

"You're right," Erica says two hours after lunch. "There's more to do this leg. The program's richer. That's the way it's supposed to be, has to be, I guess. You'd see it better if you weren't so desynched."

Erica is leaning with her hip on the couch, Collette is sitting alongside me as we watch what must be a women's

program, a cosmetics demonstration. The models are
languid women, the voice-over throaty:

> "On her face: veilessence cream makeup in
> copper with cedar mauve blushing po-
> made. On her eyes: powder eyeshadow in
> wood violet and hickory. On her lips:
> revenescence rose. Smoky grape satin-skin
> camisole leotard. And on the right, now.
> On her face, veilessence light ivory with
> blushing cream in glazed heather plum.
> Spun-gold pink; spun-gold cherry
> highlighting patina, frost-spun..."

With her own makeup, in her suede suit, Collette is as
stunning as the models on the screen, smells gorgeously of
frangipani. But the gloom clouds her face, a tired glaze in
her eyes, and her shoulders sag. She and Erica are to
report to Service Control. Their going is supposed to be
routine, still we all wonder about it.

"It's that time," Erica says.

"I'll be along," Collette says glumly.

Erica kisses us both, says she's going on ahead, leaves
the two of us on the sofa. I shut down the screen.

"We *would* be in Mexico by now," Collette says after a
moment. "What an adventure it would have been."

"Well, it's still an adventure," I say. "You'll have to
admit that."

Collette slips her hand under mine and leans on my
shoulder. I feel her warmth and my breath goes a little
thin again with the presence and odor of her. I have asked
myself if she might not still be in collusion with Taylor, or
if she's in love with me as she says; and I wonder now if it
finally matters. I haven't felt this way about a woman
since Maxine came back to me, pleaded to come back,
and I realized how much I needed her. My God, I wonder,
looking at Collette, am I genuinely falling in love with
her?

"We've been through a lot together," Collette says;
she's saying exactly what's on my own mind. "I'll never

forget the end of that afternoon in LasVenus."

I won't, either, and I sigh. I feel even worse because only now do I realize there wasn't a way to pay my respects after Massimo's death, no ceremony to attend, no way to think his passing through.

Alone. The window/wall fills the cabin with the kaleidoscopic colors of something called Pastoral Fantasy. The Beethoven is soothing, but the light show is just annoying. I clear the screen, punch up Guam again out of compulsion:

```
ATTN//GUAM STATUS//ALL TRAFFIC DOWN//ALL TRAFFIC DOWN
ATTN//GUAM STATUS//ALL TRAFFIC DOWN//ALL TRAFFIC DOWN
```

Nothing's changed. Strange to think of Guam now; I recall some of its odors, the putrefaction of the base's littered beach.

After ten minutes of playing around and using my sign key, I manage to reach into the databank of Medex. I poke around in passenger statistics and on the bottom line discover something that confirms what Collette mentioned early in the trip: the death rate on theTube is phenomenal, as high as two hundred per thousand on some all-third-class flights. That data leads me into fail-safe programs for the total hologram, into my own fail-safe program. I see that I am entered to disconnect and trauma detoxify if my heart beats at a rate of 145, or if my blood pressure reads 200/145—I'm not sure what either really means, but both seem high. My palms get clammy at the idea of trauma and the thought of the mortality rate. I adjust my own tolerances down twenty percent, then post the entry to commit when I'm switched in, hide the entry in storage. I don't want to leave footprints. The blue lights wink confirmation and I think to leave a memory code to remind Collette.

But I don't punch a memory tape. I wonder. I still do feel the slight pull of distrust about her at times, like the partly corroded edge of a razor drawn against my feelings. I don't know—I've been spooked before I came on the ship, thought it was the simple fact of my life. And yet . . .

I punch up tonight's dinner program, getting tired of this machine.

FIRST-CLASS SERVICE//

DINNER//DAY 9   Coq au Vin
                      Brussels Sprouts Bordelaise
                      Tarminochi Salad
                      Hot Bread   White Bordeaux

That's it, I think. I'll run a blind. Just what Werhner would do, I laugh to myself, I'll have to tell him about this when I see him. If I see him. The laugh doesn't last.

ENTER ENTER ENTER ENTER ENTER ENTER ENTER

PROGRAM CHANGE//MEAL SERVICE

SUBS.//new dinner program—day 9
SUBS.//new dinner program—Cannelloni
                                        Green Salad
                                        Chianti

It happens at the pool, just as I enter the water, naked today like the rest of the swimmers. My mind is blank. I am thinking only of the dive, oblivious to the colors and voices at poolside, the music. At the precise point of impact there is a burst of light, and I am diving through a hatch passageway, not through a ship, but into a white, whirling sun, flames at my feet, orange and red driven flames, the sound of rushing wind—the light alongside me is a blur of blue-white, ahead painfully white, bleached utterly, I am falling into it.

My hand on something solid: the tile bottom of the pool. I push off with my palms, shoot upward to the silvery surface, through.

I float for a moment, breathing heavily, take in the people, hear the tropical music. I dive again, but all I see is the water, the sides and bottom of the pool, green tiles meticulously grouted, smooth to the touch, sloping upward from the deep bottom. Then I hang on at the pool's gutter. An athletic woman asks me if I'm all right, is something wrong, asks if I need help.

When Collette finally returns in the late afternoon, she explains she's had a long meeting on new options, hasn't seen Taylor. She says she had some of her own business to attend to; she passes Taylor's presence off as nothing. As a matter of fact, she is exuberant—she smiles broadly, there is a glow to her that wasn't there at midday. It annoys me. I wonder if she's lying.

"I have a gift for you," she says, combing out her hair. "But you have to take a shower."

"I've been to the pool," I answer.

She puts the wide comb down, stares at me energetically. "Take a shower," she says, turning me to the bath, pushing at my bottom. "And stay in there for at least fifteen minutes. Take some good drugs."

"Collette..."

"Just do as I say. Please, Rawley?"

When I leave the bath, dressed only in a terry-cloth robe I haven't tied, I find there are three attractive women in the cabin with Collette—dark-haired, Middle Eastern women with olive skin and rich brown eyes. One is as tall as Collette, the other two have their hair in pigtails, like twins. I am embarrassed for a moment, do up my robe. They are all looking at me with suppressed, sexual laughter.

Which leaves me awkwardly grinning. The cabin lights are dimmed and I detect a new scent, the scent of myrrh; I haven't smelled myrrh since Hong Kong. Someone's hung gauzy curtains by the recliner, and I realize I can see through the caftans the three women are wearing, they are virtually transparent.

"These are three of my friends from service," Collette says softly. "I did the best I could."

I start to speak, but Collette interrupts me. "Right"— she smiles—"and that's *good*, Rawley. *Your* friend asks me strange questions, but my friends see me through. There isn't anything they wouldn't do for me."

"Look, uh, who, uh..." I say a little breathlessly. The

three women are flawless, stand with a deerlike sway watching me. Thank God, I think, I took some stimulants, not a time to feel sleepy. One of the women with pigtails crooks her mouth in a languid smile, reaches out and touches, strokes my arm under the terry cloth.

"They're your *harem*, Rawley," Collette giggles, close to me, moving behind and rubbing my neck. "Mmmm. Your skin is dry. It's this ship air, Rawley. Delia, bring some oil." Her hands around my waist, Collette unties the firm knot of my robe, then begins to bring it down from my shoulders. The twins each kneel on one knee to guide the sleeves down my arms. "Sit the master down," Collette says as the tall woman brings a cruet of oil, passes the vial unstoppered beneath my nose, then takes my hand. The smell is sweet and musky, slightly like that of bananas, it makes my head swim. One of the twins brings a long, ornate ivory pipe. Collette walks toward the door.

This moment, my mind entirely clear: one of the twins lights three candles, then draws her hands along my body, her hair brushing against my thighs. "So strong," she says. "You look so strong, Rawley." The new silk sheet beneath me is cool and the air a cool ache upon my genitals.

I watch as the woman stands at the foot of the recliner, slowly pulls off her caftan, the candle shadows moving behind her. The sight of her nakedness pierces me: she is a smallish woman, but her breasts are large, their curves not the curves of a pitcher, but of a dome; she has a cleavage even when they are naked. Her nipples darken as they come erect, her curves and hollows lapped by candlelight. I feel a sweet shock as the two other women kneel astride me, the light playing over them, and begin to rub the sweet oil on my chest and stomach, their breasts swaying as they work, their hair spilling over me. My body is aswarm with breasts, with moving lips and hands.

I open my eyes and Collette's face is near mine, her eyes slightly glazed and full of candlelight, she's come back.

"Because I love you," she says. "Because I love you,

Rawley. And because we're here. I wanted to show you what it can be like to be here."

"Hungry?" Collette says later. "The girls left some food. Couscous. Lamb. But I made a special menu while waiting this afternoon, something just for you. You can ask for it any time."

Collette hands me a pad of gold ship's stationery; this is what she's printed:

COLLETTE'S MENU

Dutch Pecks//   Hot Buttered Kisses//
Salade//Fresh Green Kisses
Entree//Hot Passionate Kisses Français
Vegetable Kisses//
Dessert//Whipped Cream Kisses//Chocolate Kisses//
Honey Kisses//

Kisses Espresso//

"And you can ask for anything," I tell her, "anything you want."

"It's close by," she whispers, touching my hand. "Love me, Rawley."

Massimo's "if one can trust such a woman" in my mind, I kiss her and tell her that I do.

Still later, after the women have gone, Collette calls me into the kitchen/bar of the cabin, she's among the clutter at the service range.

She is looking at two trays of cannelloni. "I didn't punch these up for dinner. Did you? I did a trace, there weren't any entries showing. These came through on the dinner program. Did you punch them up?"

"No," I say, my ears slightly burning. I have been mentally swimming in the self-indulgent way of a man who's fallen in love; I've forgotten what I did this afternoon.

"I thought I canceled the coq au vin we were supposed

to have, since Delia . . . I know I did."

"Well," I say, tentatively touching the sauce with my index finger, then touching the tip of my tongue. "The cannelloni looks good."

She slaps at my hand. "Are you going to eat this?" she asks. "Where did it come from? Somebody's messing with the program, somebody who knows how to cover his tracks. I wouldn't eat this food."

"What do you mean, somebody?" I ask, reaching to pick up one of the cannelloni with my fingers. Collette grabs my wrist, squeezes hard.

"*Raw*ley. Taylor—or who knows? That friend of yours died, Rawley."

I look at Collette in puzzlement for an instant, but I'm shamed utterly. And to make it worse, the sauce is terrific.

"I'll just take a bite," I mutter, taking her hand from my wrist and reaching for a fork. Collette turns away, angry with me. With my back to her back I take a sizable bite. Absolutely delicious. "Incredible," I say. "This cannelloni is incredible." I keep eating.

After a minute Collette asks me quietly how I feel.

"Great," I tell her. "I told you this was still an adventure. Try some pasta."

"No," she says balefully. "I don't like cannelloni."

"All right. I think I can eat them all."

"Well," she says after another minute, the odor of the sauce having completely filled the cabin and the cannelloni already half gone, "maybe just one." I look at her; she has the beginnings of a resigned, chagrined smile on her lips. "An adventure, the man says. Hand me that silver fork on the counter, will you? I'll eat my last meal in style."

CHAPTER 8
Vietahiti

As we descend in the morning sun, the island Collette names Vietahiti is spread out beneath us as it would be on a chart, surrounded by a rich blue sea. It is shaped into a coarse figure eight by two volcanos, their craters among the clouds. A flat saddle lies between them and contains, I see, one long, wide runway, a starship launch tower, and a group of support buildings. It is a large island, at least five hundred kilometers square. Its entire windward coast is indented with bays and coves inside small islands, and a deep green jungle stretches inland on a rising plain. On the leeward side, steep valleys corrugate the slopes, rising to a band of light green on the easternmost volcano, a forest of tropical hardwoods, Collette says. There's hardly a sign of human presence, the sight is almost breathtaking after LasVenus. We pass through the clouds just over a mawlike, moonlike crater, break through over continuous jungle, then swing back toward the saddle over the ocean to make a gliding approach. For a long moment the window/wall shows a view straight down into the reef; I see coral alleys racing by with sand bottom, like fine veins in a blue and emerald sea. Then a flash of beach, wide and almost white, then the jungle, dense and ripe, deep green.

Ah, I think, what Guam could be, without the base, without Agana—what Guam could be.

```
┌─────────────────────────────────────────────────────────┐
│                                         ▮                 │
│   TROPICAL RESERVE              ▮   "a pleasuring ground for the benefit and │
│   ‾‾‾‾‾‾‾‾ ‾‾‾‾‾‾‾                    enjoyment of people" Act 72875-83-4621  │
│  ▮                                    SoPac Congress       │
│     ENTRANCE BY TICKET          1/remain on tram, NaturBus, or within │
│     ONLY                           recreational zones.    │
│     thePleasureTube corp.       2/retain all dispoz units. │
│                  permittee      3/open fires prohibited.  │
│     A LINE                      4/passengers must strictly adhere to │
│     TICKET    ▮▮                   regulations of recreational or restaurant │
│                                    areas.                 │
│                                 5/return to ship by 0200. │
└─────────────────────────────────────────────────────────┘
```

```
┌─────────────────────────────────────────────────────────┐
│                              ▮                            │
│  / / Along with SierraNevada in North America, the island of Dominica │
│  between Guadeloupe and Martinique, and the Wadi Howar in northwest │
│  Sudan, this SoPac biosphere reserve preserves an Edenlike ecosphere off ▮ │
│  limits to human manipulation / / the ecosphere is monitored continuously │
│  and anomalies corrected by trained personnel / / here at Vietahiti the │
│  reserve is integrated with recreational zones for the widest variety of │
│  tropical activities / / shows in show areas nightly / / respect and enjoy your │
│  reserve / /                                              │
│                                                           │
│      "SoPac's NATURAL PLANT ROOM"                         │
│                    ▮▮                                     │
└─────────────────────────────────────────────────────────┘
```

Before we leave the ship, the message pager starts right in, signals live line. I flip the toggle, speak, give in. There is only a simple audio patch through the electronics to the resort; the wall screen is out. "Two-nine-two. Rawley Voorst. Patching through. I'll take what you have."

"Negative message," I hear the girl from traffic say, her voice crackling and hard to hear against the sound of steel guitars being piped through the ship. "There's somebody waiting for you."

"Traffic, this is two-nine-two. Do I read 'someone waiting'? Please identify."

"Two-nine-two, traffic. He won't say who he is."

I look at Collette, she has stopped packing and is watching me.

"What does he look like, traffic? Can you describe? A man with black hair, bushy black hair, glasses? Or short. You did say he."

There is a crackling silence for a moment, then a small noise. "Oh, no. He says I can't tell you what he looks like. He says he'll meet you at your cabana."

"Traffic, what the hell kind of message is this?"

There is another crackling silence, it sounds as if the operator is talking with someone standing offmike nearby. I swear she giggles. "Uh, that's all I'm authorized to say," I hear. "Uh, two-nine-two, traffic out."

Once through the crowded disembarkation chute, into the terminal, a Polynesian longhouse, most of the passengers filter toward waiting NaturBuses, third-class program. An older man wearing a ragged straw hat is swaggering drunkenly, jostling the crowd—nervous, I think, without spun-steel surfaces. I'm not so calm myself, wonder if now I'm about to see Knuth instead of Taylor. In the adjacent tramrun lobby the atmosphere acquires the sweet weight of the air of the tropical Pacific, a lush, flowery odor. Collette and I board an A tram for the beach; evidently the island is shared by both the tropical reserve and a resort complex. A dark-eyed, golden-skinned girl waves, smiling, as we whir away.

The tram takes us through a dense jungle that muffles its machine hum. The jungle's high canopy trees are entwined with lianas through which the sun filters down in sleepy patches the size of children. The green seems to go on and on, the air is marvelous. When we reach the palm-lined coast, the sun is barely obscured by the planet's mantle of haze—it is brighter and clearer than even the sun over Guam. Who? I wonder.

We're dropped at another Slot 9. A raffia-thatched cabana lies at the end of a synthetic path through a grove of very real palm trees and just above the high-tide line of a very real beach. Salt air. The ocean stretches away, blue and dazzling, to a vast horizon. As we approach the small cabana the sunlight pains my cabin-soft eyes.

He's sitting on the lanai of the cabana, in the shade of the thatch, his tan so deep he looks as if he lives in the place. When he sees us his grin goes from ear to ear, his hands rise in greeting.

"Surprise," he says, getting up to extend his hand in his old-fashioned way; he's laughing.

I'm laughing, too. "Good to see you, Werhner. Good to see your face. How do you expect to get back on time? How in the hell did you get here?" I shake Werhner's hand, we pump ridiculously, so dislocated yet so used to one another, we laugh at that, too. The beach stretches beyond us, the sea glassy in the morning sun, the air sweet. It's like a pleasant dream.

"Getting here was the easy part," Werhner laughs. "You loafers are resupplied through Hong Kong. I came to see your expression for myself. Have you heard the latest? Look at you, Rawley, I'll bet you haven't."

I look into Werhner's sharp, intelligent face; his smile is already hardening into something like pained relief. I tell him that Guam's been under a communications blackout, the last I've heard has been from him. "Is it about Cooper?" I ask.

"Cooper." He shrugs nervously, I notice exhaustion behind his smile now. "That's still a mystery. No, it's the whole debriefing. We're finished."

A small wave of electricity passes through my body. I ask him what he means.

"Just what I said. We're finished with the debriefing, officially terminated. Came through from the East about 0300. Full leave, new assignments in eight months." Now Werhner's grinning sardonically, his sandy hair splayed out, the smile in his eyes.

"You mean we're all through on Guam? We're through?"

"Program terminated," he laughs, pushing back his hair. "Don't even have to go back. Can you believe it? Wait till you hear why. Got the story from Tamashiro. Our blow data was misplaced years ago—a generation ago here. So we're coming back, the computer searches, the search gets nowhere—and the flow chart, a year before we land, triggers an investigation."

"So the data does exist," I say.

"The same data is in Cooper's report." Werhner

shrugs. "So nobody looks to see why the investigation's triggered, see, the data is buried. These SciCom men are well paid, right? They need something to do, important, busy. In the meantime, military does a trace, they're paying our salaries. Turns out military has the data. Meanwhile, SciCom is conducting an investigation that has no terminus, looking for that data internally, eating its own tail, while we're all drawing full military pay."

"Ooooh," I say, sitting down in a creaking wicker chair, feeling the light become brighter. "So military got us out? Is this true?"

Werhner nods.

"And what about Cooper?"

Werhner bites his lower lip. "That's what makes me wonder. Look, Rawley, it's very weird. He's not on the death list, there's no record of internment, there's no record of his staying in Houston."

"Then there's a chance he's alive. Now what in the hell . . . ?"

"If you trace him, it goes Guam to Houston to Guam to Houston through L.A. A *transit* loop. That's from closed SciCom program. Puzzling. Well . . ."

"But we're really through on Guam?"

Even with his evident exhaustion, Werhner looks better than he has for years—deeply tanned, clear eyes. "That also checks out through closed SciCom program. I'm your navigator, Rawley, I don't put you on. The results from the ship's investigation stand: 'Accidental collision with unknown interstellar material, forces tidal in nature.' The report's thin, sure. We lost all that data when program pontoon blew. But there is what there is, that's all. Now everybody agrees."

"Christ," I say. I'm slightly giddy, run my hand over the caning in the arm of the chair. "I feel like we've just landed. These last two weeks have been very strange, it was strange enough on Guam, it never quit for me. . . ."

Collette brought us tall mint juleps, we sit around a small wicker table in the shade. Palms rustle lazily, flap;

the water gurgles at the intersection of sand and shallow bay.

"I actually worried about you," Werhner says, glancing with raised eyebrows at Collette. "Now that I get here, I'm jealous. Hong Kong's not like this."

"Well, you're here now," Collette tells Werhner with a smile. "You ought to stay."

I spend a few minutes telling Werhner how I've been chased by Taylor since Guam, how Collette's been involved. Werhner surprises me again. He had a brief talk with Taylor when the ship landed, Taylor wants to see me at 1800 today in the console dome, Dome A of the ship, to hand me my official orders and to conduct an exit interview. Werhner went through his on the spot, waves his orders at me like a small fan.

"Dome A," I say. "That's fitting." I mention to Collette that Dome A was the place we worked.

"So you get to see his ugly face one more time." Werhner grins. "There's a man," he says, still talking about Taylor, "launched up his own asshole. Excuse me, Collette."

Collette says no excuse is necessary, and thanks the high heavens she's seen the last of Colonel T.

Werhner's going to stay, leaves to arrange for a cabin for the last leg of theTube's flight. After he processes in, he says, he's going to find his cabin and go to sleep; up at 0300, he's been in transit all night. We'll see him again after lunch, maybe do some diving here.

Sitting in the warm shade with Collette, I take a deep breath of salt-rich, fresh air, look out to sea across the bright sand—a few scattered clouds on the horizon, snow-white, the sky brilliant, washed blue.

VIETAHITI VENTURES//

FIRST-CLASS PASSAGE//

//shuttle trams continuously between Vietahiti Beach/BaliHi/
theTube//
//new options every hour

Vietahiti Beach//
—catamaran and trimaran
 sailing
—zodiac availability
—deep-sea transparent sub
—all aquaplease options
 continuous

BaliHi Mountain Palace//
—arboretum and jungle walk
—paradise park
—queen's garden of
 delights
—epicurean consensus

//shuttle trams continuously between Vietahiti Beach/BaliHi/the-Tube//

//new options every hour//continuous programming in each cabana//

our service is your pleasure//your pleasure our service
                                   @ thePleasureTube corp.

Collette and I join Erica and Tonio for an early lunch at the Palace Garden Club, an elegant restaurant set in the gardens alongside the large building with the red and gold roof tiles I saw when I swam out from the beach—the Mountain Palace. We are a few kilometers inland, up the slopes of the larger volcano, in a belt of high jungle. The air is noticeably cooler here, fresh and crystalline, the climate seems perfect. Peacocks strut among the tables, iridescent blue and green, clucking softly. Collette says we ought to bring Werhner here later to see.

Tonio is telling us how he managed to get an exceptional performance from a numb actress for a videon series he directed. She was, he says, the only zombied Juliet he's ever seen—she had an expressionless face and a flat voice besides. "So I put her in a grope suit," he explains, pushing back his hair with a well-manicured hand, grinning. "I had her wear a grope suit under her costume. She was fantastic—panting, her voice turned into honey—and her eyes, the *color* she got. She was just fantastic."

"Sweet Juliet," Collette says flatly. "Good God."

I look at Tonio with puzzlement. "All right," I ask. "What's a grope suit? I heard a woman say she carried one in her luggage."

"Tonio," Collette says, "you are to-the-core decadent. To the core."

Tonio gestures with his palms up, smiling. "Ah, but what an interesting play *Romeo and Juliet* turned out to be. You can appreciate that, Collette, try to imagine it."

"A grope suit," Erica tells me, sighing behind her sunburn, "is made out of latex, and where your erogenous zones are, there are bumps and things that squeeze you when you move, and mainly a knob, see, that goes in. And there are suits for men, too."

"Indeed there are," Tonio says quickly. "But look at this person—oops, he's coming this way. *She's* coming—no, don't turn, you'll embarrass me. Rawley, I think she knows you. She was looking for you."

I do turn slowly to follow Tonio's line of vision, toward the other tables between us and the bamboo bar, the monkey cages. Eva Steiner, dressed in a black jump suit, is striding our way. Beyond her, the pasty, fiftyish man with the thin hair I remember from the grandstands at LasVenus is seating two women at a circular table; they must have just come in.

"I thought it was you." Eva Steiner smiles—she's pale and a little drawn, obviously hasn't yet been to the beach. "Though this dark one I recognized first," she continues, her eyes flashing for an instant at Collette. "Captain Voorst. Rawley."

Seeing her now brings back both the final moments of our race and the grim end for Massimo. For some reason, perhaps only because she knew Massimo, I feel a pull of sympathy for her, feel bad that I didn't even respond to her invitation. I ask Steiner evenly if she's having fun, introduce her around the table.

Tonio's cocked head straightens and his slightly glazed eyes become businesslike. "Of course," he says. "Director Steiner. What a pleasure. Do sit down. May I . . . ?" Tonio goes on, giving Erica a wide-eyed glance. Eva Steiner ignores him.

"You must have heard the news by now," Eva Steiner says to me. "Congratulations. Eight months until a new assignment? I envy you."

"How do you know?" I wonder out loud. "I don't even have the orders yet."

"I was hoping you'd stop by my cabin the other day," she goes on, ignoring my question. "I was hoping you'd come. We missed you."

Who is this woman? I ask myself. Deliberately I tell her I've been concentrating on more relaxing things than she might have in mind. "I *am* on leave," I say, then notice that, for all the politeness I am trying to generate, she still returns a strange electricity. My skin prickles as her expression changes to a wider smile.

"But you owe me," she says. "It's only fair. I wanted to talk to you about this yesterday. Listen to me, Captain Voorst. My hydroplanes are here. On the west end of this island there is a sheltered bay, perfectly flat. Ideal conditions. We can race."

Collette's stare is boring through me, she has gone a little rigid. The sensation of my skin makes me shift in my seat.

"I have to turn you down," I say nervously, though she has made me feel somehow obligated. "Since Massimo died, I haven't much felt the stomach for chance like that. You remember Massimo Giroti, Director Steiner."

"You must call me Eva. Eva," she says. Now I see her own nervousness; her eyes are red, twitching slightly. "I suspect he died as he would have preferred. Doesn't the thought of how you might die excite you, Rawley?"

"No," I tell her, my skin crawling, "not at all. And something tells me Massimo would rather be alive."

She shrugs, her smile gone. "Pity you won't. They are such sleek machines, Rawley. You're making it very frustrating for me."

"Answer my question," I say. "Just how is it that you know about my orders? Just who are you?"

"Come to the bay," she says after a moment, says with a smile for everyone. Then she looks at me with intense focus. "I do want to talk with you."

"Say what's on your mind," I answer.

"I will," she says after a long moment, says flatly. But then she wheels and walks away.

Once she's well settled at her own table, I ask Collette what's on the east end of the island.

"We are. Or were," she says. "That's where the cabana is. And there's the bird preserve on the island offshore, the one they call Chinaman's Hat. But she said the west end, Rawley, that's where a bay is. Please don't."

"I heard what she said. That woman makes me nervous. No—and especially not in her boats."

"God, she scares the hell out of me," Tonio says quietly, his voice hushed in the way one speaks in the presence of a corpse. "How could you talk to her that way? What people say about her!"

"If we take off for that island this afternoon, say in a Zodiac, bring along Werhner... That island looks like a place to dive. Will we be off limits? Could we get away with it?"

Collette considers the question. "You can dive near it on an aquaplease program," she says. "I think we could get away with landing—look, they're pretty lax here. This is one place service personnel don't much care about and security's... well, security's lazy."

Beyond Erica, who begins to tell me much the same thing, lithe young women begin to slip among the tables, dancing to Balinese gamelan music, graceful as deer, finger cymbals tinkling like wind chimes. At her table, seated, Eva Steiner is keeping time to the music with her heel on the opposite woman's outstretched leg.

An hour after we leave Erica and Tonio in the cool shade of the gardens, we've picked up Werhner from the ship and loaded a boat with the help of an obese Polynesian man at the boathouse. Werhner, Collette, and I are slipping over the small incoming swells in a four-man Zodiac, headed toward Chinaman's Hat. We wind up going out past the first reef, Collette in the bow hanging on with both hands, laughing as we punch through the surf. The salty air and the spray are invigorating, the unhazed sun hot on my back as I maneuver the light boat lifting and falling with the swells. Werhner steadies the tanks; he's got some of his own gear from Guam as well.

The windward side of Chinaman's Hat turns out to be fully hollowed out, a small valley formed by prevailing weather, absolutely desolate. A white beach is at the mouth of the valley, protected by another reef farther out. Well offshore, Werhner puts on his gear and slips into the water to swim in. We power in the rest of the way, pull the boat up on the sand.

I hit the toggles on the electronics built into the center seat. Someone is paging me from the resort—my guess is Eva Steiner—has been paging me off and on for the last ten minutes.

Collette watches me unplugging the battery. "You mean business," she says.

"I didn't come here to be bothered," I say, and look around the spot, what a spot. From here the resort has entirely disappeared. Pristine beach all to ourselves, a thick grove of coconut palms and sprawling sea grape leads up the small valley. A small fresh-water stream drains to the ocean two hundred meters away, then the ridge shoulders over the sand.

I can see the bright red of Werhner's diving flag bobbing with his float on the swells; it appears, disappears, appears in the blue. The sun is booming at two o'clock, absolutely dazzling, a white-hot specter I can feel in my bones, tingling on my skin. The news about Guam is finally sinking in; I feel lighter, find myself starting to think ahead to what I might do when this trip is over. A trip to South America, I think?

"We won't be able to tell what time it is," Collette says amiably as she unloads the mats and the cooler.

"Best news I've heard all day," I laugh.

White beach, warm sand, the surf a low roar since the tide's come up. There are a few seabirds here, skimming the ocean, wheeling overhead to nesting sites on the rocky slopes behind us. We've had to move up the beach because of the rising tide, camp now on a cleared patch above the high-tide line. Collette's pouring the last of our two bottles of champagne, Werhner lies flat on his back looking up into the sky. I'm still wet, just out of the diving gear. My ears ring slightly and I have a mild sense of unreality as I squat down, dripping, at the corner of the straw mat.

"Black holes," Werhner says to the sky. "The most interesting phenomenon to a speculative mind. Rawley wisely just flew the ship. I think I began to think too much about them. I haven't been the same since. Well, neither has he."

"There's something I don't quite understand," Collette says, passing Werhner a paper cup of warm champagne. "Rawley mentioned that within a black hole, a traveler, assuming there's the slightest chance he'd live, would be free in time. Could you explain that?"

"That's a theoretical premise based on what black holes do to light," Werhner says, up on an elbow. "A black hole is so dense that it attracts rather than emanates light—and once you reverse the physics of light, you reverse the physics of space and time. Here we're free in space—we can go back to the cabana, walk along the beach, go wherever we'd like. On the other hand, we're trapped in time—we can't go backward into the past or forward into the future."

"Yes," Collette says.

"Reverse the physics for a black hole and you find yourself like light trapped in its gravity field, trapped in space; but free in time instead, since time depends on the movement of light."

"Feeling champagne," Collette laughs. "Still, you'd be crushed, wouldn't you, by its density, your own gravity? What did you call that state, Rawley? Naked singularity. You'd be pulled to the center of the collapsing black hole and crushed beyond the smallest particle of matter. Staggering to imagine."

As Collette hands me my champagne I tell her about ring singularity, the kind of naked singularity exhibited by spinning black holes. Because they spin, their naked singularity is expressed along their pole axes. And presumably, along the equator, if the black hole were large enough, a traveler could enter and survive, with enough power to orbit within. One theory suggests passing through. "Though if he did pass through, a traveler would find himself in another universe, one that shares with his universe the identical black hole. And that's not exactly passing through."

"Or just be pulsed out somewhere, maybe, pure energy," Werhner says, pushing back his hair. "I don't agree that if the Daedalus had gotten into the rotational black hole we were surveying, we'd have wound up in another universe. Vaporized and pulsed out, maybe. Levsky's idea—Levsky did the physics—is that in the right kind of black hole, with just the right orbit, you'd be caught up in some kind of loop, free in time, so your experience of the loop would be your experience of . . . Dead enough, Levsky used to say. Stone-cold dead."

"Yet in some paradoxical way always alive," I add; that's also what Levsky used to say.

"Now I am feeling champagne," Collette says. "The freedom reminds me of the hologram."

Werhner holds up his paper cup, swirls the last of the champagne. "The hologram, yes, but the hologram you can shut down. You don't come back from the black hole. Well, one last toast. Reunion of the crew. And thank God we did get back. Theoretical ideas don't get to drink even warm champagne."

After we drink the tart, flat remains of the champagne, we sit in silence for a time, listening to the surf. The rollers far out in the surf line crest and fall into themselves, one after the other, the sets growing with the rising tide. As I swam the outside reef I rose and fell with the waves, the surge and drop still with me. I am on the mat, barely touching Collette, watching a seabird skimming just over the water, so near the surface he disappears behind each crest. Collette asks me where I'd like to be, free in time. I laugh, push my hand through the sand, and say, just where I am. She says she'll file that information for the hologram.

Collette's arms are spidered behind her back, she's untying the scanty top she's wearing. Her breasts jostle free, dark nipples erect. Now she's slipping off her string bottom. "Join me?" she asks, motioning with her eyes toward the calm water inside the near reef.

"Later," I say, watching her rise, run in her side-to-side woman way to the sea. I grip the sand in my hand to feel its presence. It runs through my fingers, filters through in fine streams to the sand below. I grip so hard the sand which remains, the pain shoots through my wrist; squeeze it so tightly it is as if I want to fuse it into glass.

"Some woman," Werhner says.

"I agree." I am thinking about Taylor, though, as I watch Collette laze in the shallow water past the rubber boat, floating on her back, arms straight out, legs spread-eagled, glistening brown in the sun. "God, it's good to be alive. Do you think we're actually through with SciCom?" I ask Werhner.

"That's my guess," he says. "I've seen my new orders, so... You'll feel a little more convinced when you're holding that paper in your hands in another two hours. If nothing happens after a few days... then what difference does it make? SciCom's always watching flight crew, you know that, we'll never be through with that part of it. But this crap we've been going through? The only thing that still has me on edge is the data on Cooper. I don't understand what's going on."

"They must know," I say.

"Not according to Knuth. Knuth says if there was no transcript there was no interview, and what I pulled was probably a visit from a nurse." Werhner shrugs. "A blind? Or a..." He sighs, then smiles, looking at the Zodiac, looking past it at Collette. "You know, this is some place, this whole arrangement."

Handful by handful, I filter sand through my fingers. A woman, I think.

When I plug the electronics back together on the Zodiac, the message pager starts right in, almost as if on cue. It is the same traffic operator with a reminder from Taylor that I'm to meet him in Dome A at 1800 hours, he wants a confirmation.

"Tell him I'll be there," I say. "I wouldn't miss it for the world. Tell him that."

We have a small cocktail-hour snack, a party, at the Palace Garden Club; there are five of us; Collette and myself, Erica and Tonio, Werhner. I'm preoccupied with what I'd like to say to Taylor in an hour, but Werhner's no help. He's really taken by the place, the lush garden setting, the Balinese women dancing, the red snapper, which, he says, has never been frozen. I can see he's also taken with Erica. I think she's playing up to him, and she looks great, her blonde hair bleached by the sun, blown back. She looks as if she's lost some weight; with the food set before us in the last two weeks I can't figure out how, then I recall her bouts of flightsickness. Right now she doesn't look as if she's ever been flightsick: trim, smiling; the sun has given her a glow. She's telling Werhner she spent the afternoon snorkeling, asking him if he's ever been frightened by a shark.

"The only kind were SciCom sharks," Werhner laughs, glancing at me. "I've seen some real sharks. They never bothered me. Underwater, you have a different sense of danger, it's less direct. I think that's because the medium is heavier. Blue sharks, white tips—seen those, they're pretty common. I expect they're harmless."

"Werhner lived in the water," I tell Erica. "Look at his neck. Beginnings of gills."

"Well, it happens to be very relaxing," Erica says. "It eases your tensions. Your physical tensions."

Tonio is distant, picking at a bright red lobster. There's something as well between him and Erica. He did drag her over to the horseshoe bay at the west end of the island to watch the hydroplanes, but they only watched from a distance and went somewhere else, so that's not it.

"I saw some eels once," Collette says. "They *gave* me tensions. I'd like to try tanks someday, though."

"Didn't use tanks much on Guam," Werhner tells her. "Body chemistry sets a three-hour limit—and, well, Rawley knows the swim off Utama Bay."

"We'd always wonder if he'd come in at sundown."

"It passed the time." Werhner smiles. "The only advantage of tanks is that you can go deeper."

I see Erica guzzle a full glass of champagne, set the glass down with decision. "*Deeper*. That's something I'd like to try. Tonio didn't even put on the fins I got for him. He was too busy chasing boys. That's where we went. He said he wanted to tape the canoe racers, but he never left the beach. He barely left a certain beach blanket. Isn't that right, Tonio?"

So that's it, I think—Tonio barely looks up from his lobster, Collette is looking at me with wry, raised eyes. I am trying to stifle a smile, look at Werhner—he's turned flush, hopelessly embarrassed. A kind of dead weight falls on the table. Poor Tonio clears his throat.

"So, ummm," Collette begins. "Tell us more about, uh, Hong Kong."

"Not much to tell," Werhner says with relief. "Crowded, run-down. It's not the same. And it smells like a sewer. I was sorry I went."

"This is the place," Erica says. "Hong Kong's been out for years."

"Sure, the women here, ahh ..." Werhner begins. "I mean ..."

Tonio has folded his napkin, he's rising from his seat. He puts one palm up nervously, smiles, uses the other to smooth his white suit. "I do have to meet someone," he says to us all. Erica rolls her eyes and he gives her a sharp look. "Bitch," he mutters. "Bitch," she answers back. He manages to smile at us all. "Good meeting you," he tells Werhner. "See you again, perhaps." Then Tonio, working his fingers, walks away.

Werhner smiles nervously at Erica, she smiles back. Then a long silence falls over the table as we eat. "How did you two meet?" Werhner finally says to me, nodding at Collette. "I don't quite understand the, uh ..."

"If a woman's interested in you, she lets you know," Erica says firmly, running her statement right into the middle of his sentence.

Werhner stops for a moment, grins weakly, clears his throat.

"I'd like to sleep with you tonight," Erica says before he can say another word. "And see one of the shows."

Werhner nods a little breathlessly, looks at me open-mouthed, looks at me as if to say, thank you, Rawley, you have somehow managed to set me up. I take the credit with a grin; of course, the credit isn't mine.

"You take good care of this woman," I tell him. "She's a friend of mine, too, and she needs careful handling. Listen to what she says. There's a real woman in that bikini."

Now Erica looks at me with a grateful, romantic sigh. Collette gives me a soft punch in the ribs.

The ride up the crew elevator of the large ship is achingly familiar—twice during the thirty seconds I have the certainty I'm going on watch for the thousandth time. There's a salt scum on the edges of my lips from this afternoon, I lick them to recall exactly where I am.

As usual, Dome A is almost empty—the circular room, twenty meters across, is ringed with electronics of the same order as the Daedalus—and the consoles grouped in the center still use whole rows for vanes. The transparent dome is canted toward the center of the three-cylindered ship. Through the slightly blue glass of the dome's ground the tropical evening sky is just beginning to show; the day's light is failing, but within this chamber there are no interior lights. I spot Taylor standing in the dimness at one of the consoles near the chart table.

"Does feel like home," I say, walking over the familiar magnesium-alloy floor—and I am blithely there before I feel my blood come up, before I realize we aren't alone.

"The technology has not changed very much," the other party says crisply, her voice agonizingly familiar, absolute in the silence. "All new preprogramming, new autopilots over there. But technology develops only to a point. Beyond that point, the interesting instruments are human."

It is Eva Steiner who steps from the vane consoles. Taylor clears his throat, sets down an amber envelope with my name on it, and takes off his glasses, begins wiping one lens. "You once were anxious to meet my commanding officer," Taylor says flatly, nodding to Eva Steiner. "Well..."

The cutting edge of my feelings turns against myself. The sight of Eva Steiner, the dawning realization that she is Taylor's superior, slice through me like a knife. I had never thought this through—feel myself flush, feel the anger I had earlier today bleed through and to the sight of her, standing with a tight, thin smile before me in a shiny black flight suit, the crop she held in LasVenus at her side, the amber double loops of SciCom insignia on her shoulder, faint on the handle of her crop.

"I'm glad you are surprised," she says, her thin eyebrows raised, her nostrils wide. "So not even Massimo Giroti knew. Well, very good. I don't go on vacations, Captain. Not even on this ship."

"I don't know if surprise is the right word," I say, thinking, So that's how she knew of my orders, that's why Collette was transferred to her after the first leg. It stuns my imagination. My God, I think, the ship so familiar around me, thinking of the Daedalus crew, what did we do to unleash this?

"You look surprised," Taylor says, his full eyebrows furrowing. "You're right," he says to Eva Steiner. "It was worth it to see his expression."

I reach past him for the amber envelope he's set on the navigator's table. He draws away from my approach, as if my move were to grab him. A small wave of satisfaction runs through me, at least he knows my mind.

"We're a little embarrassed at the way things have turned out," Eva Steiner says in an oily voice as I break open the envelope's seal. "I can't tell you how much trouble this whole affair has caused between us and military."

I pull out and unfold the stiff sheet within. Formal orders: through Washington via military cable, copies to SciCom. Clean leave orders; military's worked again.

"So I'm authorized to tell you you're officially on leave," Taylor says as if he's doing me a favor.

"I've been on leave since my appeal was approved," I

tell him, folding my orders, pulling on the fold, slipping the sheet into my breast pocket. "Neither of you seems to understand that. You're going to hear from Flight, I can guarantee that."

"Oh, Rawley," Eva Steiner says, purring. "We've already heard from Flight."

I look past her pale, lined face and down the row of vane consoles, light green instruments, winking lights at rest. Microweather systems look the same, the principle of propulsion and control identical. To work again, I think, to get away—I've had to put flying out of my mind, but in this instant I find myself wanting to work a ship again, to feel the bump and roll of light-speed flight. I've been away from it long enough. Yet how little difference there's been, I think with a shock of recognition. On board the Daedalus, ship SciCom kept up a running battle with dome crew, bogged us down with Committee-Pilot, multiple logs, redundant information, five-copy corrections. In the end it's the same, I think, it's an attitude. But at least we weren't spied on then, not manipulated. Or were we? I wonder now, wonder about Cooper's strangeness to all of us.

"So we're through," Taylor says. "I'm supposed to thank you for your cooperation. I don't think I will."

"Not through, exactly," I tell him.

"I don't think so, either, Voorst," Taylor says, becoming engaged. "I'm not satisfied. There are just too many..."

"You're finished here, Colonel," Steiner says.

"We're through on Guam," Taylor says, slightly surly. "I don't see what difference—"

"I want to know exactly what happened to Cooper," I say firmly. "And I'm going to find out."

Taylor takes a deep breath, exchanges hardening looks with Eva Steiner, then tells me he doesn't doubt that I will. As for himself, he's got nothing more to say. I bite my upper lip, my heart thumping. I stare blankly at the pastel charts laid out on the navigator's table: tomorrow's launch orbit and the sunloop are plotted, overlaid with interstellar courses. What's going on? I look into Taylor's eyes, they swim behind the thickness of his glasses as if underwater. I have the feeling I've been here before, looked into that face with the same exasperation, I have been here forever.

And then Taylor's gone.

"You know something about Cooper," I say, alone with Eva Steiner in the fading light, a mauve tropical sky huge through the dome above us, the consoles in deepening shadow.

Eva Steiner turns a little pale. "There are problems," she says. "When Cooper came down, he was experiencing a gross psychotic episode. We held him on Guam for observation, then we had to ship him to Houston. He overdosed while he was there by ingesting a full gram of pure hallucinogens. We brought part of him back, part of him. And what there is of him is ours. He didn't come back quite human. The man is not a human being."

"He's *alive*?"

"After a fashion."

"What do you mean, after a fashion? What are you talking about? Cooper's alive?"

"I can show you something," she says with a thin smile. "Draw your own conclusions." Steiner punches up a security code, then a video link, on the navigator's rack of monitors. The small screen flips, then steadies in an eerie blue light to show what appears to be a cell, there's a white-haired man sitting in a cell, broad shoulders, full bushy beard—the man is Cooper. His hair is white and he is slumped over on a stained cot, behind bars. The picture is fuzzy, its resolution poor, but there appear to be a series of dark patches on his exposed forearm, an ashtray overflowing with cigarettes on the floor beside the cot. He is slumped over, propped against a metal wall, his feet on a metal floor. No, Cooper never smoked, I am thinking as I watch him raise his face—he's drooling, looks twenty years older, his eyes dark, blank sockets, horrifying.

"My God," I say. "Where is he? Is this a tape?"

Steiner is looking at the monitor intently, small beads of perspiration show on her upper lip, her eyes are wide, filled with the eerie light. "Live," she says.

"*Live*? Where *is* he?"

She switches the monitor off, leaves me looking at my reflection in the glass; before I turn away I see in my own face the horror I am trying to contain. Dear God, I think, the sight of him—think it could have been me as well, could have been Werhner. "Belowdecks," I hear Eva Steiner say; can't quite believe what I hear.

"I brought him along to question him myself, but it's been . . . useless."

"You've got him *here*? You've got him here in a damned cage?" I say. "You've got that man in a cage?"

"He's in a security cell in detention," she says flatly. "It's for his own safety."

"Taylor knew?"

"Colonel Taylor has been working since the beginning on the sensible theory that what's been missing in the analysis of the blow has been double-blind evidence. And since he was coming here, I let him know Cooper would be . . . available."

"You don't have any right to hold him," I say. "The crew's on leave. As of today, the whole crew is on leave."

"If you can say that was a man whom you saw," Eva Steiner says. "We brought him back. What's left is ours. Look, Rawley, I know there was no love lost between you. He took your woman for a time, I know that."

"You were the nurse," I say, the pattern dawning on me. "You were the nurse who interviewed him on Guam. And Christ, that's why his name never appeared on a death list. How in God's name can you—"

"Yes, there are problems, I know there are problems," Steiner says quickly. "Military's inquired because of a tracer from someone on your ship—Schole, you know him, he's a friend of yours. There are problems, but we can solve them."

I can see a strange, smoldering look in Eva Steiner's gray eyes. "Let's say this," she goes on. "He came in on a death list, he was already dead when you splashed down, a corpse in reentry. That would clear up the tracer."

"What are you getting at?"

"Military is going to find him in a few days. But if we can show that he came in on a death list, say we simply forgot to post the data, if just one other crew member, like the pilot, will corroborate that he came in on a death list... Perhaps if you talked with him, you'd see. I'm making you a proposition. Name your next assignment, your own ship, if you want. Or this ship, you see what's here. And there are more interesting places, special places."

"Did he tell you something?" I ask, my heart thumping. "Did he tell you something different from what's in the report?"

She says he told her nothing, says so flatly, begins saying that she wants to keep him, he belongs to her.

"I've heard enough," I say.

"No, don't go. Talk to me! Talk to me!"

My impulse descending in the hum of the dome lift is to leave the ship as quickly as possible, yet once in the secondary lift I punch the lower working lobby, leave the elevator there. There is only a skeleton crew for the layover; across the carpeted floor two service personnel are lazily chatting at the counter. If the ship is set up as I imagine, then the detention area is only one level up from here. I am almost right—up one level, but over in third-class hull, a man with small eyes tells me. With a coolness I did not think I still had, I turn him back to his word game with a casual wave of my hand and pass through the hatchway otherwise in his view, my mind racing as my legs carry me on what I hope looks like a visit to a drunken friend.

On the metal grating in the dim, low-ceilinged passageway between hulls, I am gripped for an instant by the sense that I am doing something foolish, that once I am in detention, the hatch lock could close with a firm click behind me and give Eva Steiner two of us to play with instead of one.

"Cooper!"

There he is, slumped against the metal wall in a poorly

lit cell, his hair white, his broad face blotchy and drawn, his eyes glazed over, unfocused.

"*Cooper!*"

He looks up slowly, looks at me without comprehension, his mouth slowly coming open with drool in the corners, gravity in folds on his face as if he has aged terribly or has been beaten up, worked over, the look of a man lost from the world, lost beyond his ability to remember. Then, making me out, his eyes widen and he begins to grin—a terrible grin, his upper lip drawn back, stretched back. No, not a tape; I shudder, thinking, How long can he have been here?

"Do you recognize me? It's Voorst, Rawley Voorst." Now I see stains on his flight suit, the overflowing ashtray on the floor, crumpled papers—and there is an odor, an odor like ozone.

Cooper's eyes are shining. "Voorst..." he says, his voice hollow, eerie, still grinning. "...you, too...dead."

"Listen to me, Cooper. I'm as alive as I'm standing here," I say tightly, gripping the cold steel bars, shaking them. "And so are you. I'll try to get you out of here, get you to a hospital. Can you understand me?"

Cooper only looks at me, his eyes narrowing, wiping his hand across his mouth.

"Do you remember what happened on Guam? You talked with a woman. What happened then? Did you tell that woman something?"

Cooper smiles crookedly, raises his hand from his face to turn a forearm to me blotched with scars. A cackle runs through his voice. "I'm a corpse, Voorst. She burns me and...I can't...feel it."

I bang the steel bar with my fist; there is a low thud. "*Cooper.* Werhner Schole is here, too. We all came back. You're as alive as I am, Cooper, there's a world outside. Listen to me. Tell me what they've done to you."

Cooper turns his haggard face away, he is chewing his lower lip, spittle at the corner of his mouth. He looks back at me; I hear him say: "Do you see things, Voorst?"

The hair rises on the back of my neck. Behind me there is a sound, quick footsteps padding on metal, nearing.

Around the corner through the hatchway comes the small-eyed security man, rushing down the passageway, paling. "Hey, no visitors. I got a call down, no visitors. Get out, you gotta get out," he says, shooing me with his hands.

It is as if there is something crawling on me, on my skin, crawling.

I take one last look at Cooper, his mouth awry with contempt, his eyes, dark with hate, directed at me or the warden, I cannot tell; I see the burns again on his forearm as Cooper raises his hands to his eyes and turns to the wall, the security man is pushing at me now.

The moon is spectral, huge. Werhner and I sit in the wicker chairs at the cabana, spooked into drinking rum, watching the almost full moon rising over the ocean. It has taken me a long time to tell the story, a long time to unwind. "It never did feel straight," I tell Werhner finally. "And seeing him... My God, man, it was like seeing a ghost."

"What did Cooper mean?" Werhner wonders aloud, wonders again. "How can he think he's a corpse? What did they do, exactly? Well, not so much difference now. But if Eva Steiner hadn't wound up needling you, if it wasn't for that, who'd know about Cooper? Who'd know?"

"Your tracers," I remind him. "She did say it seemed like a matter of days. But what might happen in the meantime?" I sigh. "Christ, am I glad we get our orders through military. Imagine what it would be like if SciCom was hooked into that."

My visions of Cooper still haunt me, the shock of seeing him blue and eerie on the monitor in the dome, the greater shock of seeing him gaunt and ghostlike in the detention cell, the weight of his presence, the strange things he said, wondering if he knew what he was saying. Having seen him, I feel vindicated somehow, though shaken: as if a bridge over which I have just crossed has collapsed behind me.

But it's hard to know what we can do for the man; I don't want to see him again. It's better, we decide, to let military handle his case than to try to do something ourselves. I really can't bear the thought of seeing Cooper; can only think he belongs in a hospital. So Werhner leaves to see what he can do—a series of tracers, asking for replies with requests to expedite.

When he returns I am still sipping rum, still watching the full moon, its light a gleaming swath on the calming sea.

"It'll take a little while," he says. "All things considered, I think it's the best we can do."

"I wonder what he told her, if he told her something in that Guam interview."

"Doesn't matter now," Werhner says quietly.

"God, I just want to forget," I tell him, Cooper's *Do you see things, Voorst?* running through my mind. I rise and stretch to shake it off. "Put this behind me. I just want to forget."

Late in the evening we are lounging at the PastPacific Show, sitting on mats at long, low tables in the center of a mocked-up village of palm-thatched huts. A Balinese ceremony has just ended and the smell of incense hangs in the air, mingles with the odors of roast pig, fish, baked taro, fresh tropical fruits. A Polynesian troupe dances into the center circle, the men in mylar lava-lavas, the women's hips furious and sensual to fast Tahitian drums, their long grass skirts small waves above their flower-circled feet. What a feast we have had, how it's cleared my mind. Werhner reclines, nuzzling Erica. I haven't felt so well in months. I lie with my head in Collette's lap, among the layers of frangipani and pikake falling in strings from her neck, looking up into her face. She is illuminated by torchlight.

She is simply the most beautiful woman I've seen in this evening of beautiful women. Her high cheekbones, her sexy big lips, catch the light in ways that seem to me magical; she seems supernatural tonight. She looks down at me with a fine, tender smile, her eyes green-gold in the light. I mouth the words "I love you." She is puzzled; I say the words. She understands and breaks into a wide grin. When she leans over to kiss my forehead, I am smothered in flowers for a delicious moment.

"You've been good to me," I tell her, thinking back over this last leg of the trip.

"I've been trying my best," she says. "Lover."

"Tell me something I can do for you. Really. Take your turn for once, Collette. You show me yours."

She laughs, looks away. The drums have shifted to a slower, sensuous rhythm, the light begins to flash as torches are whirled.

"There is something," she says.

I ask her what.

"It's something I've never done before, and I want to now, with you. It's a marriage," she says shyly. "Not a legal marriage, but a sort of wedding in the way of my ancestors. This place . . . well, this place makes me think of it. I have a few things my brother gave me, they're very old. He told me what to do with them. Will you go through the ceremony with me, Rawley?"

"A tribal wedding?" I ask. I'm not quite certain what she means. "Here?"

"No, not here. I need the ocean, there isn't anyone from my tribe. But you'll be. We can go to the island, the island where we were this afternoon. That'd be perfect. I'd have to get some things from the ship—could we reach that island in the dark? We'd have to build a fire, I'll need a fire. It's such a nice night. Rawley?"

I look up through the smoky atmosphere and see the large moon poking through the fronds of coconut trees. Really, what Collette's suggested thrills me to the bones. If we can get a Zodiac, I think, there's no problem getting to the island in the moonlight. I look over at Werhner—both he and Erica are sound asleep, arms entwined, before a massive pile of pork bones and coconut pudding.

"It's all right with me," I say. "I'm ready to go."

● ● ●

On the island's beach, above lapping, low-tide waters, in the still beauty of the night, we make a small camp around the wide mats which Collette has brought along. Collette builds a small fire from scrub and hardwood she's also brought along in the Zodiac. Once she lights it, we recline on the woven straw mat. She draws a diagram with a stick in the sand to show me what she's done, where we find ourselves:

We are in the center of the four elements, the air above, the earth below, fire and water to either side.

She's given me a loose thong, an animal-skin loincloth, to wear; she's wearing a long, sheer embroidered robe, eggshell-white. She asks me to repeat a series of phrases in a language I've never heard before. I watch her bowed head as she speaks, her voice soft and guttural, as if she speaks from the origin of language itself. Her eyes are directed downward; as she lifts her face when she is finished, the fire behind me becomes an intense spot of light in her pupils.

Then she takes my hand, holds it palm upward in her lap, and makes a small, quick incision in my wrist with an old ivory knife. The blood comes. She cuts her own wrist, a precise centimeter cut, drops the knife, and firmly pulls our wrists together with her other hand. The sensation is warm, viscous; for a moment as I feel our pulses pounding in unison I experience a strange sense of oppression and joy at the same time.

After a minute Collette sprinkles a powder on both our wrists and the bleeding stops. As she does so she tells me that her people will stand by me until death, and I must stand by them; that with her people I will always find protection, food, drink, shelter, and warmth. Her people, I think . . . there is a sadness in her eyes as she speaks, but her smile is full and sexy when she finishes, the kind of wide smile that really shows her teeth. When we next make love, she says, we will be married.

I begin to reach for her, but she stops me with her hand. There is another step, she tells me, her eyes brightening. She removes a small drawstring pouch from the basket she is kneeling beside. She tells me she will speak the *ta-ala*, a phrase she translates as "the words which must not be hesitantly spoken." As she begins I have the feeling that she has known these words for a long time.

"This is the gift," Collette says, her voice incantatory and distant, "given of the gods, which lets the eye see to behind the sun. It opens the ear to sounds which only the specters of the ancestors can hear. It opens the nose to smells which only the best of hunting dogs can smell, and, smelling, grow restless. This is the gift that gives wings to the feet for the journey to the unknown land where all totems are silent. Then shall the voice resound like the sound of the antelope and every gesture endure forever and the darkness shall be lifted and the great mysteries revealed. . . ."

As she speaks I chew a powder that tastes of bone meal and seaweed, my mouth dry. I gesture to reach for her after a prolonged silence and she says, "Shut your eyes, Rawley. Shut your eyes." When I open them again she has disappeared into the inky darkness; I didn't hear her move. I sit absolutely still, listening, but I hear nothing. I close my eyes again.

My heart is pounding. I wait for minutes and the minutes stretch; I find myself wondering how long my eyes have been closed. I lose my grip on time, look up. The sky above is a vast well of darkness, a sea of stars, snow at the Milky Way. I see Vega, the first star of the evening, a star whose light I first saw appear through the ship's dome as I talked with Taylor at sunset. And the first star of the navigator's triangle. The points of light separate themselves, they lead me automatically to a search for the Crab nebula. It is directly overhead. I look, and in looking I begin to feel the sky widen and I begin to fall through it, falling among the stars as the infinity of space opens before me like a window, like a door. I can feel the blood coursing through my veins and arteries, the rhythm of my heart the rhythm of my body.

A sound nearby. Collette steps out of the dark, naked, glistening with oil, bright beads in her hair. She holds her arms close against her body, her breasts jutting out. She kneels before me and I loosen the loincloth. When I quickly thrust inside her, she wraps her arms around my head and only her fingers move through the hair on the back of my neck. A series of jolting shocks pass through my groin, a stream of delight which does not seem to belong to me but takes the last breath from my lungs. I make no sound, do not move. Within me, muscles relax and contract, I don't even feel my breathing. Then Collette falls, lies by the fire, her eyes shut, the only sign of her orgasm an internal shudder.

After a long moment Collette rises to her feet, sends her arms outstretched to the stars. The posture resonates in my mind, brings back our first hours together. And my vision, the vision of a woman suspended in space, arms spread, enigmatic—she becomes all women, Maxine, Collette, the Spanish girl, Erica; the fright from Cooper means nothing to me now. The low fire gives Collette a golden glow, her skin glistening with the sheen of the fragrant oil as the light plays over the curves of her body.

"Collette," I say, my own voice slightly strange to me,

as if from a distance, yet my mind so clear and my heart so taken with her that the voice speaks with affection and conviction. "Collette. You are a goddess."

"A goddess," she says softly, tenderly, looking at me with a gentle smile. "Yes. And you are a god, Rawley."

I look down, gaze at the fire, watch it for a long moment. "I do feel like a new man."

"You are a god, Rawley," she laughs, holding out her hands. "You'll see."

Two hours later, long after midnight, a huge, rolling clap of thunder comes from a great distance. I turn and see a bank of faint lightning on the horizon, the first signs of a large storm that's come from nowhere. The air remains still, but now I notice the sign of weather in it, a weight. I tell Collette we have to go now, we'd better load the Zodiac. It seems a shame to leave.

"What an adventure this has been," I say.

"You think it's over?" She grins, rolling the mat, laughs. "You think this is all? Oh, Rawley."

CHAPTER 9
Trip to the Sun

We lift off through the glowering tropical storm that blew in from nowhere last night, its gusts buffeting the ship as we sat on the pad. Now, thirty seconds into launch, the winds have risen to gale force and the Tube yaws and lurches through layers of low clouds, their light gray-green. At the same time the ship vibrates with the low howl of sustained acceleration in trying to shake loose. The layers of weather swirl past the window/wall as the tidal forces of acceleration build—we are shaken one way, then another, so many rattles in the cabin a loop of soft music is drowned in this other kind of music. Something crashes in the kitchen/bar, then something larger. I manage to turn my head to see Collette, strapped into a liftoff rig at the couch, a worried expression on her face. Heavy weather, dangerous to launch. My surprise that we have lifted off at all has melted into aggravated resignation. Too committed now to abort, hanging on, the weather beyond the skin of the ship palpable and thick.

Then we punch through the last heavy layer of cumulus—vibrate still, but it is as if we go from water to air. A nice sensation of lightness, made manifest in the yellow-white light of the naked sun through the window/wall. I am finally pressed so far back into the recliner that I can no longer see.

The first thing I do once we reach stable flight, the heel of my hand throbbing again, is to check the program

through on Cooper's status. I am relieved to find that
military has a pair of high-priority tracers cross-checking
their way along Cooper's path since splashdown, SciCom
slow in responding, but the tracers moving inexorably,
step by step.

	RESIDUAL ITINERARY// FIRST-CLASS PASSAGE//	Prog.	2ndCoord.
DA12	VIETAHITI LAUNCH/TRIP TO THE SUN	bld	I/o-0600
DA13	HOLO PREP/TOTAL HOLOGRAM$_2$	bld	i/f-cont.
DA14	TRIP TO THE SUN	bl-	i/f-----

CONTINUOUS VIDEON PROGRAMMING
THE PLEASURE TUBE IS AN EXPERIENCE//INDIVIDUAL VARIATIONS
ARE COMMON AND PRECISE DESTINATIONS VARY//
CONSULT YOUR SERVICE FOR DETAILS
2, MEDICAL CLEARNACE REQUIRED

TOTAL HOLOGRAM///TOTAL HOLOGRAM///TOTAL HOLOGRAM///

//the option that is extra and extra-ordinary///medically cleared
passengers who have prereserved and preprogrammed
arrangements will receive instructions DA12//passengers are
encouraged to tune in to Videon 33 for continuous briefing on
hologram procedures, options, and benefits//shipwide total
hologram begins 0000 DA 14.

TRIP TO THE SUN//TRIP TO THE SUN//TRIP TO THE SUN//

//along with the culminating experience of the total hologram, to
complete this flight thePleasureTube will fly in a deep-space
orbit which will bring it within three million kilometers of the
sun//this orbit course, impossible without the special
facilities of theTube, is preprogrammed and self-
correcting//the increasing blue-gray shade of theTube
window/walls increases the reflectivity of the ship and should
not be adjusted//this rare experience is a standard feature for
all-class passengers//relax and enjoy the journey.

our service is pleasure//your pleasure our service

@ thePleasureTube corp.

Videon 33 displays a pleasant, young Oriental couple, identically dressed in white body stockings, seated together on a suede sofa in an elegant cabin—they're describing the total hologram, a familiar sequence I think I've seen before.

"Where brain-wave anticipation is immediately translated into full spectrum sensation," the male says soothingly, describing the hologram's loop.

"Where, best of all, you are in control," the woman adds.

"*Some*times," he laughs; they laugh together.

"In the comfort of your cabin—chemical, electrical, visual, audio, tactile—all systems. Full spectrum sensation for an ecstasy beyond compare."

"The only such system known to man is on this ship," she reminds the camera. "A hologram that's more than a hologram, controlled by you, automatically, unconsciously, instantaneously...."

"You are in control."

"Or out of it," the Oriental woman laughs, her teeth are sparkling white, her leg rising as she runs her hand from her knee down the back of her thigh, sensuous flesh electrically firm in the body stocking.

"Where brain-wave anticipation is immediately translated into full spectrum sensation," the Oriental male is saying again on the screen.

"Not for everyone"—his twin smiles—"but..."

"But riding thePleasureTube without experiencing the total hologram is like climbing a mountain and not reaching its peak."

"Like leaping from a precipice and never reaching the sea."

"The option that is extra but extra-ordinary. Come with us to the sun."

"Come with me." The woman smiles lusciously, touching her teeth with her tongue, just touching them. "Come with me to the sun."

We meet Werhner and Erica for lunch at the on-board club where Massimo and I had dinner the night he was drunk, teasing the dancer. During the day the small platform stage is replaced by more round tables, and its entire side wall opens into a bank of window/wall ports through which, now on the other side of the ship, we can view the receding sphere of the earth. Framed by bright blue seas, the storm we passed through at launch is visible as a macroweather whirlpool lying over the South Pacific—from our distance, easing into the lush-pillowed, hand-carved chairs, the storm seems as fierce as a white flower. The ship's motion hasn't quite smoothed out, though, and Erica looks a little pale, slightly glassy-eyed and staring, her lips tight. Feeling the motion, I think.

That becomes clear enough from her expression as Werhner starts raving about the looks of the curry brought to the adjacent table, nodding hello to the middle-aged couple seated there. It does look meaty, rich, though on the far side of green.

"Drink something," Collette tells Erica. Collette herself is radiant, she's been lost in her yoga all morning.

"Maybe I should," Erica says, pulling down the zip-lock of her jump suit. "I'll take another pill. Really, this leg of the flight . . ."

The service waitress arrives, a saronged woman with a ruby set in the middle of her forehead. Erica orders milk, Werhner his curry, Collette and I will split a rack of lamb.

"It's the distance." Erica takes it up again. "It's bad enough in orbit. Flying across half the solar system—I don't see why we have to. God, we've left orbit already, look," she says, wincing at the receding earth through the restaurant's window/wall. "So long to my nice, still beach. Land. Flat, steady land. Firm land."

"Construct a point horizon," I suggest, remembering how I've felt at times myself. "Watch something steady in space. Of course, that's a lot easier to do in the dome."

"You don't want to spoil your trip," Collette says. "You should eat something."

Erica moans. "How many times have I been through this?" she sighs.

Werhner's drumming his fingers on the table, says he's been offered a chance to ride up in the dome himself for a while. He can understand why the launch was rough but is curious why we are now flying with noticeable pitch and yaw—this began a half hour ago.

"It starts in the stomach," Erica says. "Then it's like my whole body, it gets into my blood. I have a hard time focusing my eyes. God, and my stomach. My poor stomach."

The saronged woman with the ruby brings our food over on a carved teak cart. Erica sips at her milk as it is handed to her, sets it down, then makes a face, a horrible face, when Werhner's curry is put on the table, steaming and ripe.

"I can't sit here," Erica says as its odor spreads; her napkin to her lips, she's rising. "I'm sorry. I have to go back to the cabin."

We watch her leave, then Collette and I start carving up the lamb. In a minute Werhner is calling the service waitress over again, asking her to take the curry and transfer it, please, to a thermos container; he's leaving, too.

"You haven't even touched it," Collette says.

"Ummm," Werhner answers sheepishly, sipping Erica's milk. Now he looks a little green himself. "Might be last night, uh, catching up with me. Going up to the dome for a while, have a look around. Anybody interested in coming?"

"Werhner," Collette says with a smile, "we haven't begun to eat."

"Right," he says, getting up with a lurch. "I'll just get my . . . curry on the way out. S'long."

Collette's foot is stroking mine under the table, feels very nice. I've eaten most of the food, on the theory that a full stomach is a good way to face instability. A small, birdlike man with prominent ears comes through the restaurant with flowers, and I sign for a dozen roses for Collette, red roses. She's touched, smiles against some nervousness that's begun to show, her green eyes are flashing.

She's explaining how one loses track of time in the

hologram, how she's pleased we'll be able to share portions of the experience, it really is spectacular. I hope the instability of the ship doesn't spoil anything for her, or for myself—I can just barely feel its effects now. And then I remember a third way to conquer motion sickness: to have sex; nothing takes your mind off a pitching ship like sex.

"It's tomorrow that it begins," she says. "So pay attention to Videon 33."

I put my hand on Collette's across the linen tablecloth. Her skin is smooth, warm, solid in a way the ship no longer seems to be.

"Let's go back to the cabin," I say.

The instability remains for hours on the ship, not a very smooth ride. I can't understand it: we're traveling rapidly, but not at speeds which create macroweather effect. Lost for a while at the window/wall, the earth's sphere far gone by this time, I gaze into the blue-black reaches of deep space, the stars blue-white, red, and yellow diamonds in the vastness; can't quite get my bearings. And then I realize the instability has gotten worse, it takes balance to walk from the recliner to the shower. In the rushing water of the shower I feel at sea, unhinged—like riding a working ship rather than a pleasure cruise. I begin to feel apprehensive, as if a chasm is opening beneath me in the white void of the cubicle. I don't stay long. Just as I am toweling dry I swear I can feel the ship shudder, and there is a live line link coming through on the videon from the ship's dome.

It's Werhner. Bigger than life and in electronically vivid color; beyond him the head-high computers, the desklike, long vane consoles in pastel blues, greens, beige. The dome looks almost deserted, Werhner intense as always with a touch of motion sickness showing in the concentration he pays to his breathing. I can see his thermos of curry still unopened on the navigator's chart table.

"Thought you'd like to know the reason we're catching the bumps," Werhner says. "You're going to find this interesting. SciCom split the casing on an aft reactor jettisoning waste—they were launching the big dispoz cans out the port pontoon, then changing the whole damned course to avoid them. *Timing* themselves, like morons. And if that doesn't shake things up enough, one of the cans hits the casing on that aft reactor, spills half the works into space. Remind you of something?"

I look up into the lens above the screen with a frown: "That happened to us once."

Werhner looks at me with a shrug. "In the Pleiades," he says. "Just like old times. Wish I would have known this was going to happen. I guess the joke's on me. Hong Kong at least kept still."

I want to ask Werhner whether he's heard anything new on the military tracers after Cooper, but know he'd tell me if he had. It's better unsaid for now, I think.

"So look what we've got," Werhner sighs. "Everybody's sick up here, we're way the hell off course. You're better off staying amidships, more stability there."

"Thanks for telling me what's going on," I say. "At least it's not serious. They should have things straightened out soon enough."

"Soon enough," Werhner agrees.

We eat again, caviar, canapés, and a very light champagne, watching the instructional transmission on Videon 33 to take our minds off the ride. The hologram's electronics are contained in a velour headrest that plugs into the recliner. A dark-haired woman, dressed in a robin's-egg-blue uniform, is stroking the forehead of a heavy, middle-aged man who's just settled in the unit. Then the screen cuts to a stark printout and the audio to a soothing voice-over:

ALL CLASS//ALL CLASS//ALL CLASS//ALL CLASS//

NOTICE OF PROGRAM CHANGE//
NOTICE OF PROGRAM CHANGE//

ATTENTION ALL PASSENGERS
AND SERVICE PERSONNEL//

NOTICE OF PROGRAM CHANGE//
NOTICE OF PROGRAM CHANGE//

//DUE TO TECHNICAL DIFFICULTIES THE SHIP IS
EXPERIENCING TEMPORARY INSTABILITY
//THESE DIFFICULTIES ARE IN THE PROCESS OF
BEING CORRECTED BY THE COMMITTEE PILOT//

//AS OUR WAY OF SAYING THANK YOU FOR YOUR
PATIENCE, ALL-CLASS OPTIONS BECOME IMME-
DIATELY AVAILABLE WITHOUT ADDITIONAL
CHARGE FOR THE LENGTH OF THE DELAY//EAR-
LY HOLOGRAM ENTRY IS ALSO AVAILABLE
WITHOUT ADDITIONAL CHARGE//

Our service is your pleasure//Your pleasure our service

I moan; Collette asks if this means something else has
gone wrong. She's been annoyed with me because I
haven't taken the damage very seriously; but I know well
enough that it can be fixed, they only need to blow that
reactor away.

"It's not that," I tell her. "It's just that they've started
using the Committee Pilot. Now it'll take a day to reach a
half-hour decision."

"Well, we can plug in," she says. "We can enter the
hologram now or just after dinner. We can eat and use the
hologram all night."

"Tonight, then," I say.

Collette tells me that once we start, we'll be consumed
for the remainder of the trip. She asks me if there's
anything I want to do beforehand, if there's one of the
other programs I want to run through, anything else on
the ship I want to try.

I mull the matter over for a long moment. "No," I say.
"The only thing that seems unfinished to me is Massimo's
death. I wish I had had the chance to pay my respects
before we left LasVenus. I wasn't thinking very clearly, I
guess, too interested in getting out of there. But I wish I
had gone to where they took his body."

"I haven't been thinking very clearly, either," she says.

"I should have thought to tell you. His body is probably on the ship."

"On the ship?"

She nods, looks at me seriously. "Passenger remains are taken back to L.A. They always are."

"Is there a way I can...see him? There must be."

"There is a morgue on the ship, he's probably there. But you have to get clearance, we'd have to make a request."

Collette does the checking for me. Sure enough, Massimo's remains are in the morgue. But she says no requests for downship activity are being authorized because the main lifts are out of operation for the duration of the instability.

"Is there a back way, a way through the superstructure of the ship? I'd like to go now."

"Without clearance?" Collette asks, checking the time by punching it up into a corner of the screen. "Well...I suppose there's no reason to worry now; what can they do, after all? Sure, there's a way. I'd have to show you."

"Just give me directions," I tell her. "You can get the electronics set up for the hologram. I'll go alone. I've been through ships before, just tell me where it is."

"Well, I'd have to get you through a hatch. Are you sure you want to do this just before we plug in?"

"I'm sure," I tell her, cracking off a piece of flat bread, spooning on the last of the caviar. "And the hologram after will be just the thing. I'm the sort who lays one on after a funeral."

Before I leave the cabin, Collette pulls a soft, stylish leather coat from the narrow closet off the kitchen/bar in which she keeps her clothes. "It's going to be cold," she says, easing the coat from its hanger, passing it to me.

It is a man's coat, a warm golden shade, like a flight jacket. It has the supple texture of glove leather, fits as if it had been cut for me, less a kilo or two. I admire the coat and thank Collette—it really fits well.

"It was my brother's," she says. "I didn't want to sell it."

I put my hand on the leather. I want to ask her about her brother, she's mentioned him before, yet I can see pain in her eyes. I hesitate, but my curiosity is too great. I ask her why he didn't want to keep the coat.

"He died," she says quietly. "He was given the wrong drugs. Who knows why."

The man who said that paranoids are survivors, I think.

Collette takes me back to the pool area, where the air turns chemical and humid. We pass the thinning crowd, slip into the locker room, and she leads me across the thick carpeting to a door marked SERVICE ONLY/DO NOT ENTER. She opens the heavy door by slipping her blue card into a lock slot on the satiny metal door frame, tells me to go all the way down, kisses me goodbye.

Once through the doorway, I pass from rug to metal grating, from the sleek redwood benches to ranks of bare metal pipes, valves, and scaffolding. The door shuts behind me with a slam. She was right when she said it was going to be cold: I can see my breath. I am in the cavernous maw of the interior of the ship, just alongside the works for the pool. Beyond the pumps lie vacant stretches of space between this first-class hull and the other two hulls that make up the second-class and third-class sectors of the ship. The Tube is constructed just like a tripled starship with a skin—three long starship cylinders, three domes, each with its port and starboard pontoons high overhead. I guessed something like this, seeing the ship on the pads in LasVenus; still, I am startled by the sight. When I consider for a moment where we will be flying, I know I shouldn't be. Yet in the bowels of this ship, each hull so resembles the Daedalus that I have an eerie sense of never having touched down, of walking in space.

I've already climbed down the flight of steep metal stairs past the pool works, enter a series of hatch passageways in the hull on the next level; the stairway continues down, narrow, there are hatches at every level,

stenciled numbers. I clamber down more steps, read 022.
It is a long way to go, I guess two hundred meters beneath
me.

I reenter the ship sector through the very last hatch. I
open it, a little rubber-legged from the descent. The
morgue is achingly stark white, dispassionately institu-
tional. I am struck by its size once inside it, for the single
level I've reached through the service door descends two
levels further through wide inside elevators. Instead of
two or three mordant attendants, I find the office area is
staffed by a half-dozen people. I'm told to go below by an
angular-faced, pale woman in white.

A chemical odor seems to radiate from the smooth
walls and tile floors, from the interior of the elevator in
which I descend. The lowest level is again dazzlingly
white. Leaving the elevator, I have the sensation that I am
inside the white heart of a vast machine—ducts, pipes,
fittings, valves, line the ceiling of the hallways and the
racks on the walls. I recognize hatchways leading to the
engine room of the ship. A hum seems to come from
everywhere—the long thin tubes of lighting, the machine
fittings and ducts, the thick steel doors leading to rooms
visible through small squares of wire-reinforced glass,
rows upon rows of oversized drawers tagged at their
handles. Collette was right about the number of deaths. I
feel a formless blindness creeping into my vision, a
nervous tremor runs through my body—slightly spooked,
I guess, at the atmosphere of this place, raised to an
unknown power by its size.

I cannot escape the notion that Massimo still has
something to tell me. I recall our first meeting on the A-
line tram, the sense I had then of being impelled with him
toward something new to me yet known somehow; we
never arrived at it, yet we seemed sure to, I could feel it in
my bones. And the idea of his intercession intrigues me.
Judging from the way he orchestrated a connection for
me with Eva Steiner, he could very well have seen to my
appeal without telling me, had it taken care of even

though he didn't know who Eva Steiner was. The hygienic chill seems cruel and unjust, just as his death still seems wrong, the gorgeous Ferrari smeared along the wall, its orange-red fireball a young, seething sun.

In C-1 there is a two-man crew seated at a desk playing chess on a magnetic board—the vault beyond stacked ceiling-high with drawers that recede down a corridor bathed in light.

"Well, let's see," the older of the attendants says, moving his fingers through a card file. He looks queasy from the motion of the ship. "Giroti. G.G.G.G.G.G.G. You say you're not a member of the immediate family?"

"I'd just like to pay my respects. The man was a friend of mine."

"You can see what we have," the older man says, peering at the card he's pulled.

"What do you mean by that?"

"Looks like he was pretty well busted up. He's in drawer thirty-three, right down there. I guess we have effects, says here personal effects are in there, too."

I stare at the attendant blankly, stupidly; I don't know what to think.

"Look," he says, pulling his chair up against the desk so he can hunch over the chessboard, "you want an interfaith minister or something? We can call upstairs."

"No," I answer. "I'll be just fine."

In the chilly air I stare at the pathetic sack on the slab, the body bag from which wisps of CO_2 rise like smoke from a dying fire. I wonder why I've come. Now it seems so useless. I stand silently, lost in my thoughts. I recall Massimo's kindness to me on the last day he was alive, the enthusiasm with which he seemed to lose himself in his cars—to be utterly lost, in the end, in a blur of acceleration in the Ferrari. That is what he might have preferred; I accept that, it makes his death sensible to me. Yet it reminds me of the ways in which I've lost myself, reminds me of the moments before the blow four year ago. In the instant before I blacked out I thought I was dying, remember experience becoming an all-consuming blur, passing into something from which I never thought I'd recover. I sigh. Well, friend, I think, peace be with you.

After a while I look through Massimo's scattered effects. Behind the separator in the body drawer lie his tagged leather luggage, suit bags, several briefcases. I stare for a while at his unfamiliar things. There is a tagged video cassette lying alone, which I pick up, examine. It is dated the second day of the trip, and in the title box are written the words "To my survivors"; the handwriting must be Massimo's.

I anticipate its contents, guess a dozen things on my short trip up to the morgue's first level to run the tape, expect an explanation to a question I can't quite formulate. I'm given a machine without signing for it; nothing I've done has been logged. When I run the tape I look with infinite sadness at Massimo's smiling, animated face, see his sly kindness and sense of his own end evident even before he speaks. Of course, I think, he was coming on against medical advice, he knew that he might well die. What he has to say has nothing to do with his Governorship, or with SciCom, or with the trip; it is a message to his household, and to his friends. "You belong to a new age," he says. "Go in pleasure and in peace."

I stare at his still image fixed on the final frame.

I am passing back into the bowels of the ship when it happens. The chill intensifies, the brightness of the morgue goes, and in its place is the shaky dimness of the hatch passageways. I am lost in thought, vaguely wonder how Collette is making out. I still have a long way to go, stop at a hatch only one flight up to take another look at the superstructure of the ship.

I unseal the hatch, push to go through—and it swings open to a howling bright light, the white light of a whirling sun, intense, overwhelming, incredible. A screaming rings in my ears, the light is blinding me. I wonder if I've been hit, if the ship's been hit, my arm is still on the hatch lock, I shade my eyes with my forearm and slam it closed.

Silence. The dim light. My heart is pounding, the blood banging in my ears.

A morgue attendant who's heard the slam is at my side, asking me what happened, what's wrong.

The hatch swings open at the touch of his hand. I had not set the lock. Beyond it lies another metal stairway, the dim light of the ship's interior, the pall of machinery, nothing else.

"Look at you, man. What happened?"

"I don't know," I say, leaning back against a metal stair. "My God, I don't know."

The cabin's soft brown walls, the faint hexagons of its carpet, the Rubens, pink and fleshy, comfort me with their familiarity. Collette is in the kitchen/bar assembling dinner. I catch a whiff of piquant sauce, feel my stomach tighten, put one hand on the couch to steady myself against the ship's motion. God, what is it, I wonder, the instability of the ship, the last days of the trip, or what I saw, what I saw? I notice now the velour headrests for the hologram sitting on the carpet near the recliner; they connect to the recliner's base through an array of gray cables.

"I'm really having problems," Collette says, coming out empty-handed. "The béarnaise sauce keeps separating on me, it's curdled twice."

"I'm not really hungry," I tell her, see now she seems a little pale herself.

So we sit on the couch sipping Cinzano for our appetites, watching the last of the instructional programs for the hologram on Videon 33. The white-haired physician I've seen twice before is summing up a long, personal theory. He says in the end, translating from archaic Greek, that the highest pleasure of an organism consists of its return to its own true nature.

"My nature at the moment doesn't feel very steady," I tell Collette, think I need to do something, to get myself occupied. I go with her to the kitchen and we try the sauce again—once more wind up with thickening butter and specks of egg. When I tell Collette I'm not interested in eating, anyway, she says the motion is getting to her as well, she isn't particularly hungry herself. She says she thinks we ought just to enter the hologram, plug in. The electronics are ready and it's always worked for motion sickness for her. I wash my hands at the metal sink. I just want to forget. I tell her that now seems as good a time as any other, and so we clear away the aperitif glasses, set the cables into their racks, change into robes.

I have a pleasant moment as Collette sets my head in the headrest before a pastoral videon screen, nervous as I am.

Then a severe, searing pain begins at the tips of my fingers, shoots straight to my sinuses and teeth, grips me in the spine. My stomach muscles contract to double me up, but I can't move. The pain is razor-sharp, burning, takes my breath away, my fist flails out and slams into the side of the recliner. I am out of the headrest, doubled up now, gasping for breath, the pain receding. "...Jesus."

"I'm sorry, Rawley," Collette says, biting her lip. "That had to be done to clear your neurology for contrast. I'm sorry. But if I had told you, it would have been worse."

"Worse?...Jesus."

"Lie back," she says.

"Oh, now..."

"Trust me," she says. "Lie back."

Collette self-induces her own initial neurological clearing with a timing mechanism—I can hear her catch her breath. Then she tells me everything is ready, makes herself comfortable on the couch, her full hair spilling over the headrest. I'm not at all certain what to expect. Despite my apprehension, with the ship unstable I do feel far more comfortable lying down, I'm sure now I won't be sick. I lie there watching a pastoral scene on the videon screen, rolling hills, cultivated land, a farmhouse, and a young man and woman doing something by its door.

"Say, Collette, when will I—"

Suddenly there is a flash of white-yellow light, I am blinded, not unpleasantly, but I am consumed in light. The vision quickly passes, fades in diminishing visual echoes, then my mind, my senses, go blank—my vision utterly obliterated, I cannot hear or see a thing. Slowly my mind fills with a color, pure, throbbing red, then pure, cool blue, then a deep, iridescent green, the colors fill all of my senses, seem to saturate every cell in my body, I have never had a sensation such as this. It is both frightening and compelling at the same time. It goes on and on, the colors begin to mingle and shift, swirl into unutterable combinations.

The light shifts to yellow-white again, fades, and I find myself transported to a beach. A beach? I wonder, reach out and touch the sand. Its grains slide between my fingers, smooth, weightless as dust. I inhale—salt-rich air. I turn and Collette is lying on her side on a mat, boosted up on her elbow. She seems as vividly real to me as she did on the day we lay just this way on the beach of the island off Vietahiti; the surf is booming out at the reef with a deep roar I can feel in my bones. I reach out to touch her—she seems real, but my hand passes through her arm with a tingling sensation—not Collette, but a holographic representation.

"What would you do?" the specter of Collette asks in an eerie, hollow voice. "What would you do if you were utterly free in time?"

"I'd put myself somewhere pleasant," I answer, laughing because I know we've had this conversation once before, giddy at the sound of my own voice, queerly unreal. "I'd put myself right on this spot."

A feeling is spreading throughout my body, a rich, warm, pleasant feeling, a feeling like orgasm, but broader, wider, suffused into every limb, reaching into every part of me, permeating every cell.

I reach out to touch Collette again, concentrate—focus my eyes, move my arm slowly. There is a sensation in my hand, a sensation like the soft touch of her skin, but cooler. The moment of touch extends itself, seems to last forever as the warmth grows inside me, seems to lift me higher and higher....

I have no idea how much time passes—the moment of touch modulates, all my sensations undergo a shift through odd, funny exchanges with one another. I taste the color pink; a moving pattern of lines sounds like running deer. Then a series of scenes begin to pass through my mind, complete with all their sensations. One instant—or is it hours?—I am holding Collette for the first time, feeling the warmth and weight of her, the firmness of her back muscles, their modulation as she moves against me; then I am reclining with her on the soft loam of woods in broken sunlight, hear the murmur of a stream, feel the soft caress of her hand stroking the back of my neck, my shoulders. And then I am turning in my cabin, watching the window/wall open into another cabin, Erica turning simultaneously, Erica's smile wide and arms rising; then I am moving toward Collette in the cabin, to music that is everywhere, above, beneath, beside me. Again I am pressed against the leather seat of the Ferrari as the car, its steering wheel in my hands, curls with smooth adhesion around the hairpin; the thrust of its acceleration coming out into the sun goes on forever; and I am sitting with Collette, her lips full and shiny, her loose hair backlit by the sun, her face inches from mine, the odor of gardenias everywhere. The experiences seem simultaneous, yet each has a full integrity, seems separate, through swimming in the soft bulk of the Pacific over an involuted reef, walking through the green mansions of palace gardens among rainbow blossoms and clucking, iridescent blue peacocks. At times they seem distant, at times so present in each detail the effect is overwhelming. In one sequence I bite into a piece of filet and see the fibers snap as in a blown-up picture, follow the process of its saturation with saliva, the chewed bit sliding with a scraping sound down my esophagus and falling with a splash into the cave where gastric juices swarm over it like foam from a wave. Collette hands me a glass of red wine and I smell sugar, grapes, the sunlight of the vineyards; she wipes my lips and the sound is like skis on fresh snow. And then I am watching myself from a distance again, the Ferrari from above a smooth blur of red, bright in the sun. The pleasures amplify, intensify, in these and other ways. The pleasures seem to grow, a surge of pleasure which, like my first moment of touch, extends itself, sweeps me away, loops me into whirlpools of memory, timelessness, sensation, a rush I have never known.

The scenes recur, roll into and through one another, green mansions and blue water, the curves of a woman, the sweet freedom of flight; they go on and on, I am in and out of them, they roll on and on.

The sky above is motionless, a sea of stars, snow at the Milky Way. The Crab nebula is overhead. I look up, and in looking I begin to feel the sky widen and begin to fall through it—falling into it, falling among the stars as the infinity of space opens before me like a window, like a door. I can feel the blood coursing through my veins, the rhythm of my heart the rhythm of my body.

A sound nearby. Collette steps out of the dark, naked, glistening with sweet oil, her breasts jutting out. She kneels before me, and when I quickly thrust inside her, she wraps her arms around my head and only her fingers move through the hair on the back of my neck. A series of jolting shocks pass through my groin, a stream of delight which does not seem to belong to me but takes the last breath from my lungs, continues, continues, continues. . . .

Finally Collette rises to her feet, sends her arms outstretched to the stars; the low fire gives her a golden glow, her skin glistening with the sheen of the fragrant oil as the light plays over the curves of her body.

"A goddess?" she says softly, tenderly, looking at me with a gentle smile. "Yes. And you are a god, Rawley."

She laughs, wrinkles at her eyes, holds out her hands. "You are a god."

Her eyes are jade-green, striking. Her broad face is framed by black, loosely waved hair. Her tongue touches the edges of her teeth as she laughs. I kiss the soft hollow between her shoulder and her neck, chocolate skin lushly warm, smooth, soft. She moves from me, whirls away, stops. "You think this is all? You think we're finished?" she says breathlessly, Collette says breathlessly. "Oh, Rawley."

Her eyes are jade-green, striking. Her broad face is framed by auburn, loosely waved hair. Her tongue touches the edges of her teeth as she laughs. I kiss the soft hollow between her shoulder and her neck, pinkwhite skin lushly warm, smooth, soft. She moves from me, whirls away, stops. "You think this is all? You think we're finished?" she says breathlessly, Maxine says breathlessly. "Oh, Rawley."

I see Massimo's face, broad and radiant, the radiance seems to come from deep within his bones, his eyes smiling, his lips cherry-red, his shock of white hair and white beard brilliantly white.

"You belong to a new age," he is telling me. "Go in pleasure and in peace."

Each scene comes again, recedes, these and others, they shimmer through one another, whole scenes and fragments freeze, their images recombine: green mansions, summer wheat, the gulf of space, a sun of ice. They freeze again for a time I have no sense of, then expand into vivid swaths of pure, electric color, roll on, memory and desire mingled into a timeless rush of ecstasy and delight, roll on and on....

Then there is a jolt, a jolt like no other. It shakes me whole and violently, fixes itself in time to the thumping of

my heart, reverberates intensely, then reverberates again.
It is outside me, a severe jolt as from a ship, a jolt through
the recliner, through my body, a jolt of massive weight
and inertia.

For a moment I don't know where I am. My heart is
thudding in my chest, my blood is racing, a terror laces
through the incredible sense of well-being that I
have, my body feels lusciously pleasant but for the
throbbing in my hand, the fright in my heart. I am
struggling for consciousness, struggling to bring my dis-
location under control. I feel the light pain my eyes
as I open....

"Wake up," Collette is saying, holding a glass of
orange juice to my lips, her hand shaking. "Something's
wrong. Something's wrong with the ship, there's an
alarm. Werhner called down from the dome."

The cool liquid runs down my throat, its sweetness
heavy on my tongue. "How...long...?"

"We've been under all night, it's day fourteen, Rawley.
Here, drink more. This will detoxify you. There's an
alarm. He wants you to come up to the dome."

My eyes blink, I see Collette, robe open, perspiring,
fear in her face, I reach out and touch the pulsing vein in
her neck. Turn to see the cabin, its edges sharp—the
paintings askew, utensils tumbled from drawers in the
kitchen/bar, the closet door hanging open, the lights dim
and flickering, coming steady.

"There was a jolt, Rawley."

My mind comes awake; the drug, I wonder, the fright. I
am sitting up and rubbing my face for a long minute, feel
the blood rise to my cheeks and temples. I look up to the
videon:

ALARM   ALARM   ALARM   ALARM   ALARM
ALARM   ALARM   ALARM   ALARM   ALARM

"He wants you to come up to Dome A."

I have slipped off my robe, pulled open my bag, and am
pulling on my flight suit, stop with one arm remaining to
shove through and punch Dome A on the console:

ALARM ALARM ALARM ALARM ALARM ALARM ALARM ALARM ALARM
TRAFFIC DOWN TRAFFIC DOWN TRAFFIC DOWN TRAFFIC DOWN
ALARM ALARM ALARM ALARM ALARM ALARM ALARM ALARM ALARM

The ship is terribly unsteady. I run my hands through
my hair, the ship pitches, and I have to reach out for
support against the recliner. I see Collette wiping her face
with a towel, reaching for a silver jump suit.

"Look, Collette..."

"I'm coming along," she says.

On the lift to Dome A I hold the cold handrail so
tightly I know without looking that the back of my hand is
white—with my other arm I hold Collette against me, her
silver jump suit slides against the palm of my hand, her
body warm beneath.

"Kiss me," she says, her face close to mine, she's barely
smiling. I look down at the glistening of her lips, into her
liquid green, frightened eyes.

I meet her lips, her tongue, lose myself for a moment in
the flesh-and-blood warmth of her, run the back of my
hand over the soft chocolate skin of her cheek. I don't
know what to tell her, how to articulate the terror I feel
lacing through the pleasure of her presence. What was it
that I saw, I am thinking now, what was it through the
hatch, familiar and strange at once? The question mingles
in my blood with echoes and reverberations from the
hologram, the eerie sense of its unreality and the vividness
of its visions.

My hand grips the handrail even more tightly, aches.
The fingers of my other hand run their course through
Collette's black hair, twist together before they have
passed through. I pull Collette's head back by the hair
down her back. Her eyes widen, her mouth opens, her
gaze is directly into mine. Her neck muscles tense, her
head seems an upward weight against the pull of my
twisted fingers.

Smile lines creep from the corners of her eyes. "Ahhh,"

she says, "You have an im-agination."

"I do," I say, releasing my fingers, relaxing my hand. "I have an imagination, all right." Collette shifts her weight against the accelerating upward pull of the lift, leans against the spun-steel wall still watching me, smiling. How odd, it wasn't my imagination, but an impulse to feel the simple, present reality of her that made me cause her pain. Even as I think this I begin to lose it again in our distorted reflection on the opposite wall, the vague soft map of ourselves which moves even as we both move to unlock our knees and stand flat to the wall behind us against the abrupt deceleration of the lift as the panel light begins to flash DOME A.

Something's wrong. As the lift doors open I am feeling the ship's slow roll to steady, feel for a moment that odd sensation of leg muscles ready to move for balance when there is no need to, suddenly steady on, I almost fall stepping from the lift. As the lift doors close behind I can see in the amber light of the hatchway to port pontoon a large, blue-suited figure across in program, yet the dome seems deserted—a half-eaten sandwich on a near console, equipment out of place, a thick oil seeping over the magnesium-alloy floor from the high bank of condensers. As if by habit I close a slowly swinging locker door, only then look across and see Werhner seated at the navigator's console, absorbed, intent on his instruments, digging into his curry, so absorbed he isn't looking at his plate but eating heartily. I feel a temperature change on the exposed surfaces of my skin, cold. I look up.

Through the concave hexagons of the dome itself an expanse of spectral, brilliant light lies across the port quarter, something huge—and on the starboard side nothing, not a trace, starless, an inky void. A chill runs down my spine, I feel something crawl across my lower lip. The lull. The ship's instability has passed; we are in a lull so motionless I can feel the blood coursing through my veins. Only once before have I had these sensations, seen what I am seeing now, only once and forever—four years ago.

"Rawley, look at the instruments. Look."

Werhner is waving me over to the vane console without glancing up; in a daze I make it over to my station, lean on the vane console with both hands. Lull figures, absolute lull figures, the needle of each instrument pinned by its own thin weight at zero.

"SciCom cricuits overloaded," Werhner says. "Even Committee Pilot's patched out to give them more room. Christ, Rawley—the ship was blind-sided. Something came up faster than we are, came up from behind us, the other two hulls are gone. The other two hulls are gone. And I show . . . this . . . configuration, a ring singularity entry horizon, that's what I'm showing, Christ, just . . ."

Now when he looks at me I can see how wide Werhner's eyes are, his cheeks seem stretched back, an aura of light around his head the wildness of his sandy hair. Neither of us wants to say it, to think it, but I can smell it in the burned insulation in the cold air, feel it as a tingling on the back of my neck, see it in the array of the dome: the presence of the Daedalus beneath my hands is as palpable as the pads on my fingertips; I can feel it in the rhythm of the faint vibrations running through the console.

A hand at my shoulder: Collette. I move my hand to her shoulder, squeeze. I can see my own distress in her face, my horror; she asks weakly, what's wrong, what's wrong. Yet I sense she sees in my face a staggering weight to the answer, doesn't want an answer. For an instant an afterimage from the hologram returns to me, the metallic voice of a calm, old man, saying that the highest pleasure of an organism consists of its return to its own nature, the afterimage of a searing burn of launch seen up through a ship. Feel swept away, I am being swept away, feel obliterated as I felt in the early hours of the hologram today, or was it yesterday. . . . And why not the same trip? My experience with Maxine translated in Collette, an ongoing tension with SciCom, each launch a course correction to lead me here.

I am still holding Collette, she is pressed against me, her warm body tender and firm, the warm dampness of her breath on my neck.

I turn back to the instruments.

"It's a flight simulation. Werhner, this is a flight simulation."

"A flight simulation? God, I've been so damned sick, I... But Rawley..."

"We're being set up, Werhner."

"A program in the hologram," Collette says breathlessly. "It isn't possible, they can't do *this*...."

"Rawley, if she's right. But the hulls are gone, the other hulls."

I release the thruster safety, switch toggles for alternate readings from secondary and tertiary mag and grav systems, stare, my eyes widening, at the readings: zero, null, zero, null; rap meter faces with my knuckles.

A high-pitched laugh pierces the faint machine hum from across the dome.

A man. Collette screams. Cooper. Cooper is in the dome, moving from the amber light of the hatch to program our way, Cooper, blue flight suit disheveled, the bulk of his form backlit by the amber light, his snow-white hair glowing like spectral flames.

The hair on the back of my neck rises at the sight of him. Werhner's turning slowly, I can see the awe of recognition on his face. Collette stumbles alongside me, a blur of brown and silver, clings; a thumping begins somewhere deep in the ship. The thumping of overloaded reactors and slipped vanes, I've heard it only once before.

"Cooper," I say. "Stand fast."

Cooper is supporting himself at a low tape rack, his laugh maniacal. "They're all below," he says, a whine to his voice. "We're the only ones up here."

"They told us you were dead, Cooper," Werhner says. "They told us you'd committed suicide in Houston."

Cooper's high-pitched laugh starts again; he looks mad, insane. "Look at your instruments, Voorst."

"Coming up again," Werhner says firmly, wide-eyed at his instruments, his fork suspended above his plate. "I show a pulse on the port side. Fucker's coming up again."

My eyes are wide on the monitors before me, grav and

mag sensors show a massive, swift front near the center of the inky field starboard, we're still otherwise blind. Something catches my eye from the periphery of my vision. Red, the blind-sided panel going red across the dome, the red sweeping across the consoles this way, Cooper five meters away clutching a downhatch ladder, the strap of a liftoff rig. "Thrusters," I call to Werhner, urge Collette to hang on, the panel's red—my stomach heaves and folds, snaps into a knot. I am blacking out, moving my hand in an impossible slow motion for the thrusters, suspended, the panel entirely red, a jolt, a bone-shaking jolt is beginning to run through the ship . . .

ALARM ALARM ALARM ALARM ALARM ALARM ALARM ALARM ALARM

EVENT INTRUSION EVENT INTRUSION EVENT INTRUSION ALL AUXILIARY SYSTEMS A & B SEQUENCE ALL AUXILIARY SYSTEMS A & B SEQUENCE ALL AUXILIARY SYSTEMS A & B SEQUENCE DAMAGE CONTROL DAMAGE CONTROL DAMAGE CONTROL

ALARM ALARM ALARM ALARM ALARM ALARM ALARM ALARM ALARM

I've blacked out, or close to it—my consciousness swims with fragmented visions, a nightmare of déjà vu and the momentary conviction that I am coming awake in my cabin, a woman kneeling at my side, the sweet odor and warm sight of her—I reach out my hand to touch her face, feel the throbbing pain, see the blood running crimson as Collette grasps my wrist and turns my hand palm upward.

There is a gash in the heel of my hand, a deep gash, bleeding steadily; I touch the spot, am startled by its sticky warmth.

At Collette's knee is the dome's first-aid kit, scattered contents. She quickly pulls a wide bandage around the heel of my hand, thin, translucent, medicated—the pain sears to the bone, bone numbed.

"Rawley," she says, her eyes moist, her long hair loose on her shoulders.

The ship is screaming under power. I rise groggily, see blood splattered at the thrusters, turn to the sight of

Cooper grinning horribly five meters away, hear him grunt. "Now you know," I think he says; there is a thumping. The ship's gone rocky, unstable; Werhner's curry and rice smear the navigator's table, he stands at a console intent on a monitor, curry smears the chest of his flight suit. I look to the dome, check for port pontoon—still there—look into a foggy white field of radiating lines on the starboard side, upward, and a void, an inky black void, where the other hulls should be. I feel as if I'm falling, feel in this flash of time as I felt when I blacked out and came to in the Ferrari during the race, falling.

"And we die," Cooper says hoarsely. I see Collette's hand rising to her mouth. "And we die, we always die."

Instinctively I key in the auxiliary thrusters, wondering what, what, an electricity in my body like I've never known, look to Collette, her living, breathing body, thinking, Cooper... "*Know* what? Did they tell you to say that, Cooper? Do you remember?"

"Get into program," Werhner says to him sharply. "We need—"

"Yaas, we die," Cooper says. "The loop, the same nowhere and everywhere, we always die—look where we are, Voorst, you can't believe it. If you'd known you'd have paid, I've been paying. The data was wrong, Voorst. We were never well off."

... here before, I am thinking, overcome by a sense of both pure freedom and crushing oppression at the same time, recalling my own log: *holding vane angle in the lull and watching Werhner eat... violently ill, I first thought it was from watching him; then focusing on the panel, I saw lull figures then everything red—instantly, I don't know if it was a trick of vision, but the red seemed to sweep the panels right to left along with the first strong jolt...*

Collette's horror mirrors my own, her green eyes welling with tears. "No, no," she says. "It's all in the program, it's your imagination. It's this place, Rawley...."

"*I'm flying the ship,*" I say, the pain in my hand the throb of my pulse, my body's blood oozing at the bandage, warm at my palm, the ship under my hands.

"Yes, you're always flying the ship," Cooper says, "that's one of the languages. We die, Voorst...."

"Damn it, *coming up*," Werhner says firmly.

"I'll prove it to you," Collette says, out of breath. "It's all in the program. We won't die, Rawley, no, not us. They've put it in the program. We live, Rawley, don't listen to him. This is just what they wanted...."

ALARM ALARM ALARM ALARM ALARM ALARM ALARM ALARM ALARM

EVENT INTRUSION EVENT INTRUSION EVENT INTRUSION
ALL AUXILIARY SYSTEMS C & D SEQUENCE ALL AUXILIARY SYSTEMS
C & D SEQUENCE ALL AUXILIARY SYSTEMS C & D SEQUENCE
DAMAGE CONTROL DAMAGE CONTROL DAMAGE CONTROL

ALARM ALARM ALARM ALARM ALARM ALARM ALARM ALARM ALARM

EVENT INTRUSION EVENT INTRUSION EVENT INTRUSION
ALL AUXILIARY SYSTEMS C & D SEQUENCE ALL AUXILIARY SYSTEMS
C & D SEQUENCE ALL AUXILIARY SYSTEMS C & D SEQUENCE

ALARM ALARM ALARM ALARM ALARM ALARM ALARM ALARM ALARM

"Where's the woman? Where is she, Werhner?"

"She's in the port pontoon, she ran into program." Cooper laughs hoarsely. "She's right, Voorst, the loop is your imagination. She's your imagination."

The hatch is sealed, the wide, ribbed hatch to program slammed by the blow or by Collette. I shunt up program on the monitor, there's nothing showing but gray snow on the screen. I bang the key with my fist, the monitor hissing, showing nothing but gray snow.

"Clear the port pontoon," Werhner shouts. "We have stress markers, another pulse in fifteen. Cooper, get your ass..."

I push past Cooper, stumble across the dome, pull with all my strength at the hatch lock. The hatch will not turn; I hear Werhner saying sharply that it's sealed and won't respond. Cooper is laughing low and hoarse behind me. I make for the thrusters, but reaching Cooper, stop short and grab him by the throat, the muscles and sinews of his neck tight but giving in to my clenched hand, the blood through the bandage bright red against his windpipe, I am straining, holding his weight. "What do you know, you bastard? What did you tell that woman?"

"Eight."

"*We're all on the death list,*" he says, his eyes widening, his teeth glistening white, eerie, his voice half choked. "*We're all on the death list from the blow. That's what else I destroyed.*"

"Six."

The ship is beginning its yaw, I can feel the pulse coming up beneath us, the console a phantasmagoria of lights.

"*Initial on number three,*" Werhner says. "*Go with it.*"

I lurch to the console, push the thrusters with my wounded hand, shove through the bandage into blood and bone, burned insulation in the atmosphere, my vision swimming, the pulse a mirror of the hologram, I think of Collette, Collette, Collette.

"*Three, gonna hit it.*"

"The woman, Werhner! The woman!"

"What . . . woman?" I hear Werhner say and I begin falling, falling. I see Cooper ripping at the cable rack from program, his large frame hunched in dim light, ripping.

"*Two.*"

"*Alive!*" I scream.

"*One.* Coming . . ."

ALARM ALARM ALARM ALARM ALARM ALARM ALARM ALARM ALARM

IMPACT EVENT IMPACT EVENT IMPACT EVENT IMPACT EVENT INTRUSION EVENT INTRUSION EVENT INTRUSION DAMAGE CONTROL DAMAGE CONTROL DAMAGE CONTROL

ALARM ALARM ALARM ALARM ALARM ALARM ALARM ALARM ALARM

IMPACT EVENT IMPACT EVENT IMPACT EVENT IMPACT EVENT IMPACT EVENT IMPACT EVENT IMPACT EVENT IMPACT EVENT

ALARM ALARM ALARM ALARM ALARM ALARM ALARM ALARM ALARM

IMPACT EVENT IMPACT EVENT IMPACT EVENT IMPACT EVENT
IMPACT EVENT IMPACT EVENT IMPACT EVENT IMPACT EVENT

ALARM ALARM ALARM ALARM ALARM ALARM ALARM ALARM ALARM

The hatch to program blows open with a rushing scream, hangs open like a tongue. Through it I see a howling, whirling sun filling the gulf of night, a huge sun, growing larger, a whirlpool of light bleaching my vision in the fine atom snow of the cosmos into which I spin orange flames at my feet, falling, falling. My bones are exploding, yellow-white to white light vision, pure white, white light vision.

Still image: a woman frozen in space, fixed in inky blackness, the funnel of infinity pierced by diamond points of light, stars in the celestial sea. She floats as a swimmer, her palms flat and forward. Her hair streams behind—yet no breeze. Her expression intense and incomprehensible, lips slightly parted to show the glistening edges of teeth—a kiss or a cry—silent in the void.

SCIENCE FICTION BESTSELLERS
FROM BERKLEY!

Frank Herbert

THE DOSADI EXPERIMENT   (03834-3—$2.25)

CHILDREN OF DUNE   (04075-5—$2.25)

DUNE   (03698-7—$2.25)

DUNE MESSIAH   (03940-7—$1.95)

THE GODMAKERS   (03913-6—$1.95)

THE ILLUSTRATED DUNE   (03891-2—$7.95)

DESTINATION: VOID   (03922-6—$1.95)

Philip José Farmer

THE DARK DECISION   (03831-9—$2.25)

THE FABULOUS RIVERBOAT   (04315-0—$1.95)

TO YOUR SCATTERED BODIES GO   (04314-2—$1.95)

NIGHT OF LIGHT   (03933-1—$1.75)

Send for a list of all our books in print.

These books are available at your local bookstore, or send price indicated plus 30¢ for postage and handling. If more than four books are ordered, only $1.00 is necessary for postage. Allow three weeks for delivery. Send orders to:

Berkley Book Mailing Service
P.O. Box 690
Rockville Centre, New York 11570